BLUE BOSSA

BLUE BOSSA

Bart Schneider

Viking

VIKING
Published by the Penguin Group
Penguin Putnam Inc., 375 Hudson Street, New York, New York 10014, U.S.A.
Penguin Books Ltd, 27 Wrights Lane, London W8 5TZ, England
Penguin Books Australia Ltd, Ringwood, Victoria, Australia
Penguin Books Canada Ltd, 10 Alcorn Avenue, Toronto, Ontario, Canada M4V 3B2
Penguin Books (N.Z.) Ltd, 182–190 Wairau Road, Auckland 10, New Zealand

Penguin Books Ltd, Registered Offices: Harmondsworth, Middlesex, England

First published in 1998 by Viking Penguin,
a member of Penguin Putnam Inc.

10 9 8 7 6 5 4 3 2 1

Grateful acknowledgment is made for permission to reprint excerpts from the following
copyrighted works:
    Anyone's Daughter: The Times and Trials of Patty Hearst by Shana Alexander, Viking,
1979. Reprinted by permission of the author.
    "Black Coffee" by Sonny Burke and Paul Francis Webster. © 1988–92 Sondot
Music Corporation and Webster Music Corp.
    "You've Changed" by Carl Fischer and Bill Carey. Copyright © 1942 by Melody
Lane Publications, Inc. Copyright renewed. International copyright secured. Used by
permission.
    "Journal for My Daughter" from *Passing Through: The Later Poems New and Selected*
by Stanley Kunitz. Copyright © 1995 by Stanley Kunitz. Reprinted by permission of
W. W. Norton & Company, Inc.

PUBLISHER'S NOTE
This is a work of fiction. Names, characters, places, and incidents either are the product of
the author's imagination or are used fictitiously, and any resemblance to actual persons,
living or dead, events, or locales is entirely coincidental.

LIBRARY OF CONGRESS CATALOGING-IN-PUBLICATION DATA
Schneider, Bart.
Blue Bossa / Bart Schneider.
p. cm.
ISBN 0-670-87695-X
I. Title.
PS3569.C522374858 1998
813'.54—dc21   97-24276

This book is printed on acid-free paper.
⊛

Printed in the United States of America
Set in Bembo
Designed by Sabrina Bowers

For Patricia, with the fine ear and the full heart

You say you had a father once:
his name was absence.
He left, but did not let you go.
—Stanley Kunitz

BLUE BOSSA

Early Morning

Early on a cool February morning, two weeks after Patty Hearst has been dragged screaming from her Berkeley apartment, Ronnie Reboulet sits bolt upright in bed trying to remember the faces of his mother and father. It's been a long time that they've been gone. Longer yet, his twin brother, Natty.

As a boy, Ronnie often woke with a charge. He'd rush to his bedroom window and look out into the treeless street. Nothing but parked cars and taut, black telephone lines. A bone white mist rolled up Balboa Street as the foghorns separated into minor thirds—a blast of blue notes to warn the world.

He'd throw on pants and a jacket and creep outside before first light, to some small adventure, only to sneak back under the covers again before his brother had to be shaken awake for school, poor Nathaniel cursing the world for robbing him of his sleep. Sometimes Ronnie walked to the end of Balboa, peeking into Playland at the Beach, a ghost town at that hour, with the flutter of pigeons and gulls, stutter-stepping through the morning debris as their voice boxes broadcast a coiled babble.

He'd sit against the ocean wall—as ships sailed to the Orient, and madmen, chugging from pocket bottles of port and sherry, crowded around a bonfire in a swell of laughter and indignant shouting—and think of Natty, safe in bed. It was hard to understand how a boy his same age needed twice the sleep.

Now Ronnie clears his throat and leans over to kiss Betty's cheek.

"What's the matter?" she says from an agitated corner of sleep.

"Not a thing, darling, but that's a funny question for someone who's just laid a kiss on you."

"Nice," she says, her eyes still closed, her face rounded by sleep, "that was nice."

Mr. Hearst

By a quarter after five Ronnie's showered and dressed. He halves a fat Texas grapefruit for Betty, cuts the fruit into sections, gives it a sprinkling of brown sugar. He scoops three measures of coffee into the bleached filter and sets the Mr. Coffee for 8:00 A.M. The bereft gurgle of the coffeemaker will be what wakes her. Ronnie packs his gear into the boot of the Alfa and returns to the doorstep for a look at the *Chronicle*. He studies the face of Randolph Hearst, Patty's father, a sad-looking fellow with large black-framed glasses like Clark Kent. Mr. Hearst doesn't look like a man who's ever been uncomfortable in his skin. Despite his money, and the power of the family name, the poor man cannot change into Superman to save his daughter.

Today he is willing to distribute two million dollars' worth of food to the poor to get his daughter back. Ronnie imagines Mr. Hearst in his cotton underwear, practicing composure in front of a floor-to-ceiling mirror, the electric shaver buzzing patiently around his chin. The man dabs on an aftershave he doesn't like: English Leather from Patty, a Father's Day ago. He really shouldn't blame himself. He's done nothing wrong. They keep telling him that. It is what he cannot do that is driving him crazy.

Secret Love

Before he's out of Half Moon Bay, Ronnie hears himself on the radio. "Secret Love," something he'd recorded twenty years ago, when he was in his late twenties. It wasn't a tune he'd wanted to record, because he couldn't get Doris Day's fetching rendition out of his head. He called it out at a ridiculously fast tempo and the band nailed it after a few takes, at which point the A&R decided he wanted a ballad. They took a break, got loaded, and did the song like a sweet spoof of Doris. The A&R asked him to sing a couple of choruses, so he stretched the lyrics wide enough for them to melt.

They make more of his singing, now, than his trumpet playing. But he's never been moved by his own voice. It's too easy to hear the con in it, the easy-does-it, the here's-what-you-want, baby, here's everything you could ever want. A man goes through his life and people miss his point. He cared about the trumpet, the sharp and blatty, hard-driving piston work of the horn. The utter impossibility of it. Sometimes he closes his eyes and sees three fingers working the valves. The fingerings as a secret code. He'd seen old trumpeters try to mask their finger combinations by dropping a handkerchief over the valve hand. He'd never done that. He wasn't a technician, he had nothing for anyone to steal. But he liked the image of the hanky, a weightless silk square fluttering over his workingman's fingers.

It's been more than five years since he's put away the trumpet, but he can't stop the tunes from drifting through. Sometimes he catches himself scatting in the shower, juking through the innards of a Tin Pan Alley ditty he wishes he could forget. Or he's sitting on his high stool at work, whistling four-bar riffs like a happy-go-lucky fool.

Back in the fifties, he went around with a girl who'd tried to teach him Zen meditation. "The only trick is to keep yourself from thinking, keep yourself from thinking, keep yourself from thinking." He'd never been much of a thinker, but just tell him that he couldn't and he became a thinking fool, stringing together all the lyrics he'd ever sung.

Some nights, Betty wakes him up from tortured singing-dreams. She shakes him lightly. Says, "Easy, Ronnie, easy now," as if he were driving too fast through the dark. And some nights he reaches into the gauze-light, wishing the silver trumpet were there.

He's tried to wean himself from stations that play jazz and keep the radio tuned to news. The idea is to imagine himself as a normal man or, at least, a facsimile thereof. That had been his goal when he ran off—to become a reasonable facsimile.

Ronnie mouths the final chorus of "Secret Love" over the top of his recorded relic, then catches his eyes in the rearview mirror, half-closed, full of feeling. Fucking crooner. To hell with it. He switches off the radio and keeps his eyes fixed on the centerline, like a man driving through a bad storm.

Flower Heart

Rae walks into the sleeping boy's room and listens to his breath hiss and lurch in swells. Quincy has always been an easy child. Despite the fitfulness of his sleep, if he were awakened he could easily fall back into his zone of active sleep. When he was an infant, she and Darnell woke him late at night, to play with or show off to a friend. They'd put him on a blanket on the floor where he'd gurgle pleasingly and go about the business of discovering his hands, and when they dropped him into his crib again he'd sing himself right back to sleep.

A doctor at the clinic told her she should have the boy's adenoids removed. He would sleep more comfortably. The doctor claimed it was a minor operation, but her catastrophic insurance wouldn't cover it. There was some consolation in having a problem in her life ruled out of the realm of catastrophe.

She bends over Quincy's red metal bed and looks into his brown face, the skin still puckered in sleep. She kisses him awake. "Happy birthday." She scoops his face into her arms. "Take a ride on your birthday?" He opens his eyes and stares blankly at his mother.

Ever since Darnell left, the boy opens his eyes hoping that her face will be his father's. Roused this morning from a deep enough sleep, Quincy's eyes register neither hope nor disappointment. For that she's grateful.

She and Quincy have each other, and that's about it. Wherever they go people stare at them. Shirtless men stroll arm in arm through the Castro, with earrings pierced through their nipples, but they don't seem as peculiar as a white woman holding the hand of a little brown boy. Straight white men either regard her as trash, or as a wayward creature worthy of their sympathy. Black guys look right through her, or pretend to know her— "Hey, how you doing, girl?"—as if the first thing on her mind is making more brown babies. To black women she is a pale vixen.

She lifts Quincy in a blanket and carries him to the car. He is small for four, with delicate features and long eyelashes that the delivery nurse said were too fine for a boy. Rae sets him down in the backseat and picks up her neighbor's *Chronicle* from the doorstep.

No news on Patty Hearst, but still a bevy of stories. Rae is less fascinated with the mysteries that surround Patty's captivity than with the show of grief by her confused boyfriend and father.

Teary in his stiff suit, the father is impressive. Until the kidnapping, he'd been able to live his entire life apart from the rabble. Rae wonders if he's ever had a ride on a public bus. Now he's required to declare his love for his daughter, and to offer a part of his fortune to get her back.

Rae doesn't like the looks of the boyfriend, Steven Weed. She doesn't mind his mustached handsomeness, but could you trust him? Has he really loved Patty, or was he only screwing her and fantasizing a spot for himself in the family empire?

Rae studies her sleeping boy, all creamy brown and cozy in the backseat, and starts the engine. She drives out Fell Street into the park. A giant heart and arrow, left over from Valentine's Day, is fashioned from primroses on a mound outside of the Conservatory. It is a city of love birds and broken hearts. She drives past Speedway Meadows, past the fenced-in buffaloes that you can't see from the car, and her favorite willow tree, at the chain of lakes. Even though it's cold, she rolls down the window, like the surfer boys do, as soon as she hits the ocean highway. She just doesn't let out a surfer's yelp.

Half an hour later, she parks in front of a bakeshop in Moss Beach called Heavenly Delights. Quincy is still asleep, so she locks the doors before hurrying in to get donuts.

Disarray

On her eighth birthday she walked too early into her parents' bedroom. Her father was just back from a long time on the road. He said he'd come back special for her birthday, but she wasn't sure she believed him. Life with her parents was always a matter of careful timing, and she never managed to be careful enough.

This time she dressed slowly. She pulled on a sock with a pink fringe, and softly sang a song to herself before pulling up the other. She strapped on her patent leather Mary Janes and sat at the foot of her bed for a long time brushing her hair.

Her parents' bedroom was in *disarray*. Her mother used the word often, as if she'd made peace with the condition and had no expectation of its changing.

"Things are in *disarray* here," she'd say to friends on the phone, "but come on over."

One of her mother's breasts sat atop the white sheet while she snored a sizzle of pressed air. Her father was a tight package under the covers. The room had the sour smell of old Chinese food. An assortment of glasses, and whiskey bottles, and containers of pills was scattered among the wobbly stacks of newspapers and magazines. Only her mother's mirrored tray of perfumes seemed immune to chaos—the small cut-glass bottles held their ground in quiet dignity. Rae looked at the face of a beautiful, sweet-as-a-daisy blond woman on the cover of a record album. The name Rosemary Clooney was printed in large red letters. It was the prettiest name she'd ever heard. Much prettier than her name, Florence Rae. Rosemary wore a white chiffon dress. As Rae counted the plastic spoons and forks and wooden sticks poking out of gooey take-out packs, she whispered, "Rosemary . . . Rosemary . . . Rosemary." Her father startled her. "What are you doing?"

"Nothing."

"What time is it, honey?"

She didn't know what time it was, but thought she might cry. Her father pulled the sheet over her mother's breast and sat up in the bed. Rae stood straight as a soldier, biting her lip. She watched his eyes open in stages, like a pair of bamboo shades being raised inch by inch up the face of the windows.

"How come you're all dressed up, honey?"

"It's my birthday."

"I know *that*, Rae. Hey, turn your back a sec."

She heard her father climb out of the bed.

"It's okay now," he said.

He had on his boxer shorts and looked a little like a bashful boy. He looked like anything could hurt him. Everybody said how handsome he was. He had the looks of a movie star, strong chin and high cheekbones. Her mother thought he was dreamier than Montgomery Clift, and called him Sweetness when she wasn't mad at him. Once she heard her mother say, "What are you going to do with all that sweetness?"

He winked back at her, "Spread it around?"

"Wrong answer," her mother said, whacking him playfully across the bottom.

"Save it for you?"

"That's right." She gave a little jump and went girlish, as he buried his lips in her neck.

Her father cleared a path through the clutter of newspapers and take-out packages. "This place is a disaster area."

"It's just in a little disarray," she said, mindful that her mother could wake at any moment.

Her father had two kind of moods, talkative and silent. He was like a store that kept strange hours. Some days everything would be bright and chatty. You'd barely have to push the door and it would swing open, and the man behind the counter would be lovely. He might say, "Come on in here, honey. How are you? Pick something out for yourself, whatever's mine is yours." Other times you could tell from a block away that the place was dark, and when you got up close a big old padlock hung like danger off the door. Only a fool would stand in front of that door and shake it when it was closed. It was scary to see her father like that.

He could sit for hours, hands and mind empty, on the living room sofa. Sometimes he smiled from that distance, but it was never a welcoming smile.

Friday the Bigamist

On the morning of her eighth birthday, her father grabbed two bottles of Coca-Cola from the fridge. They sipped Cokes while the streetlights were still on, driving out Turk Street in the Alfa the color of honey. It was a drizzly morning and there weren't many people out yet. Past Arguello, they cruised down Balboa and her father came alive, chattering about his old neighborhood.

"See there . . . see that over there. That's where my father used to have his hair cut. Beautiful place, I mean, for what it was. Half a dozen barber chairs going at once. Look at that dump now. What are they selling out of that dump? Hey, I kissed your mother on that corner . . . and that corner, and right there, and over there. See that building . . . that pink stucco job on the corner? I used to know a fella, a bass player that lived in the upper flat there. Can you imagine hauling a bass up all those stairs? He was a bigamist. You know what that is? A guy that's married to a couple of women at once. It's rare, but not uncommon." Her father laughed, flashing all his big, white teeth.

"See, it's an illegal thing. A man is only supposed to be married to one woman—like me and your mother. But some guys, they get all mixed up. It may start with a little lie that multiplies into a hundred. If you're going to commit this kind of crime you've gotta be clever. And this fella that I'm talking about—his name was Friday, by the way—wasn't so clever. He was living with one wife high up in the stucco flat on Third Avenue, and the other wife was stranded across the park on Kirkham. A fifteen-minute walk between the two. This does not show great intelligence. Suffice it to say the poor man was caught, and thrown out into the street with his bass."

Her father had an endless stream of stories about men and women she'd never meet, that perhaps nobody had met outside of the winding dash of his imagination.

Her mother tired of these stories. She called them his improvising. "Don't pay attention to what he's telling you now, he's just improvising." Rae liked his "improvising" because it was something, a story or a song, that he made for her.

Only once did she meet somebody he'd mentioned in a story, a small black man in a beret who walked into the poolroom at the musicians' union on Jones Street. Her dad hollered, "Well, look who's here," and introduced her to Junior Reese, the trumpeter who'd lost his lip. She'd always laughed to herself when he spoke about Junior Reese, because it seemed so odd, the idea of a trumpet player losing his lip. And here came Junior Reese with both of his lips, shouting back at her father, "Hey, Ronald, you got your girl here to show you how to shoot some pool?"

Her father started up again when they got out of the car. "Another funny thing about this Friday was the way he walked. Slow . . . as . . . a . . . dead . . . man . . . in . . . carpet slippers. He said it helped him remember who he was and which wife he was going to. I guess you better go slow if you're spending your life hauling a string bass back and forth across Golden Gate Park, from one wife to the other."

He grabbed her hand and led her on a hunched, dead man's walk toward the door of the Sugar Bowl Bakery. Then he sat her down at a table by the window and walked normal speed to the glass cases, where he whispered something to a pretty woman behind the counter. She watched her father follow the woman through a swinging door.

It was early yet, and there were no other customers in the bakery, except for a bleary-eyed paperboy with a transistor radio that played "The Monster Mash." The paperboy really seemed to know his way around the place. He dropped a couple of coins on the counter, poured himself a cup of instant cocoa, and chose a powdered-sugar donut from the cooling racks.

Rae put her head down on the table and fell asleep for a moment.

"Hey, sweetie girl," her father said in a voice like a warm hand on the side of her face. She looked up to see him standing between a baker and the counter woman, all three in giant chef hats. Her father held a cake lit with birthday candles. They sang "Happy Birthday," her father's sweet voice rising above the others. "Okay now," her father said, "time to make a wish."

Sand Dollars

Rae holds one of her son's hands and watches his bare feet pad out in front of him in the hard, glassy sand at the water's edge.

"It's nice to wake up at the ocean, Quincy. Don't you think? Especially on your birthday. I want you to always remember this birthday."

What is it, she wonders, that she wants the boy to remember? Living with a quiet child, she is always trying to fill the space. She can't help herself, and extends her arms toward the ocean. "I want you to remember this."

"Okay," he says, and kicks at a strip of seaweed that has gotten tangled around a couple of his bare toes.

The tide is out and, as they walk up the beach, Rae stoops among clusters of sand dollars. She picks them up, and brushes off each side to see if they are perfect. She's never seen so many perfect sand dollars at one time, and can't keep herself from stuffing them in the deep pockets of her canvas barn coat. At first she shows Quincy the sand dollars as she picks them up, but he seems indifferent to the lot of them, and runs ahead, poking with a long stick at washed-up jellyfish and dried sand crabs the size of his toenails.

The pockets of Rae's coat bulge with sand dollars. She's happy at her good fortune, and laughs out loud at herself—a young woman walking a slow dead man's walk at the ocean, her boy hollering in delight as he skips ahead of her, in and out of the white-water foam.

"What's in the bag?" Quincy asks.

"None of your business."

She leads Quincy away from the water and up, over mountains of soft sand, to a tarry log that had had an earlier life as a telephone pole. Sinking a crooked path through the sand, Quincy seems more a midget boy than he had at the edge of the ocean.

"Close your eyes now, honey," she says.

She lines up a couple of cupcakes on the log and drops four miniature candles into the cake closest to the boy. The first match blows out in the breeze. Quincy opens his eyes on the spectacle.

"Keep them closed."

He smiles at her, not mischievously, but with what seems a knowing pity, and then dutifully closes his eyes. After several efforts she is still unable to light the candles. She looks at Quincy, his eyes still closed, smiling in anticipation, and wonders if our eyes move under their lids when a memory is made, just as they do when we're dreaming.

Quincy's eyes open wide as she sings "Happy Birthday."

"You just have to pretend the candles are lit."

His cheeks puff immediately and he begins to blow.

"Hey, hey, hey, did you make your wish?"

Rae lets him eat two cupcakes and watches the smears of chocolate gather at the corners of his mouth. She pulls a few sand dollars from her pockets and lines them up on the center of the log.

"What is a sand dollar, Mama?"

"A kind of shell?"

"An animal does live inside it?"

"I s'pose so, honey," she says, wishing she knew something about the natural world.

"How do we know that it did die? How do we?"

"We're just pretty sure it's dead."

"But what if it's still alive?"

"Then we'll figure out a way of dealing with it."

"How?"

Rae doesn't answer. She gathers up their things and leads Quincy back over the dunes toward the car.

"Mama," he says, and tugs on her coat, "does hot lava come to this place? Does it?"

"No, not to this place."

Rae stares beyond the receding tide. An arched bank of fog sits forward like a big boy on the horizon's broad shoulders. She closes her eyes. After she leaves, this will be one of the moments *she* remembers.

The Letter

Ronnie shares a desire with Mr. Hearst—to be reunited with his own daughter. And yet, in the year he's been back in the Bay Area, he's made little effort to find her. Once, he called Rae's mother. It had been five years since they'd talked. She was a wreck. Cat. Catherine. She hollered at him on the phone, drunk at ten in the morning. He hung up on her. He'd once loved her more than the world.

During the first hour of his shift, Ronnie resolves to write her a letter of apology. For what? Running off? For ruining everybody's life? For hanging up on her as she slung drunken queries at him?

> *Dear Cat,*
> *I wanted to say . . .*

In the next half hour, he smokes half a dozen Viceroys and rips through a Value Pak of Red Hot gum. He chews each of twenty sticks deeply, but as soon as the sweet flare of cinnamon and sugar subsides, he wraps the spent sticks in foil and plunks them into a metal wastebasket.

> *Dear Cat,*
> *I've been meaning to write . . .*

Golfing Fools

Ronnie pushes the letter aside as the golfers come up to the starter's shack, in twos and threes, to pay their money and get their time. The golfers are like big boys, no matter how aged and calcified they've become, decked out in their oranges and kelly greens, showing off their paraphernalia, brimming with chatter and false optimism in the idle moments before they tee off. The only pleasure to be gained from these characters comes after hours, when Ronnie, allowed to play the course, hustles a few dollars from the regulars who like to be hustled.

Ronnie is alone most of the day in the starter's hut, a soulless

shack with nothing but a cash register, a telephone, and a radio.
The sound of the scratchy public address speakers surrounds him
with his own voice, not lyric crooning but the barking out of
foursomes: "All right, we have Smith, Hendrickson, Swoboda,
and Sawyer on the tee . . . Rose, Williams, Burroughs, and
Cartier on deck . . . and in the hole, it's Hooper, Groaty, Quirk,
and Reasnor."

Ronnie is expected to pass as a member of their tribe, from
the lower order. He is supposed to embody the chipper, all-is-
right-in-the-world motto of golfers everywhere, to carry on like
a certifiable bawdy-boy, with a treasury of please-pass-the-salt-
and-pecker jokes.

But he's always hated golfers. As a boy the game came easily
to him, and his father forced him to play every Saturday with
parties of grown men. The idea was to give him seasoning, to
teach him about the everyday culture of the game. The men
gasped over the pint-sized kid who had a short game like
an angel and could drive his Maxfli out beyond theirs. He was
well mannered, like a boy singer with a god-given talent. He
studied the men—each a compound of tobacco and sweat, good
cheer and temper, preening and deference, high manners and
coarseness—until his fear of them turned to a recognition of
their weaknesses, and he saw the way each of them could be
beaten as a golfer, and as a man.

The Father

Ronnie studied his father as closely as anything in his life, but he
never understood the man. Years later, well after his father was
gone, it occurred to him that the measure of a man corresponded

to his enthusiasms, and Roger Reboulet, called Rust for his red hair, had none. Of course, there were isolated moments of excitement—when he brought home a new style of beer in a package of six, or took the boys to a ball game at Seals Stadium, or the strange night he strolled in with free tickets to *Salome*. But could a man live sixty years in this world and find nothing that gave him sustained pleasure?

Rust Reboulet was a small, wiry man with a double-jointed body always twisted into an ungainly position, so that he looked as if he were on his way somewhere even when he stood stock-still. And he was always on his way. He could fix anything. Could take apart a broken watch or the motor from a Frigidaire and get it running again. He could wire a house, plumb it, put a new roof on it.

He was a housepainter by trade, a union man, who lurched around on a scaffold with frightful abandon. There were times when Ronnie, bringing a forgotten lunch box by a painting job, spotted his father three stories up, bobbing without a safety, one foot on a windowsill, one in midair. He was in a world of his own. Another painter on the job would spot Ronnie and holler up to his father, "Hey, Reboulet. . . . Frenchie, your kid's here!"

For the longest time, Ronnie was certain his father would die falling from a scaffold. (It turned out to be a ladder, years later, when a heart attack persuaded him to change direction between the scaffolds of a stucco house in the Marina.) But in the years that Ronnie lived with him, his father arrived safely back home by 3:30 in the afternoon.

Rust Reboulet would change into his khakis and yellow slicker, and recruit Ronnie, never pale Nat, to haul his clubs around the hilly course, as he played a half-dozen sour holes of golf before dinner, cursing the wind and the fog, cursing the stupid duffers on the next hole who thought, because they paid to play, they could dawdle, cursing Roosevelt and taxes and his French Canuck papa for abandoning him and his mama in 1908, cursing the ocean for being so damn beautiful that it made him lose his concentration.

If Rust Reboulet had any enthusiasm it was for his twin sons, and when Nat, the loyal one, the one who looked like he might amount to something, dropped dead, at twelve years old, shooting baskets in the rocky alley, Rust Reboulet zipped the last flap of his tent. He had reservations about his surviving son, Ronald, the one with the strong heart, that everyone took to calling Ronnie, a moniker better suited for a sweet, sucking candy than a boy or a man. Ronald was made for trouble, any dumb fool could see that. The boy had a nice touch on the golf course, but it came too easily for him. Everything came too easily for him.

Rust Reboulet devoted his excess energy, and there was plenty of it, to molding Ronald into a championship golfer. By fifteen, the boy's short game was like radar and he could outscore nearly everyone in the city and county of San Francisco. If he wanted to blow his silver trumpet a little on the side, that was all right, as long as it didn't interfere with his golf game. After he won the All City tourney, Ronnie saw a glimmer in his father's eye. Rust Reboulet talked about taking the boy on the road, playing him in a few tournaments around the state, to get the boy's feet wet. The day before they were to drive the new Hudson out to Stockton, he told his father no. He was sixteen years old. Two months later, small as he was, he got himself into the army.

The Nineteenth Hole

As soon as he walks into the Nineteenth Hole, Jeanette, a round-faced waitress who's barely climbed out of her teens, brings him two crumb donuts, a thermos of coffee, and a glass of ice water with a floating sliver of lemon.

He and Jeanette carry on a benign flirtation—she blushes whenever he says anything to her, and he acts courtly in return. Her blushing aside, she is a smart young woman, reading whenever she has a minute. Standing, sitting, leaning over a counter, she is always holding a beat-up paperback that's been dipped in dishwater or catsup. What else is she going to do? Make small talk with a bunch of nickel-and-dime tippers in a tacky clubhouse? So she reads.

Ronnie's always been taken with serious readers, folks whose posture has been altered by having spent so many hours staring at a string of words. He reads the newspaper or the racing form once in a while. He's always loved words and used to keep a dictionary around the house for deciphering smart-guy lyrics. At one time, he read poetry. Not a lot. He carried a little book in his trumpet case. Charlie Parker did that. Ronnie found poetry almost as easy to memorize as song lyrics.

But books, he could never sit still long enough to read a regular book. He used to try and imagine the lives of readers, and figures this young woman must have something special blooming on the other side of her book. He's surprised by the interest she takes in him. But, Lord knows, he isn't looking for puppy love. All he has to do is subtract her age from his.

Subtraction has become his most common exercise. In 1956, and again in '59, he scratched days and weeks from short prison terms. Now he subtracts spent years from life expectancy, fallow years from those that might have been productive. His mind has become a calculator, deducting the distance of his tee shots from the yardage left to the hole. All he ever seems to add are afterthoughts. The things he should have said or done. He learned an old idiom in Paris: *Idée de l'escalier*. The idea on the stair. The thought that occurred to you too late. The meaning you wished you had conveyed. He nods toward Jeanette and she comes up to his table and gives the coffee thermos a little shake.

"How's this holding up?"

"Fine." She has a pretty face, with the taut, scarred skin of an acne survivor. He must have a good twenty-five years on her.

"So what do you hear from Patty Hearst?"

"Not much, Ronnie. For some reason she didn't call last night."

"She must have been out partying. No, I think it was her bowling night."

Jeanette laughs. "Bowling. You're funny, Ronnie. Anything else I can get you?"

He shakes his head. The room is nearly quiet. A solitary golfer reading the *Chronicle* sips coffee at the counter. A puff of Muzak, or the infernal sound of KFOG, drifts through the room like a damp and sorry climate. Mantovani plays "Hi Lili, Hi Lili, Hi Low." Music this lush might kill people, like ants drowning in sugar, if they actually listened.

Jeanette has been hanging by his table. "You okay, Ronnie?"

"Oh, yeah." He smiles at her, flashing his false teeth, a picture of high cheer. A golfer's smile.

You've Changed

Back at the shack, he wants to be wrapped in something familiar, and switches on KJAZ, turning the volume high enough to blast the golfers coming by his window to pay their money and get their time. Dexter Gordon's stately tenor fills the starter shack. Dexter-man blowing "You've Changed"—a statuesque solo of rising arpeggios, wanting to break your heart with its soaring.

You've changed . . .
That sparkle in your eyes is gone.

Ronnie shrugs to the golfers, as if to say, *Ain't it a bitch the way this radio's gone out of control.*

"You've changed" . . . it used to be Billie Holiday's song. Dexter knows that. You can't play the song without playing it as a tribute to Billie. He knows that it's a junkie's song more than a love song. When you're a junkie, everybody's watching, asking questions. Has she changed? Can she change? Will she change? What happens if she doesn't change? Billie changed every time she sang it. Dexter changes whenever he plays it. Ronnie Reboulet's changed for good—he doesn't sing or play anything.

That's the way his mother changed. She didn't have a habit, except for sitting down most nights at the basement piano and singing a few traditionals. But when Natty died she stopped singing, and only went to the basement to do laundry.

It wasn't much of a piano, an Everett upright with a few chipped ivories, but she took good care of it, had a bald-headed man come out to tune it every six months. Every Saturday she gave each boy a little cup of milk and a dipping rag to clean the ivories. They started at either end and planned to meet at middle C. Natty liked to bang up from the bottom, but Ronnie milked his way down the keys quietly, only letting himself strike every sixth or seventh note, trying to hear the bottom of each wide interval before he played it.

His mother had a lovely voice, a warm, head voice with just a trace of vibrato. But she sang sad songs, or so they seemed to Ronnie, even when she may have been her happiest.

He used to wonder what happened to her voice when she stopped singing. Was it like the notes in the piano that he chose not to play, that he could hear without playing?

It isn't particularly cold in the starter's shack, but he puts on his heavy pea coat. He'd like to bundle into the car with the waitress Jeanette and drive. It is that simple. He has no desire for her. He would swear to that in a court of law. He wants to drive with the music up high, and pull over at a turnout by the ocean and ask if he can put his head in her lap, if she will hold him.

The dope had been a long cashmere coat with a silk lining. Sometimes he misses it like it was his mother. The stream of well-being coming through the open door. The way it held him and kept him warm. The quiet efficiency of the thing, not bothering with talk, or the endless chatter everywhere, the yap yap yap that follows every song on the radio, the damn chatter while you try to play in a club, all the chatter about nothing, a supermarket of chatter, the constant chatter that seems the highest price you have to pay for living in this world.

Oh, Betty

"An old junkie will give you a hundred reasons why he used the stuff," he'd told Betty when she first started going out with him. "But there's nothing romantic about it," he said, and went on to make it sound romantic. "A dope fiend will tell you whatever you want to hear. Dial up as much poetry in the telling as you'd like. One thing for sure, the glories of being clean make a bad story. Don't talk to a junkie about that. Don't call him cured unless you're handing over some money so he can go out and get high. Only hams are cured. That's the truth. If you stud a junkie with a handful of cloves he'll figure out a new way to get high. Better to call him lapsed, like a man who's temporarily given up his membership, who no longer subscribes, who's forgotten a little part of his original religion, but who's always ready and willing, with the slightest nudge, to join up again. Clean or not, he'll never stop hustling you. Like, right here—with one hand I'm warning you, pushing you away, but with the other I'm pulling you closer. Pretty soon, I've messed you up so bad, you don't have a choice but to stay."

"Don't be so sure," she said.

"Oh, I'm not sure of anything."

Five years now, she's stayed. She bought him a three-year-old Alfa Romeo, a gorgeous machine the color of a juicy blood orange. Gave up a good nursing job in a Tampa hospital. Moved away from her native Florida to live a nomad's life. She'd done her best to make a home, with curtains and tiny glass containers filled with dry herbs and spices. She'd fed him cubes of sugar as if he were a horse, and watched him gum them into liquid; baked countless cakes and pies. She helped him stay clean, petted him, stole dope from the hospital to tide him over, left him space to pout, asked no questions unless invited. When he decided he wanted nothing to do with music, she stopped singing in the shower. She made love to him in the middle of the night when he couldn't sleep, and gave up sex when he lost interest. She played cribbage and Scrabble and rummy, rubbed his back with hippie massage oil that smelled like old berries, softened his feet in the bath with a pumice stone. She taught him manners, like he was a man that grew up in a cave, which was close enough to the truth, the way his mother let things go after Natty died.

Manners, Betty once told him, are nothing more than treating people with respect. And if you're cool, you learn to do it with a little style. He thought of some of the black musicians he'd played with—Bird and Hampton Hawes and Dexter—who all had a courtliness passed down from their mothers. They were little black church boys grown up, dressed in their Sundays for a whole lifetime; dead-gone junkies who always seemed to have a clean handkerchief sticking out of their coat pocket. They could talk enough trash—motherfucker this and motherfucker that— to make you want to bury your head in sand for the quiet. But let a lovely woman walk into the room, or an older person deserving respect, and they'd turn to sugar.

Ronnie went to school at the table with Betty. A lapsed junkie, with a new set of choppers, he learned how to chew his food with a closed mouth, to look at her as she spoke, to excuse himself before leaving the table. He was devoted to Betty. He told her how lovely she was, left her little notes around the house, brought her flowers, sang her a song he'd written twenty years before. Only two things about Betty wearied him: her goodness, and the fact that she could see straight through him.

Bird

A Charlie Parker tune comes on the radio: "Bird of Paradise." Young Miles blows the faintest fanfare—a breathing thought, a pencil line of sound, elegant and perfectly deferential. Bird bursts onto the scene, brash yet intimate, his broad, burnished alto burning a fevered rash, a streaking ripeness that breaks time into a vapor of sound, until he smacks his line back to the simple beat, and slowly bends a note, and you can breathe again, realizing that he's only playing the blues.

The first time Ronnie heard him, Bird had just gotten into town and was auditioning trumpeters for his West Coast swing. Ronnie had gone down to the club reluctantly—he really wasn't able to wrap his mind around the idea. He stood in the crowded doorway of the Blackhawk, gasping as Bird pitched a swell of notes into the room and called them back again to circle in a perfectly staggered formation. He was like a boy on the roof commanding a flock of pigeons.

Somebody must have mentioned Ronnie, because Bird called him out of the crowd, in a funny French accent, "Is Ronnie Reboulet here?" He slunk up to the bandstand with his silver trumpet, a pint-sized white boy in a borrowed sport coat, the sleeves reaching halfway up his thumbs, and moon-faced Bird, his kinky hair glistening with sweat in the stage lights, counted "Scrapple from the Apple" at a rocket tempo.

There wasn't time for dread to set in. He stood beside Charlie Parker, forcing an open-faced blast through the bell. He didn't have the confidence yet to blow as quietly as Miles—he needed to establish himself.

After he blew a chorus, Bird said, "You've got some sweet apples, Reb," and played a regal solo himself, a rosy desert flower bursting open in the room. A couple of songs later, Ronnie had gotten comfortable and blew a lilting solo on "Star Eyes." Bird laughed through the piano chorus, and said, "I'm telling you, you're the eighth wonder of the world."

Ronnie blew a quiet obligato à la Miles, as Bird took "Star Eyes" out with neon brightness.

Bird paused after finishing, and Ronnie thought he was about to be dismissed from the stage.

But Bird said, "Hey, Reb, you know a place where we can get a nice chicken dinner?"

"When?"

"Right now."

When Charlie Parker bowed to an audience he seemed to nod to every soul in the room. "Thank you so much. You're very kind. Exceedingly kind. At this time . . . nature, being what it is . . . we are obliged to heed it. Which is to say . . . it's only a slight ache, and we'll be right back after the break."

As Charlie Parker walked off, somebody shouted, "You coming back, Bird?" And Bird, the horn still hanging from his neck, turned back to the crowd, opened his arms like St. Francis himself, and said, "In . . . dub . . . it . . . tab . . . ly."

A minute later, he and Bird were out the back door of the club, cabbing the fifteen blocks to Grisson's House of Chicken on Van Ness. Bird was a man who knew what he wanted. He bowed to the maitre d' and handed him a five-dollar bill. "Maestro, would you be so kind as to seat my worthy associate and me as close to the chickens as you can."

And when the put-upon waitress finally got to their table, Bird caught her eye. He seemed to sympathize with her plight—having to work a room full of swells and old ladies expecting to be pampered, then turning around to serve this mixed-race dog and pony show.

"Nice of you to come by, my dear. I see that you serve your chickens by the half. Would you kindly bring us four halves. We need to get some flesh on this poor fella's bones."

With all the excitement, Ronnie had lost any appetite he might have had, and watched Bird carve his way through three of the chicken halves. The man was amazingly dexterous with a fork and knife, and didn't even consider picking up a piece of chicken in his hands.

Ronnie finally worked up his nerve to ask Bird when he might choose his trumpeter. And Bird started laughing.

"You're shitting me, Ronald. Who do you think *you* are? Why do you think I'm buying you this motherfucking chicken dinner that you aren't even eating? You better have yourself at least a little piece of this chicken to consummate the marriage. I'd hate to leave behind this bird, but I don't subscribe to no motherfucking doggy bags, not when I'm wearing a good suit."

Pretty soon a young white woman recognized Bird, and started waving. She pulled a girlfriend with her over to their table.

"Are you really Charlie Parker?" she said.

"Matter of fact . . ." Bird said, and flashed his boyish cheek-to-cheek smile.

"Oh, I heard you were in town."

Bird shook hands and signed a couple of autographs.

He gestured toward Ronnie. "Surely, you must know this beautiful young man. He's the golden one, your native son."

The girlfriend looked over at Ronnie and bit her lip.

"He is pretty, isn't he?" Bird said, pulling a twenty-dollar bill from his wallet, "but you must excuse Monsieur Ronnie

Reboulet, my tuneful associate and me, regretfully we must return to an earlier engagement."

"TURN THAT SHIT DOWN!"

Ronnie looks up to see the fat face of Reg Garheart, the club pro, filling the starter window.

"That's not shit," Ronnie says flatly, as he recognizes Charlie Rouse, running a mild tenor solo over Monk's "Pannonica."

Reg Garheart is waving his Ping putter. "What the hell you doing, Reboulet? You been juicing or something? Can hear this shit out far as the ninth green."

Ronnie flicks off the radio. From all to nothing but the chatter of golfers and Reg Garheart's simple face in his window. Ronnie turns toward his microphone. It is always better to contribute to the din than to be the sole person absorbing it.

"We've got Ebinger, Stewart, and two Herreras on the tee; Scott, Marshall, Hobby, and Stinger on deck; in the hole it's Jacobs, Rabinowitz, Asher, and Haas."

The Art of Hustling

Ronnie is standing on the seventh tee with a big fuck named Harter who slices everything out of the lot. He's always enjoyed playing with the big guys: Nothing bothers them more than having a little man take their money. The jumbo fellows will wager on anything—who can dig the deepest divot on a ninety-yard pitch, or drill the tightest fade on a dogleg right. And when you finally let yourself whack a drive a few yards past theirs, with a hundred bucks riding on it, you break their backs, you make them cry.

His round with Harter began innocently enough—Ronnie

won several five-dollar holes and a few side bets, and managed to lose a couple. Things were as predictable as pudding. He'd never have guessed that Harter would leave the eighth hole a dead man.

On the seventh tee they both light cigarettes as they wait on the foursome ahead of them. Ronnie pulls a comb out of his pocket and drags it back through his greased, sandy hair. He's always made a point of keeping his hair neat. He likes combing it back through the thicker tines because then his hair takes on the rugged look of wide-wale corduroy.

Betty always tells him how much she likes his hair. She's even got a theory about it.

"It's clear you wear your hair the way you want it, and that's good. Getting older, it's important to show your intentions, or at least create the illusion that you have a plan."

"Yep," he says, not bothering to tell her that he's worn his hair like this since he was a teenager.

Harter sneers at him: "Hey, Reboulet, you got some money invested in Brylcreem?"

"Vitalis."

"Greasy kid's stuff."

"Each to his own, I guess."

Harter, impatient, sits back in the golf cart, tilts over onto one fleshy buttock, and passes a booming trail of gas.

"Indigestion," he offers by way of apology.

"You don't say."

The first rule when hustling a fool is to never get greedy, to take only what's offered. The second is to respect your man's arrogance and find benign ways of feeding it. Ronnie overcomes his desire to call the man Farter, instead of Harter, because it won't serve his purpose. He tries to engage his man in conversation.

"So what do you make of the latest Patty Hearst business? I'm impressed that the old man's willing to give away a couple million bucks to get her back."

"That money's nothing," Harter says, "it's a drop in the bucket. Anyway, I think she's set up the whole fucking thing."

"How do you mean?"

Harter looks irritated. He slouches down in the golf cart, lights up a smoke, coughs, then lobs a mouthful of phlegm toward the bushes.

"She's a clever little bitch, just trying to drag the old man through the mud."

Patty Hearst is a simple victim, as far as Ronnie can tell, but he isn't about to argue with Harter. Ronnie drops his Titlist into a ball washer and corkscrews it through the suds and brushes a few times. He finds himself thinking of Rae all the time now. He can't quite imagine what she looks like. She's darker than Patty Hearst. Beautiful like her mother.

Harter has finally hit a ball down the center of the fairway. He stands majestically before the ball and bellows, "Fifty dollars, I put it on the green."

Ronnie nods. Harter hasn't hit a green yet. This time the five iron spins in the fat man's hands and he shanks the ball into the spiky ice plant. He tosses the club twenty-five feet up a pine tree.

"Aw, fuck!" Harter shouts, and kicks at one of the cart's tires a couple of times.

Ronnie grabs a nine iron and walks toward the fairway trap where his orange ball sits nicely in the sand like a sunny-side-up yolk. He wonders what it would be like to go through life as an oversize character like Harter, a foolish fuck who can never keep his shirt tucked in. The big man, less his five iron, has dug himself a seventy-five-dollar hole, while Ronnie's ball is plattered nicely in the sand.

Harter scoots up in the cart. "Why do you play those ugly orange balls?"

"The eyes aren't what they used to be."

"Twenty bucks, you can't put it on the green."

Ronnie nods. He likes having a guy try to psych him out. Especially this guy. He thinks of blasting his ball over the green to offer Harter a little momentum with which to destroy himself on the back nine. But as he settles into the bunker, Ronnie forgets that he's hustling and pops it out cleanly, six or seven feet from the hole.

"Hey, Reboulet," the big man asks on the eighth tee, "when's the last time you cracked a smile?"

"I believe it was during the Eisenhower era. Not much of a golfer, Ike. Lots of pomp and circumstance. He brought a smile to my face. Matter of fact, he had a slice something like yours."

"Fuck you, you little prick." Harter pulls out his wallet.

"You don't have to pay now, Harter. I'm sure my luck's about to go to the dogs."

"I'm not sticking around, you bastard."

Harter counts the ninety-five dollars he owes and drops the bills so that they flutter on either side of one of the white blocks that mark the eighth tee. "There's your money."

"Hand it to me, Harter."

"Fuck you."

Ronnie thinks about driving a rabbit punch into Harter's fat throat. "Pick the money up, Harter."

"Shit," Harter mutters, and looks around to see if the threesome approaching the seventh green has a savior among them.

"You waiting for an audience?"

"I'm going to get your ass fired."

"Pick up the fucking money, Harter, and hand it to me."

"You goddamn bastard," the fat man shouts.

Harter's face turns as blank as a block of yellow cheese. He bends over with a grunt and passes gas once more, then seems to hang for a second in mid crouch, the air around him fouled, as he topples forward, collapsing directly onto the white block, forcing enough air from his chest to keep a normal man alive for a moment, but this one's dead as soon as he hits the ground.

He should have seen it coming. But who expects a man, half the size of the clubhouse, to collapse before he's had his supper? As Ronnie's luck would have it, a five-dollar bill rises like a feather while the larger denominations lie pinned under

Harter's oversize body. Ronnie considers turning the fat man over, not in hopes of saving him—he is clearly dead—but to free up the rest of the money that has killed him. Instead, he waves his driver in a mad circle above his head, and hollers, "HEART ATTACK!" The three guys putting out on seven jump at once. Two scramble to their carts, the third hauls ass up the hill to the eighth tee.

"What's going on, Reboulet?" shouts Bob Macey, the running man, a husky old plumber, panting on the tee under his Giants cap.

"Turn him over," commands Zack, a wiry man in a green parka, who stands straight up in the cart as it zips to the scene.

"He's dead," Ronnie says.

Zack and Macey and Macey's teenage boy bend down and press on Harter's torso. A couple of twenties pop up from under his thick shoulders. Ronnie forces himself to look into Harter's fleshy face which, muddied and grass-stained, appears, in death, less empty of character.

"What's his name?" Zack asks.

"Harter."

"Family?"

Ronnie shakes his head in ignorance. He takes a deep breath, inhaling great draughts of cut grass, pine, and eucalyptus.

The Dead

He was at school the day his brother died, and he didn't get to
see him until he was in his coffin. Natty's pale white skin was
shaded a waxy peach, but he appeared strangely alert, even if he
was dead, in a starched summer suit that he'd never owned. He
looked like the picture of health in a horror film, or a man-child
who was about to be sent door to door, by his grandaddy, to sell
little newspapers praising the Lord. They told him that Natty had
died shooting baskets in the rocky alley. But Natty never shot
baskets. Sickly and small, he was not a sports boy. That week
he'd been home in bed with German measles. They said he
snuck out to the garage hoop while their mother was napping.
He wanted to see what it was like, they told him, to launch a
jump shot.

Ronnie remembers the hands and shoes of the first fresh dead
man he saw, a drummer named Spence who sat in after hours
some nights, laid out in an alley behind the Tin Star, with a
cashmere coat over his face. Ronnie had gone back to cop
between sets and here was this dude Spence with his enormous
pair of black-man hands, fat rings on every other finger, a coat
over his face, and a pair of brown wingtips, shined but without
laces. Ronnie stood in the alley, getting anxious about where he
was going to cop, yet fascinated with Spence's wingtips. What
the hell happened to his laces? Had the dude gone out of his
house without laces? Did he buy the shoes off somebody that
way? Was that his chosen style? If it was, Ronnie had never
noticed. He stood there musing until Hobie Rodgers, the manager of the Tin Star, came out the back door and hollered at him

to get the hell out of there before the police came. He wandered down Ellis Street into the Tenderloin, cold without a coat, looking for dope.

Ronnie stands beside the plumber, Macey. The plumber's son, a teenager with long, blond hair pulled back neatly in a ponytail, stands off by himself whimpering.

"What's all this money doing floating around here?" Macey asks.

There were now four twenty-dollar bills on the loose.

"He was paying off a bet."

"To you?"

"Yeah."

"Better pick it up."

Ronnie looks over at Macey and then at Macey's son, who is crying openly. "His first dead?"

"I s'pose it is."

The plumber walks over to his son and lays a hand on his shoulder.

Ronnie stands apart from the father and son, as the late afternoon fog, a visible shroud that neither drops from the sky nor rises from the ground, deepens around them.

Inquisition

"Was he always my grandpa, was he?" Quincy asks when they get back into the car in Santa Cruz.

"That's right," she says, and begins humming some nameless ballad, trying to discourage the next spurt of questions.

"How could he be my grandpa if I never did meet he? How could he?"

"That's the way things work when people go away."

"How come he did go away?"

"I'm not sure."

"Did he know my dad?"

"No."

Quincy's small face is twisted with urgency. "How come I never did meet he?"

"Because he was gone."

"How come?"

Rae shakes her head. "I don't know, sweetie."

"Did he see me when I was a baby? Did he?"

"No, but I'm sure he wanted to."

Corn Dogs and Fries

Rae had driven down to Santa Cruz for the famous roller coaster which she'd always heard about but had never seen, as a special treat for Quincy on his birthday. She parked as close to the roller coaster as she could get. To Quincy, drowsy from the car ride, the massive steel structure loomed like the beginning and end of the world. He curled into a ball in his seat.

"What's the matter, honey?"

"Hold me, Mama."

He wanted no part of the amusement park. "It's got too many things," he said.

"Are you hungry?"

He rubbed his eyes.

"What do you feel like eating?"

"A cold meat sandwich."

"How about a corn dog?"

"What's a corn dog?"

She walked Quincy into the pavilion and ordered corn dogs, fries, and root beer, and held Quincy up so he could see the man swirl the hot dogs on sticks through corn batter and drop them into the hot oil. Quincy made a lisping sound like snakes as the corn dogs cooked.

Rae spread a blanket on the beach and watched him eat, a little man going about his business, dipping french fries into a big splat of ketchup on a square of wax paper. He chewed his way slowly down his cooled corn dog, never straying far from his root beer straw which seemed to double as a lifeline.

Rae had no appetite. She hummed a song her father used to sing to her, and told Quincy about him, that he was a singing man who played a trumpet.

"He went away like your daddy, except he left a long time ago."

A few months after he left, her father started sending money orders, in brown Western Union envelopes with a window cut in them where her mother's name and address appeared. The money orders were almost always for a hundred dollars, never for more. Her mother complained as she tore open the envelopes.

"Hey, sweetness, how about a cost-of-living raise?" Cat shook the money order from the envelope. "Bastard sends me cigarette money."

Her mother hoped for something else to fall out of the envelope, but he never sent a note or return address. Sometimes the money order, signed Ronnie Reboulet, R. Reboulet, Reb Reboulet, R. Reb, sat on her bureau for days. Rae was more interested in the ripped envelope, postmarked Kansas City, MO, Austin, TX, Baton Rouge, LA, Mobile, AL. She wondered how he knew that they were still at the Jackson Street apartment. Cat said he was not a man to send his money to the wind. Then half a year passed, and nothing. Her mother said good riddance, until the money orders started coming again from Florida. Now, after all this time, he calls.

Half Moon Bay, CA

Bunker Avenue is a block of humble bungalows, two streets from the beach. Rae parks beside a grey Plymouth Duster, out front of number 65, a small, white A-frame with a pair of window boxes, one filled with red geraniums, the other scattered with a mix of bright tuberous begonias, fire orange and pink and canary yellow. The two open windows are covered with witty curtains, flecks of red checkering their way across the sand-colored fabric, as if the designer had made her marks with a shaker of hot sauce. The curtains balloon like a skirt in the breeze of the open window. Rae sits in the car a minute and watches a woman peek out at them from behind one of the curtains.

Quincy asks, "Is this where grandpa does live?"

"I think so . . . I think that's grandpa's house."

She leads the boy out of the car and before they can get to the concrete steps, a woman in her mid- to late forties, a graceful woman with high cheekbones, stands in the doorway.

"How do you do?"

"Hello, ma'am. I'm Rae Reboulet and this is my son, Quincy." She wonders what the woman makes of the two of them—the little brown boy with his bushy, caramel blond hair who, despite her best efforts at brushing him down, must look like a sweet pastry that's been rolled in sand, and herself, an apparition with a toothy smile, half hidden in her washed-out barn coat—coming to call.

"You're Ronnie's daughter," the woman says, not unfriendly.

"Yes, I am. We've come to say hello."

"He should be back soon. Oh, he's going to be very glad to see you."

"Thank you." Rae laughs at the picture of herself with Quincy, standing before this regal woman. Quincy hides his face and pulls on his mother's coat as she tries to remain calm.

"Quincy is a little shy."

"Hello, Quincy. Would you like to come in? I'm Betty Millard." The woman reaches a hand out to Rae.

"Pleased to meet you, Betty."

"Well, I'm pleased to meet both of you."

Betty leads her guests into the kitchen, and invites them to sit at one of the red counter stools.

Once Quincy is in place, dangling his legs from a stool, he fixes a suspicious glance on Betty, and mumbles a dozen words so closely on top of one another that she doesn't have any idea what he's saying.

"Pardon me?"

"Betcha don' know wha' day is."

"No, I don't."

"My birthday."

"You're kidding."

"Ask she," he says, pointing to his mother.

"How old are you?"

Quincy closes both fists into balls. He will not hold up fingers. "Four years ole."

"How about some ice cream to help you celebrate your birthday?"

Quincy mugs to his mother.

Rae nods. "That's kind of you."

She studies Betty as she pulls open the small freezer compartment of her fridge. The woman is a little younger than her mother and far better preserved. She's taken care of herself.

"I've got chocolate chip and strawberry, peppermint and rocky road. See, we like ice cream in this house. Ronnie Reboulet happens to a have a mouthful of sweet teeth."

Save Our Fake Rocks

As they drive up Skyline Boulevard, Ronnie finds a certain comfort in the deepening fog. Jeanette is tense in the seat beside him. She's been quiet since he told her about Harter. A couple of times he's thought of putting on the radio. Does she feel like a kidnap victim? Patty Hearst herself, obliged to ride off with a strange man in his Italian car? He opens his window, letting the fog and salt air creep in, as Jeanette looks out into her own whiteness.

"You're not cold, are you?"

"No, I'm fine."

He drives up Great Highway, past Fort Funston, a heap of sand dunes and ice plant, reminding him of Fort Ord, on Monterey Bay, where he'd been forced to run around with a rifle performing military exercises, a couple of lifetimes ago. He remembers the weight of his boots, and the way his legs ached. Despite chewing five packs of Juicy Fruit a day, he'd carried a certain metallic taste in his mouth that he counted as rage. Rage to be thrown out there, one more fool with a rifle. Nobody told him this would happen. 1947. Peacetime. A trumpet player signed up for the military band. What the hell was he doing out there? No reason but to break him.

Ronnie wonders what it is that's making Jeanette so tense. The dead man? Being alone with a man the age of her father?

"Go for a drink?"

"Sure," she says, "but it probably shouldn't be a very fancy place, I'm still in my uniform."

Ronnie drives along the open strip between the ocean and the fenced-in dunes, where Playland used to stand. On the beach side is Kelly's Cove, home of a thousand early morning bonfires. He points to his right.

"This used to be Skateland at the Beach. And right next to it over here was a Mexican restaurant called the Bull Pup. It had a take-out window and people would come out from skating, or run over from the beach and order enchiladas. Everybody stood in front of that window squirting hot salsa out of old ketchup containers. It wasn't until I was about fifteen, and I'd been eating take-out at the Bull Pup for years, that I realized the window was connected to an actual restaurant, and that you could go in and sit down. This was a real revelation—there was another class of people inside the Bull Pup. I wondered why anyone would want to sit inside this place when you could stand at that window, dripping salsa on your bare chest, and look across at the ocean. It kind of ruined the place for me."

As he drives the twisting hill to the Cliff House, Ronnie notices that the false mountain has survived. The mountain, constructed decades before to limit erosion and to civilize the steep dunes spilling down from Sutro Park, looked like a tunnel from a Lionel train set. When the wrecking crew came to level Playland, Ronnie noticed that some hippie had spray-painted the bald face of the mountain, in a lurid orange, with the words SAVE OUR FAKE ROCKS.

A Saucer of False Teeth

After Quincy is set up in the TV nook, Betty leads Rae into the living room, a tidy space with coved ceilings, a black leather love seat, and an E Z Boy rocker, covered in a plush forest green corduroy. Rae doesn't want to get too comfortable and opts for the wicker side chair. She looks around the room for some trace of her father.

"He sits in the rocker," Betty offers.

Rae nods, nonplussed by her circumstance. Is she supposed to ask this woman questions, or offer reasons for why she's come? She bites her lip and listens to Quincy's laughter coming from the other room.

"He's a doll."

Rae nods. She couldn't begin to say why she's here.

"Ronnie should be home anytime. He had a golf game . . . but anytime. And then I get going to work. We're like a couple of ships passing . . ."

Rae stands. "We'll leave."

"No, please . . . can I get you anything . . . coffee?"

Rae shakes her head. She looks into the older woman's face. Betty has moist, brown eyes and a smile that leaps up at the corners of her mouth with the slightest provocation.

"Your father and I have lived together a little more than five years now. It hasn't been the easiest thing in the world. He was something of a wreck when we met, but he touched me like nobody had for years. I sat your father down and said, 'Look here, I'm too old and tired to be treated with anything but love and respect.' He said, 'You and me both.'

"My strategy was to try and scare him off early. 'There's something else,' I said, 'I lost one of my breasts to cancer.' He looked me right in the eye. 'That's nothing,' he said, 'my mouth met up with a kinda plague and all my teeth rotted out.' He took his teacup off its saucer—we were sitting in my kitchen in Tampa—and he closed his eyes, put his hands inside his mouth, as if he were going to draw out a sword, and he yanked out a whole rack of big white teeth and set them on the saucer like a trophy. I looked at him, and I looked at his teeth sitting in a puddle of milky tea.

" 'If you think I'm going to do something similar,' I said,

'you've got another think coming.' And pretty soon we were both laughing as hard as schoolkids, really as hard as I'd laughed in years. It may have been the first time that a woman fell in love with a man at the moment he pulled out his false teeth."

Betty's mouth stretches into a wide smile.

"Your father and I decided, just like in the movies, that we wouldn't talk much about the past. He's been good to me."

Facial

Rae stands before a wrought-iron mirror, adorned with a pattern of roses, and studies herself. She's never cared for her small, upturned nose, or her thick lips that occasioned a crude classmate to call her Liver Lips. The boy had a crush on her, but she despised him. "Hey, Liver Lips," he'd say, "give me a kiss."

She does like her eyes, they're such a forceful green they seem to have a life of their own. Her eyes have a hardness that she likes to see in herself. Everything else about her is too soft.

At twenty years old, she still has a face full of freckles. Once she asked her father, "What happens to a girl with freckles when she grows up?"

"What do you mean, what happens?" he said, puckering his lips in a silly imitation of her pout. "What happens is that her freckles either fade away, or she becomes a lady with freckles."

She couldn't remember ever seeing a woman with freckles.

"What happens to a lady with freckles?"

"Nothing happens to her. Everybody thinks she's kind of cute."

Rae brushes a few grains of sand from her forehead and

loosens the braid in her hair. She runs her fingers over the wrought-iron roses.

"You have nice things, Betty."

"Thank you. When you get old enough . . . you've picked up a few things."

"My father?"

"Well, no, he's not a person much interested in things. He's got a box of old stuff that he never looks at, but that's about it."

Rae shakes her head so that her hair falls free, then makes the dizzy, sweet smile of someone who knows she's being watched looking at herself. Cute.

Cat's Game

As soon as his mother nodded off, Quincy climbed from his pile of pillows in the TV nook. It was as if he had radar, Betty thought. He became a nervous little boy, worried that he didn't have a waking person to look after him.

Betty whispered, "Hey, you know how to play tic tac toe?"

He shook his head.

"You know how to make your exes and os?"

She sat him up on the stool with a couple of sharp pencils and several sheets of laundry cardboard from Ronnie's shirts.

Betty showed him how to make the letters and he marked up the cardboard with a dizzying series of fat exes and os. He was very pleased with his cardboard sheets.

"You're a smart boy, Quincy. You know what this one looks like?"

He shook his head.

"A pirate map."

"A PI-RAT map," he echoed, "yeah." He forced a clipped pirate laugh.

They filled several sheets of cardboard with tic tac toes. Quincy liked saying "Cat's game," in his pirate voice.

Now Quincy jumps up and down as he watches Betty come out of the bathroom in her nurse's uniform.

He calls to his mother. "Look at she!" He grabs Betty's hand, ready to play a new game.

"I have to go to work, honey."

"No," he says, and pouting, turns to his mother, "I don't want she to go."

"Ronnie'll be here anytime now. You two make yourself comfortable. There's food in the fridge."

Rae shakes her head. "You don't know me from Adam."

Betty looks at Rae and the boy. There is something hollow about each of them.

"Are you going to steal from me?"

"No."

"So, there you have it. You've gotten this close to your father. I don't think you should leave now."

World in a Jug

Once Quincy is asleep, Rae walks through the bungalow looking for signs of her father. She discovers a framed picture on the bedroom bureau and curls up in a yellow butterfly chair to study it.

His hair has hardly thinned and is still combed back in wide streaks. But his cheeks have collapsed, caved in on him. The actual bone structure, especially his fabled jaw, looks severe matched with the sunken cheeks. The landslide hasn't taken the spirit from his blue eyes. They stare straight from the center of the wreck into the eye of the camera.

Rae used to keep a publicity photo of Ronnie from his glory years in her day pack. His album covers were the only images of him that her mother allowed in the apartment. They were dreamy shots of the boyish, dimple-cheeked charmer with his trumpet, leaning against a tree in dappled sunlight or sitting at a Parisian café table with some Mediterranean beauty.

After it became clear that he had left for good, her mother defaced each of the women on the album covers with red and black markers, but she never marked up Ronnie's image. He looked absurd enough sitting beside a woman with a long red beard, or a Salvador Dalí mustache. And yet, her mother never tired of describing his beauty.

"You should have seen him the first time I laid eyes on him. He was playing at Fack's on Bush Street. He'd been on the road a few months with Stan Kenton, after getting out of the army. Leaving Kenton, he used to say, was like getting out of the army for the second time. 'The freest moment in this man's life,' he said. He must have been feeling free that night. Boy oh boy. He walked into Fack's in a Hawaiian shirt, a pair of pressed dungarees, and shined penny loafers. He carried his trumpet in a black leather case, stamped REB in gold letters.

"He was an amazing sight, you know. A small man who was the biggest thing you ever saw come into a room. He walked into the place, flashing his big white-tooth smile at everyone, as if he was saying, 'Okay, you heard I was pretty, what do you think, honey? I mean what do *you* think?' He could walk into a crowded room and seduce twenty-five women without saying a word. He may have been small, but he had a very beautiful build in those days—that's the one thing the army gave him—and women, they just wanted to touch him.

"And when he took the trumpet out and blew those sweet and easy lines, the sound so fresh and intimate, it was as if little doors and windows had opened everywhere. He had that effect, he could intoxicate a hundred people in a room at once. All those rich and looping trumpet lines made you feel like you were alone with him in a room by the ocean. You could hear him so well, you became a little foolish and thought that he actually understood something about you. Sometimes I don't know how I got him."

Although only in her late thirties when Ronnie left, and a good-looking woman who could still get modeling work, Cat gave up her forward-moving life and got to drinking in gulps. All of her life, she'd have you think, was spent in the fifties and early sixties. She'd remember odd things, all the places around town that Ronnie might be hiding out. She even recalled the phone numbers, with the old exchanges, where she tried to track him down.

One drunken night she forced Rae to sit and listen to her recite phone numbers. Her mother had a gauzy look in the eyes and smiled like a girl at a spelling bee.

"First place I'd try would be the Rosy Bowl barbershop. If he had his way, your father would spend his day high as a kite in a colored barbershop. I don't know what he saw in that society, but I still remember the damn number. TUxedo 5-5257. In the evenings, if he didn't have his own gig, I'd try the clubs. The Blackhawk, GRaystone 4-9567; Fack's, PRospect 6-6360; El Matador, GArfield 1-3348. Sometimes I'd find him at the counter at New Joe's on Broadway, EXbrook 2 . . . or having his shrimp noodle soup at Sam Wo's, YUkon 2 . . ."

Rae goes through the drawers of Betty's bureau, fingering underwear—rows of cotton panties, a red and a black satin chemise, sachets of lavender and potpourri, which she picks up and sniffs, admiring how finely the woman who keeps her father, keeps her things. In the third drawer down, among apparel of lesser intimacy—T-shirts and walking shorts—Rae finds a large pile of notes written to Betty. They are tied in a length of wheat-colored yarn. She recognizes her father's large, curling hand. The undated notes are written on lined index cards, scratch paper, and sheets from a printed pad that reads Pacifica Golf Club. She wonders when he wrote the last notes, and whether Betty ever unties the yarn to read them.

Rae flips through a dozen notes and reads them out in funny voices.

Dear one, I'm thinking kindly on you this morning.

. . .

It's daytime, and there's you—that's my blessing.

. . .

Imagine this is a kiss, or a whole train of
little kisses, traveling slowly across your eyelids.

Her father's singing voice had been famous. The liner notes describe the voice as dreamy. She knows his voice from the records but can no longer remember what he sounds like talking. It wasn't like she was a baby when he left. Fourteen years old. Two years later she'd have her own baby. He used to say, "I got the world in a jug and the stopper in my hand." He pretended it was his anthem, but even when she was young she knew he was pretending, that it was just a line. She knew he had a quiet side. She'd see him sitting alone at the kitchen table with his hands folded in front of him, the skin of his forehead bunched in a hundred thoughts that kept him far from the world of jugs and stoppers.

Sometimes she tried to understand what the words really meant. What was the world he held in the jug? Was it just him in there, or everything he could imagine? How about her mother? How about herself? Was she somewhere in the jug? Could he stop her in there if he wanted? What would it take to let herself out?

Rae pulls a fancy, pink cocktail napkin from the pile of love notes. She unfolds it and reads: *How did I get so lucky, sweet one, to find you?*

She lies down on the bed and reads a few more notes. No

voices this time. Just the sound of words in her head. Anybody's words, that her own father happened to write. Rae is certain that one of the notes has been written for her, but she doesn't know which one. She chooses an old lyric, copied out in a red pen with a little heart drawn in place of a signature, and folds it into a pocket of her jeans. She knows the lyric, she's heard him sing it on one or another of his albums, but has no memory of how the song goes. She forces out the words in a breathy chant.

> In a sleepy world, on a sleepy morn
> when I wake to birds and blowing horns
> it's you I think of
> you I love.

She pushes the note deeper into her pocket and tries to make a song, this time, whispering the lyrics into the gentle push-and-pull of a Latin beat, willing for a moment to be charmed with herself.

Eyes for You

A bashfulness creeps across Jeanette's face, a tender smile full of teeth and gums. She lets her eyes rest on Ronnie. His lived-in face has such deep ruts and ridges that she imagines the glory a blind woman might have climbing it with her fingers. She keeps a steady gaze on Ronnie as she sips her Watneys. One important thing the blind woman would miss is the man's sprightly blue eyes.

Ronnie takes a large gulp from his Coke. "You want another beer?"

"Sure. Don't you drink?"

"Coke, a lot of Coke. You know, I used to drink too much, everything a little too much. Now, it's just Coca-Cola."

Ronnie pushes his captain chair back from the window and stretches his legs.

"You seem relaxed, Ronnie."

It is the first time she's used his name since they went driving. He bares his teeth in a half-smile. "Me? I'm never relaxed, it's only an illusion."

"You're not thinking about the guy anymore."

"Harter? What's to think? He was a genuinely unpleasant guy, but I'm sorry he died. Even sorrier that I had to witness it."

Ronnie pulls a cigarette from his shirt pocket and knocks the filter end against the table a few times. He looks across at her. "You're a very lovely young woman. But this is not about me having eyes for you. You understand?"

Ronnie waits for her to nod and tries to imagine himself as her protector, the girl's uncle arrived late in the day from another state. "Otherwise, we're operating under false pretenses. I'm old enough to be your father's older brother."

"My father doesn't have a brother."

Ronnie flicks a long ash. He pulls in his legs and curls himself into something small in the captain's chair.

Jeanette looks across at the gnomelike man with smoke streaming through his nostrils. He sits with his small hands, palms up, on the table, projecting the gaunt-yet-noble appearance of a religious man. Jeanette isn't sure whether Ronnie is making or receiving an offering. He holds the pose for a long moment, an expert at being appraised, then snuffs his smoke and smiles at her like a shy boy.

"Should I take you back home?"

"I'm not in a rush."

She drops her hands to the table, closes her eyes. "Ronnie . . ." She holds on to his name, unsure what she is going to say. "I think I do have eyes for you."

The restaurant, all its windows to the fog, is like a private room, a small ship in a dream.

Night Picnic

All he wants from Jeanette is a couple of hours of quiet companionship, and to be held for a long moment. But you can't expect a young woman who has eyes to put her arms around you and have it mean nothing, any more than you can ask a whore to make love to you for free.

Jeanette has switched from beer to wine and emptied most of a bottle of Wente Grey Riesling, in steady sips. She watches him across the table. Even though he lights one cigarette off the hot end of the one before, and drums with his fingers, rap-tap-tap, on the table, he is the calmest man she has ever seen.

He pours a can of Shasta Cola over a sliver of lime and notices how she relaxes into her body the more she drinks. Between sips of wine her tongue slides across the flesh of her lips. Her lips turn pouty. He is not without desire for her. She is sweet and has a nice shape, and would give her life away if he kissed her gently on each eyebrow.

She tilts her head and smiles at him as if they were old paramours. It's a look he's seen in the face of countless women, so many starved souls. At one time he may have been a decent-looking man, but far more was made of his looks than they deserved. His easy neutrality was mistaken for charm. A woman attached to the idea of love will give away plenty if she's allowed to think what she wants. When he was on the road, he saw a half-dozen women each night with a ravenous look in their eyes: anorexic waitresses who lived on a daily cup of cottage cheese and prunes, beatnik girls with their nipples popping through their black leotards, rouged and powdered babes who pretended to be singers or dancers, secretaries that looked like dressed-up cakes or birthday presents, the way they poured themselves into frilled office clothes, topped with big white ribbons. The worst were the wives of hotshot business guys and doctors, women who'd been cheated on for years. They made much of what they owned, they asked about his Alfa and brought their own sports cars for him to drive them around in. Some came up to the bandstand and put their hands in his hair and would just as soon screw him with the top down, right in the middle of town.

Jeanette has a moony look on her face as they wind back down the road, past the fake mountain. He wants to tell her that he's lost interest in sex, which is true enough. That he owes his life to a particular woman and wouldn't do anything to make her feel soiled.

She takes hold of his right hand as he's driving. "Can I show you something?" She leads his hand under her uniform skirt and damp panties, and he feels the familiar, hazy excitement that demands a duty to pleasure, spreading the sweet, supple lips, stroking her soft spot that is really as hard as a bean, fucking her with his fingers, the god-almighty arousal running away with him like a car he can't stop. All he wanted to do was go driving, maybe tell her about a few old movies that she wouldn't have seen.

Now he's trying to picture a clearing where they can throw down a blanket, and he remembers the Dutch windmill near Beach Chalet. The windmill hasn't worked for years. He turns left where the park ends and finds the wreck in the disappearing light. It is a beautiful thing, the windmill, driven crooked like a Monterey cypress by the stiff gusts off the ocean. The blistered surface of the tower hasn't been painted in a generation. One of its blades is a stump, twisted out of its socket. But still, rising out of a grassy knoll, planted in red and yellow tulips that have closed up for the night, the windmill is something to behold.

There is no blanket in the boot of the car, just the damp towel attached to his golf bag. Even his towel has had a long day. He spreads it on the soft grass between sprinklers. Jeanette climbs on top of him and lifts up her pink uniform skirt. Nobody would believe him, but he really wanted to pretend they were on a night picnic and that she had brought an apron full of goodies from her job. He thinks of Cat—how in the early years of their marriage, often drunken or drugged, they'd make wild love and little Rae would run into their room at the first sound of her mother's come cry. In an instant one thing changed to another—Cat pulling up the disheveled covers around their daughter, whispering a line from Mother Goose.

"Wait, wait," he says as Jeanette unzips his fly.

"What?"

"Not here."

"You put the towel down," she says, as if his complicity is sealed for life. She pulls his cock out into the cold air.

"Jesus."

"Lay back," she commands.

He doesn't have the will to fight her. Her hands are in his hair. Gentle, they move slowly across his face as if they are trying to find something. She is crouched over him, on her way, so he lies back and lets her ride him. She bites into his neck, goddamnit. He lets out a howl and reaches under her blouse. He pushes up her bra, and grabs each of her breasts. Two breasts. Two warm breasts. He thinks of squeezing her nipples until he hurts her, but all he wants to do is cup her breasts and feel how soft they are. She works in cross rhythms, her hands float above him while her hips grind with greased purpose. Aaggghhh, she practically tears his hair out, coming. His mouth opens to a wide O, a tunnel halfway up his spine, when he lets go. There's a streak of blue in the night sky. He looks up at the windmill's rotting arms and imagines them turning.

Warm Milk

It's after two by the time Ronnie drives up. His cock is frozen in half-erection, it throbs unpleasantly and burns a little as if sand has been poured down the urethra. A rusted, beige Valiant is parked in front of the blue bungalow. Ronnie expected someone would come if he let his whereabouts be known. Someone with an eye to a reckoning—a creditor coming to collect for a thing Ronnie doesn't remember ever having. He wasn't counting on a grown-up woman with a braid of blond hair sticking out of a sleeping bag, and a little black boy, his small head haloed with sand dollars, snoring under a pile of blankets. Once he peeks in on sleeping Betty, and looks to see that the rest of the place hasn't been ceded to visitors, Ronnie stands for the longest time, watching his daughter. Grown-up girl.

He showers until the water goes cold, trying to wash away every trace of the waitress. Do his visitors exist in anything more than his imagination, he wonders, tiptoeing out of the bathroom.

His daughter lies peacefully enough on her back, her spirit running flush in her cheeks, even as she sleeps. A marvelous smear of brown freckles spills each way over her small nose. He looks at her hands, woman's hands now, with neatly trimmed nails that remind him of how she always had her fingers in her mouth, nibbling across the nails as if they were miniature ears of corn. She wears a single ring, a small moonstone mounted in silver on her right pointer, and she has a tattooed garland of miniature roses curling around her left wrist. Her hands are crossed in benediction over the sleeping bag, the very bag that he and Cat had given her for a camp-out.

How he'd fretted about her going on an overnight with a group of twelve-year-old girls and one outdoorsy mom. It rained all night and he pictured Rae either drowned in the bag, or struck by lightning. He cursed himself for letting her go off on a drizzly afternoon, and tried to wake Cat out of a drunken slumber, to share a moment of worry and grief about their daughter. Cat would not be disturbed from her own night business. He called Samuel Taylor State Park and listened for a while to the telephone buzz-buzz in the woods.

Rae returned the next afternoon, cheery and full of stories—after the tent began to leak, the girls had gone to the bathroom for an hour in the middle of the night, and played rummy with a deck of naked-lady cards that the disheveled mom pretended not to see. He thought it was boys who played with naked-lady cards. "Girls can be naughty too," she said, and they laughed together at the naughtiness of it—five pubescent girls sitting on sinks in a large bathroom, holding hands full of ladies with crossed legs and pointy breasts.

Two years later, he considered running off with Rae. She would do no worse with him on the road than staying in the care of her poor mother, in an apartment with dying houseplants and a steady diet of frozen potpies. But he was in miserable condition himself. Nearly toothless and strung out on heroin, his livelihood rotted with his teeth. He left to stay alive and, in the lost year that followed, lived among other broken men, sleeping in two-dollar rooms, in parked cars, beside bonfires on the beach.

In Phoenix he delivered circulars at five in the morning, sold plasma, carried rags and a bucket of sudsy water behind an old Swede window washer who never stopped complaining about the heat. He worked two jobs in St. Petersburg Beach, swabbing bathrooms during the day at the Orange Palace, the vintage gangster hotel, and pumping gas at night. He saved enough for a mouthful of new teeth, a set of used golf clubs, and a rusted white Rambler with ninety-seven thousand miles on it. (The '63 Alfa, his last trace of glory, had been impounded by the police in

Laredo, when he'd slipped across the border for a few days, and he hadn't been able to summon the energy to claim it.) He bought himself a set of knit alligator shirts for three dollars apiece (fresh, he guessed, off the back of a dead man) at the carriage-trade Goodwill in St. Petersburg, and looked so sharp when he finally hit the links that he stood a moment with his Walter Hagen driver in front of the clubhouse mirror, smiling like an immigrant at his first photograph of himself in a new country.

But he hated Florida. People moved there to die and con-gratulated themselves every day on having come. He shaved his head and spent hours in the early morning and evening hitting practice shots, saying fuck you to the hovering ghost of his father who wanted him to hit still more shots. After three months of it he was playing scratch golf again, and able to make half a living hustling old sots who, after all the sun and cocktails, began imag-ining themselves as Billy Casper.

It was in Florida that he made the point of banishing music. He cast it out, isolated it like a disease from the rest of his one-foot-before-the-other life. He slipped it into an unlined case, his strongbox for all things gathered that would not of themselves dissolve. He tried to reenter the world with the peculiar posture of the tone deaf. He felt confident that he could join the tribe of shambling gracelessness without incident. His speaking voice, which had once registered as a singing, if husky, whisper, now became a commanding bark, and people who, in the old days, may have sidled up and pretended to be his buddy, now kept their distance. His disguise may have succeeded, if it hadn't been for Betty. She recognized him, not as Ronnie Reboulet, former jazz star, but as a kindred soul.

He climbs into bed beside Betty. Gently, he touches his feet against her bare calves until she rouses.

"See who's come?"

"How'd you get her to stay?"

"She wasn't going anywhere till she saw you. Where you been?"

"I had business . . ."

She can smell through the cigarettes and the breath mints, through the toothpaste and almond-honey shampoo, to a burnt-coffee and patchouli scent that is not his: The skin of a woman. How much he has been with her, Betty doesn't know. She can see their carefully prescribed life of mild comforts and affections coming apart.

Ronnie swings his arms and legs around her and feels how warm she is under the covers.

"She okay?"

"I can't tell you that. She's a nice girl, though."

"She is," he confirms, enjoying the rare authority of applying the past to the present. "And the boy?"

"Hers."

"I figured that. She must have got pregnant at fifteen."

"I wouldn't know."

"A black boy. What's he like?"

"Your grandson. He's precious." Betty turns to face Ronnie. In the dark she can make out the lean outline of his face, the cheeks drawn after the dentures have been plucked. She does not suggest that he wake up his daughter, nor does she offer to make him a cup of warm milk, though she knows that the small animal motor in him will chug for the rest of the night and he will not sleep. She wonders how far along he is with measuring guilt and justice. Years ago, in one of his more foolish moments, he talked about being a man who felt no guilt. She hadn't believed him for a moment. She touches his face now, the tight skin around his jaw standing at attention.

He turns away from her onto his side. He has vowed that no one will know him this well—his mystery reduced to a cup of warm milk they both know he wants, but which neither will acknowledge until he asks for it. He lies there, his balls throbbing. He imagines Jeanette, awake in her bed, and closes his eyes, thinking of warm milk. He hunts for a single breath, a soundless low A, deep enough to keep his breathing even, as

Betty spoons around him. She moves a hand along his ruddy throat, and will hold it there until morning, wanting not to squeeze the life out of him—although the thought occurs to her—but to grab ahold of any sound, from hum to ragged wheeze, that he might make.

A Single Tree

The next morning Betty waters her window-box plants, watching the small pools of water disappear into the soil. Surprisingly, the herbs are in good shape. Days go by and she forgets them. Sometimes one dries up, or goes to seed, and she's sorry to miss its transformation. She grabs a long, healthy shoot of Russian sage, slides her fingers up its height and smells her hand. It has the scent of a mild-mannered foreigner who wears wool scarves and speaks a slightly twisted English.

Ronnie once told her about the Japanese—the little space they had to live in and how that affected their attitudes. A single tree stood for a forest. It gave them more room inside. Ronnie had spent two weeks in Japan, traveling on fast trains between concerts. He knew nothing about the people or the place. His few cultural "facts" came courtesy of a sax-playing acquaintance who had taken three lessons on the *shakuhachi* from a Japanese flute master. And yet she loved the rare moments when Ronnie offered "knowledge." It made him sound as familiar as any man, pawning platitudes, or utter foolishness, as fact.

When they moved into the Half Moon Bay cottage, Ronnie brought her a bonsai in a dark green ceramic pot. She put it into the bedroom and looked at it every morning, wondering if she might be growing more space inside as her outer world narrowed.

Strawberries

Betty looks over at the boy and his mother and grandfather, dipping strawberries into the bowl of sugared whipped cream she's set before them. They sit on the counter stools, a quiet group of three, fixed on the big bowl of fruit. Ronnie looks downright studious in his wire-rimmed glasses, a curiosity he employs more for the purpose of disguise than vision. He asks Quincy questions and the boy twists himself into shy contortions.

"What's your favorite food, Quince?"

"Hamburgandcheez."

"What did he say?"

"Cheeseburgers," his mother pitches in.

"How about you?"

Rae, without an answer, shrugs.

Betty fights the instinct to smooth things over, and allows the three of them to stumble through the wide pauses.

Despite it all, Ronnie seems happy. He sits, his hands folded, admiring his company. Rae and Quincy have their heads down, eating strawberries.

"Betty, come on over and join us," Ronnie calls.

"I don't want to crowd you guys."

"Come here, Bet."

She stands behind him a moment, dropping a hand on his bare neck.

"Aren't they lovely?" he says, nodding toward Rae and Quincy.

It seems as if he is prizing two young children, rather than one with his mother. The form of affection isn't lost on Rae, who looks up and grins at Betty.

"You two have become fast friends," Ronnie says.

Betty lifts her hand from his neck. "We haven't had enough time to do it slowly, Ronnie."

He dips a strawberry and smiles at his daughter. "I'm proud of you, Rae."

Tom Dooley

Betty backs away from the tableau, and says a little prayer to herself. She thinks of her son Adam, who did not come home. Adam, baby-faced as a boy and young man, spent his early life being shuffled between remedial classes. He wasn't stupid, but scared.

"Sometimes I know the answers, Mama," he told her once, "but I'm afraid to tell."

She told him it was all right to make mistakes.

"But what if I open my mouth to answer . . . and no words come out? Then they'll think I'm really dumb."

"But you're not dumb, honey."

He nodded and sealed his lips.

Before Adam, she hadn't been much of a worrier. She'd not been fearful about her first two children. But when this boy was born she became tense and watchful. Her husband, Marty, ran off two years after Adam was born, to devote himself to the ponies at Hialeah. Before he left, he swept his hand through the colic in the center of Adam's blond head. "This child's all right," he said, "you're the one that's nervous. You're the one that will turn this boy into a wreck." Maybe Marty was right.

When it was too late, Adam wrote home to say he wasn't scared anymore. He awoke every morning with a sense of peace, no matter how hot or rainy it was, how muddy or dark, no matter his weariness or the look on his partner's face, no matter what animals woke him, even if they crept in camouflage and planned to toss grenades in his direction. For the first time in his life he greeted his mornings blissfully unafraid. He'd sit up in his bag and take a long and peaceful breath, just like she'd told him to do a million years ago. She'd write back to the middle of a jungle she couldn't begin to picture, begging him to get scared.

When the young military officer drove up in his official Ford, Betty pushed straight through the screen door to wave him away. She knew what he had to say, but he kept coming. He offered no details, which suited her fine. Was she wrong to have no interest in the details? What comfort did it bring to find out, as she later did, that Adam, a razor in hand, was whistling "Tom Dooley" at the moment the grenade exploded?

Family Tradition

The boy sits on a pink booster chair at the Hippopotamus, facing the two halves of his Jungle Burger.

His mother says, "You don't have to eat it all, Quincy."

His grandfather says, "You don't have to eat any of it."

Rae gives her father a censuring glance.

"I'm just trying to put him at his ease."

The boy begins to swill his strawberry milkshake.

"They sure set you up with the works."

He looks at his grandfather. "What is the works?"

"All those fries and the Jungle Burger, and that milkshake you practically have to climb a ladder to get to the top of."

Quincy takes up his straw and forces a few cackling bubbles out of his strawberry shake. He seems tremendously pleased with himself and starts giggling. It is the first time Ronnie has heard the boy laugh. He blows a few bubbles in his own milkshake, making as if he were behind a powerful motor giving chase to the boy. Quincy screeches with delight, and tries to make a bubbling getaway.

Rae smiles at her father.

"The kid's a gas," he says, "a really beautiful boy."

"Thank you."

He leans toward her. "So what's the deal with the boy's father, if you don't mind me asking?"

She shrugs. *None of your fucking business,* she thinks, but doesn't say. *What's the real question here? What do you want to know? How did I let myself get knocked up by some black punk who has no interest in me or my child?* Her face goes blank.

Ronnie pushes aside his milkshake. "I'm sorry." He shouldn't have asked. It's not his right. He looks across the table at his long-haired hippie daughter, that's what she is after all. He considers her big green barn coat that she wouldn't let him hang, even though the restaurant is so toasty he wishes he could strip down to his undershirt. He imagines she has a pack of neatly rolled joints in one of her coat pockets. A Sucrets box filled with joints. He wonders what it would be like to do a little weed with his daughter. Just a taste.

She wants to hurt him. "I didn't think about this as much as you might guess. Seeing you again. I've always tried to be philosophical about your leaving us. I told myself it was less personal than selfish. I never expected I'd see you again."

Her mother had always crowed about how he'd be dead soon enough from dope, or driving his Alfa into a tree. Some act of convenience or other that would make the mourning complete. They stopped hearing about him. Nobody that actually knew him was in their lives anymore. Murray, her father's longtime friend and manager, forwarded the dwindling royalty money when any of it came his way. Once Murray had her mother and her down to his Carmel Valley ranch to meet his young wife, but nobody said a word about Ronnie Reboulet.

Her mother had a favorite phrase: "He might as well be dead." She carried on incessantly about the Alfa. How much did he spend on that car anyway? It was just criminal the way he cared for it. Like a baby. Out there waxing it every Saturday. Spending more time waxing his car than making love to his wife.

Cat always had him driving too fast with the top down. He'd have some girl with big tits in his lap who thought she was in love with him but who was really looking for her own father. He wasn't even interested in the girl. Sure, he'd screw her, sooner or later, but all he really cared about was the idea of having a girl with big tits driving around in his car with the top down. Rae spent years trying to hate him, but her mother seemed to have exclusive rights.

"Well, *I* did," Ronnie says. "I thought about seeing you all the time, though I doubted I'd get the chance. Not that I deserve it."

Rae smiles again at her father. The man has a special talent with angry women. She looks into his beautiful face, the blue points of light, alert like a man driving in heavy traffic. His skin is bunched like a pachyderm's, in deep, leathery wrinkles, but his expression is calm, simpatico. He's struck a winning pose.

Rae looks toward her boy, in his own world with a faceful of french fries, and back at her father.

"I'm afraid that I'm going to leave him," she says.

"Why?"

"Maybe it's a family tradition."

The lean waitress, who wears a cardboard hippopotamus hat, curls her nostrils at Quincy and offers a special hippo wave. "How's everything here?"

Quincy chomps through the herculean mound of fries with a certain fury. A tiny bit of french fry hangs miraculously from his cheek. His entire face is smeared with ketchup.

Ronnie nods to the hippo waitress. "I bet he's never met a french fry he hasn't liked."

Solitude Times Three

Six months earlier Rae was sleeping with a man older than her father, a black man named Wallace Henry who was not her boy's father. Wallace still had his own teeth. He was a lovely man, a gentleman, and she fell for him hard.

He wooed her, not by telling her that she was beautiful, but by listening to her sing. She had a little job singing for tips, Monday nights, at a piano bar on Haight Street called Relax with Evone. It was the last prehippie bar left on Haight Street. An oasis for old lushes. Nobody much listened to her when she sang.

There may have been a dozen people at Evone's who noticed that the music was live. One misfit or another was always ogling Rae, sizing up her breasts. She didn't notice Wallace until she'd begun singing "Solitude."

She'd sung three or four songs already, and there'd been a smattering of applause, the slightest evidence of a collective heartbeat. But after "Solitude," a lovely, brown-skinned man in a tweed coat stood up and said, "That was very nice, miss, would you mind singing it again?" Rae nodded to the man and then to Jamie, the fey piano player, who flashed her a silly smile before chording the intro. She had trouble knowing when to come in after the intro and suspected that Jamie was trying to mess her up. Jumping into a song was more difficult than running into the cold ocean. But she carried on.

After she'd finished her second time, the man stood up again. "I know it's a lot to ask, but, if you wouldn't mind, I'd love to hear that song again." By the time she finished singing it the third time, her dress was soaked through and she felt like crying. The beautiful hunk of brown man was already on his feet. She was at the point of saying, "Please, mister, don't make me sing that song again," when the man mopped his brow with a white handkerchief and said, "Thank you, miss, that was lovely, absolutely fine."

Two weeks after she sang to Wallace for half the night, she went out to dinner with him. He said, "I've never taken a hippie woman to dinner before." Rae didn't know whether to be insulted. She had never thought of herself as a hippie. That night she wore a close-fitting aubergine dress in velvet. She'd picked it up at the Bargain Mart on Divisadero, and it cost more to have it cleaned than she paid for it. It was a genuine find. She wore a white linen coat over the dress and stood in front of the mirror admiring her understated elegance.

Wallace owned a three-story Victorian on Laguna Street in the Western Addition. It was neither a fancy painted lady nor a splintering wreck, but a dark, serviceable house, with heavy curtains and absurd chandeliers, that he said had been in his family for a long time. He walked her through the long hallway, pointing out framed photographs of his family. Everybody in the pictures was dead. Grandmothers and aunts and plenty of cousins; strict-looking men in suits. His father and grandfather had both been undertakers. "I broke the mold," he said, and asked if she wanted to see his books. He pushed open a pair of walnut doors and walked her into a room lined with law books.

She asked what kind of law he practiced.

"I'm a whore lawyer," he said.

She couldn't keep herself from smiling at his answer.

"Somebody's got to get 'em out. I look after a lot of girls, a lot of individuals. I'm a person of certain renown in this community, strange as that may seem."

"That doesn't seem strange at all."

She told him about Quincy and what it was like to be a nineteen-year-old white girl with a three-year-old black boy to raise.

He said, "You must like black men."

"I like you," she said.

They sat in their clothes on his bed sipping from snifters of Courvoisier.

"This is an estimable VSOP," he said, "Very . . . Special . . . Old . . . Pale. Just like you, except for the fact that you may not have the required age."

"I'm old enough."

"Yes, in the legal sense, you are."

"How come you're playing with me?"

"I'm not playing, darling."

Rae took a gulp from her snifter and sneered at him.

Wallace refilled her glass, chuckling. He told her how slowly a good cognac should go down. "It's gotta be chewed to appreciate its richness."

Every time she began to take off her clothes he slowed her down.

"This is not about being in a hurry," he said.

She had her linen jacket off, and he'd slowly run his hand over the velvet dress, across her breasts, along her side, her narrow belly. She was ready to jump on him.

He smiled at her and grabbed a handful of velvet fabric near the hollow of her belly. "You have a nice, soft skin on top of your actual skin."

Rae *was* in a hurry. How to tell a man that you're in a hurry? That had never been her problem. This would be the first time she'd cheated on her husband, even if he wasn't her husband. The father of her little boy, the man she sometimes shared an apartment with, when he came home from his mother's little house which he found infinitely more comfortable. Still, this was not a casual business, even though Darnell had been catting around on her from the start.

"Hey, sweetie," he'd say, coming in some nights after midnight, rank with gamy perfume. He'd fan away the stink, and say, "Hey, I'm out here trying to keep my nose clean, but I got to follow my heart." That was a favorite line of his.

She'd arranged to have Mrs. Herrera stay late with Quincy, that night, in case Darnell didn't come home. She imagined him either tucked away in his boyhood bed, or screwing some girl who kept telling him how pretty he was. He probably had a load of beers in him, and would crash through the door of her apartment at two in the morning, finding the boy in his bed and old Mrs. Herrera, with her shoes still on, asleep on the sofa.

When Wallace Henry finally jiggled down the skinny zipper of her dress, and the cool air hit her back, she felt as if she'd been cut out of some false body, freed to her genuine skin. He rubbed her back and her breasts and the flat of her belly with a vanilla-scented massage oil, and fucked her long and hard, saying, "Mmmm . . . mmmm . . . mmmm . . ." like a drummer flicking his hi-hat on the after beat with a pair of wire brushes.

The next morning Rae sat up in the bed, sore and worried. The street outside was noisy with traffic. She thought about Quincy waking in the strange morning with Mrs. Herrera on the front-room couch, perhaps his father marching around the house cursing her, "Fucking whore. Fucking whore." Wallace walked into the room, dressed in another dark suit. He didn't say anything to her, but smiled. She wondered how many minutes could pass before one of them spoke. She faced a shelf of African carvings, little totemic men and pointy-breasted women. A re-touched photograph of Wallace's mother as a young woman hung beside the carvings. Rae was grateful for the silence. She tried to spill the worry off like a warm liquid. *Hot lava:* Quincy's favorite words for tantalizing himself with the dangers of the greater world. Wallace stood at the mirror knotting his tie. Of course, there were many dangers in the greater world. Rae buttoned herself into one of Wallace's starched white shirts and stood beside him.

Bulldogs

Four weeks after she first went to Wallace's house, he sent her away. He waited for her happiest moment—a Saturday morning in which she suspended worry because she knew that she was in love. Wallace sauntered into the bedroom in his blue terry robe.

"You have your choice," he said, "breakfast in bed, or you can come out to the kitchen and sit with me."

He had a way of keeping her jaunty. "I'm not going to tell you, mister." She grabbed his banker-stripe shirt from the day before and jumped up and down on the bed, flapping her arms like a mad bird, the tails of his long shirt flying up around her nakedness. Two or three times in her life she had let herself have a happiness like this. She opened her throat like a bird and sang the first line of "I Loves You Porgy" with a solemnity that perfectly balanced her joy.

Wallace stopped what he was doing in the kitchen and came into the bedroom where she was singing. "Don't sing that song, darling. Sing something else for me."

Wallace had gone back to the kitchen. She opened her mouth but no longer wanted to sing.

Rae sat at the kitchen table.

"You look like you're ready for a big stack," he said.

He brought a plate of the fancy buttermilk pancakes that he called bulldogs, and a large linen napkin. She watched him pull a bottle of sorghum out of a saucepan of bubbling water with a bare hand.

She didn't touch the food, but looked into his broad face, with its smart eyes and serious brow.

"You have a lovely voice, darling. There's no mistaking that. But what you're singing—that's not your stuff. This is not about black and white, you understand. Anybody's free to sing that song, the way I see it. Was a white man that wrote it."

She held her hands folded in her lap. He sat down across from her and forced her to take a plate of butter.

"Put something on those bulldogs. Don't leave those things bald for too long."

She didn't budge.

"That's anybody's music. It's the way you approach the songs. Like you're trying to force significance into a song that's already got it, because you don't believe in your own. That's why I had you sing "Solitude" all those times, that first night. I thought you'd get so sick and tired of it, you'd end up singing your own way. But you'll find out about that soon enough."

Rae made herself go dead. She'd heard enough of what Wallace was saying and could tell it wasn't going to get any better. She felt a little short of breath and tried to dig to the bottom of her lungs for a breath that she could ride awhile. Wallace was not a cruel man, not like Darnell, who'd get a gotcha grin on his face whenever he had something smart to say.

Wallace smiled at her. "You better put something on those bulldogs, darling."

He tucked his napkin into his collar like a bib and carefully carved through three thick hotcakes as if he were cutting a steak. "The other thing . . . well, I've been watching you. You know that. 'Course you know that. You're a very beautiful young lady, and you've had this glow of happiness about you that I hate to take away. But I'm way too old for you, darling, too old and too black."

Rae heard his words and stood up absently, as if her name had been called off a list in a crowded room. She looked down at the stack of hotcakes and the bottle of sorghum.

"Come on, sit down, finish up your bulldogs, darling."

"I've got to run," she said, and took a quick look around the room, at the man in his blue terry robe, at the little framed pictures of his relatives, at the stack of bulldogs with the pat of butter he'd just spread across the top dog, and picked up her coat, and picked up her bag, and didn't breathe again until she was out in the crisp air, running up Laguna Street, with Wallace's banker-stripe shirt still flapping under her jacket.

Dumb Promise

Ronnie doesn't return to the golf course for two weeks after Harter's death. A day after the incident, he got a phone call firing him for his questionable behavior. They said he'd abused his rights as an employee. There'd been allegations about his gambling with the paying customers. So, what else is new? Time to clear his locker and pick up his final check.

Walking into the clubhouse, he's feeling chipper. He waves to golfers he barely knows, keeping up a steady banter. "Nice day out there. Hey, Ray, what do you say, Ray? Sumptuous day, to go out and play. Fog had a job to do and it looks like it's gone and done it. Hey, Harry, you going a full round, Harry, or just nine?"

Nobody seems to know that he's been fired, that he's a ghost in the place, paying a final visit. "Hey, Donny, hey, Donny boy, how you hitting with those Pings, Donny?"

At the moment of his departure he becomes the solid citizen of good cheer and empty chatter that they always wanted him to be.

"Hey, Phil, nice sweater," he says to a man decked out in an orange pullover with a golf-club-swinging Tweety bird stitched over the left breast.

"What do you say, Ronnie?"

Ronnie ambles over to Phil Dozniak, addressing him in a conspiratorial tone. "Didn't you hear, buddy? I'm out of here for killing Harter on eight, a couple of weeks ago. You know, the fat guy, always walking around farting, guy with the temper who threw his clubs, and shit. The golden spike exploded in his chest, man. Better be careful, Philly, you look like a ripe candidate. Don't get carried away out there. Got to be careful what you eat, Philly. You know what they say: not too much salt, but a lot of pecker."

"Hey, you bastard," Phil Dozniak says, his face suddenly red, his mouth full of spit. Ronnie watches him huff off in his cleated white shoes, clanging down the hallway like a nervous herd of small animal.

He clears out his locker. There are a few stray clubs he didn't carry in his bag, including the ancient Walter Hagen driver, with the mahogany shaft, that he calls his Peckerwood. He pulls out towels, a couple of caps, a slicker, two umbrellas, a nylon rain suit, a pair of rubbers—everything imaginable against the damp. He knows he's going to miss playing in a late-afternoon rain, or as the fog thickens. The only one out there. The real beauty of the game.

He's tried to explain to Betty what it is like, a man walking a part of the earth by himself, hitting a ball every couple hundred yards, or less, the course shrouded in heavy weather, the ocean just beyond your seeing. It's silent, aside from the moan of foghorns and his own chatter and song. How to explain to somebody who hasn't grown up playing? As a kid his father made him hate the game. But when he got out there by himself he was just a boy walking the earth. He played the course with a mastery that most grown golfers could only dream about. The game was an afterthought. You hit the ball when you came to it. You concentrated on where to put it. He liked to talk to himself, and sing Irving Berlin songs, and broadcast a running commentary on his future life as a man.

Jeanette lets out an audible sigh when he walks into the Nineteenth Hole. The woman has more than eyes. Ronnie has come to say good-bye. It's been a long time since he's been the cause of shorted-breath hysteria in a young woman.

"You're not . . . you're not leaving the area?" she says.

"I may be," he says.

"Why?" she mouths, not quite giving sound to the words.

"Gonna miss you," he says, and remembers how cruel he used to be, taking a girl like this by the hand when he didn't even want her. She'd do anything for him. He'd known plenty of musicians who could keep a string of girls whoring for them by giving them that look and keeping their habits going.

Jeanette is searching his face for the look. He doesn't want to give it to her, it won't do her any good. She stands stock-still with a dirty hamburger platter. Despite himself, he feels his lips stretch back from the shiny dentures, grinning a dumb promise that he has no intention of keeping.

Frozen in a Tree

In the month before his daughter and grandson came, Betty spent a lot of time watching Ronnie. Evenings, he'd sit in his chair, pretending to look at the TV, or leafing through a golf magazine without noticing anything on the pages. She imagined that he was buried inside songs he used to play—frozen, like a mythological spirit in a tree trunk, into the form of "Lover Man" or "Green Dolphin Street."

One night Betty came home with a new coffeemaker, a French plunger, and a pound of fresh-ground beans. She polished off a pot of vanilla nut brew by herself and proposed the idea to Ronnie—that he was frozen inside a tree of unplayed music.

"What the hell are you talking about? Frozen in a tree."

She circled his chair. "Just think about it . . . think about it a minute . . . think."

He laughed. "Sit down, you're making me nervous. You don't know what you're saying, it must be the coffee talking."

But then he nodded his head and looked around the bungalow, as if he were trying to get used to the idea. He surprised her with a series of literal questions. What kind of a tree did she imagine him locked inside? Was it a hard wood like oak, or something soft like eucalyptus? He asked about the origin of the myth, but she could tell him nothing, except that it might come from the Greeks or Romans. She remembered a character in *The Tempest*, but couldn't recall the name of the character.

Betty circled the room, wired. She was wearing nothing but a black slip and an embroidered camisole.

Ronnie sat back and watched her as if he were watching a parade. What sort of tree had his mother gotten herself trapped in, he wondered, once Natty died and the life went out of her?

In a while he climbed out of his chair and crept after Betty.

"Stand clear," she said, and stepped up her pace.

He grabbed hold of her and wouldn't let go. "Now who's trapped?"

Finally, she settled into his arms. "Tell me the rules of this thing," he said. "Can a person locked inside a tree free themself, or does it take someone on the outside to do it?"

Once, when she'd been trapped within her own body, he'd freed her. It was the time she'd told him about her cancer. She had no left breast. She'd known men that couldn't handle an empty flap of skin, cross-stitched over her chest. She told him how she'd thought of it at first, as a parking lot with an empty stall. A space to pull the car in.

He nodded and took her hands. "I don't care how many breasts you have, I care about you. I have eyes for *you*."

She'd brought him home and mixed a pot of Darjeeling. He sat down at her small kitchen table, stacked with copies of *Good Housekeeping* and *Gourmet*, and calmly took out his teeth. The teeth were poised in the center of *Gourmet*'s cover dish—Paella Valenciana. She made a point of studying the festive platter of saffron rice, studded with clams and mussels, roasted lengths of sausage, and gleaming dentures.

He offered her a wide, gummy smile. "This is not something I usually do when I'm out on a date. But then I haven't been on many dates lately. Do I remind you of your grandaddy?"

"No, my granny."

"People used to make quite a fuss over the way I looked when I was a young man."

"You were beautiful."

"How would you know?"

He took off his baby-blue denim sport coat, an absurdly modish affair with showy white seams, and unbuttoned his white shirt. "I want you to see how scrawny I am. Also, I have an ugly tattoo from my army days. It says 'Mitzi,' which is the name of a girl I knew for about two weeks in 1947. Sometimes I try to remember her face, but I don't have a clue."

Betty sipped her tea and looked at Ronnie in his ribby tank top, a little used up but still very beautiful.

"One thing that I should point out, besides the ugly tattoo, is that my arms are messed up, scarred pretty bad from all the years of shooting dope."

He turned his hands palms up, and held his arms out in front of him, a man used to being inspected, and capable of the rarest sleight of hand—she looked away for a second and his dentures had moved from the paella Valenciana to his saucer, swimming with milky tea.

The old tracks on his arms had left bleached, shadowy scars, like the sides of a frame house that have had their ivy vines ripped away. He pulled off his T-shirt. His hairless white chest reminded her of a boy. Her own baby boy, Adam, had been a hairier beast than Ronnie Reboulet.

Citrus

After Adam died, Betty kept expecting a woman with a young child to show up, someone come to recite all her dead son's promises. Adam had no girl, though, would probably never have had a girl. But here was this young woman, at her door with a little black boy, wanting help getting her life together.

One Saturday morning, hours after Ronnie has gone off to hustle golfers at Sharp's Park, she makes a stack of french toast. She slices little fingers of toast for Quincy and he smiles at her and walks off with a plate to the television nook. A few weeks in and he's colonized his corner, operating the TV remote with a stiff-armed authority.

When Rae has finished her french toast, Betty asks her if she'd like to have her hair brushed out. Betty's mother had pulled a brush through her hair, a hundred strokes a day. Her mother's perfume, a faint citrus, traveled on little feet like a civilized crea-ture, out on its own. With the perfume, they were three in the room, collapsing into one. She'd closed her eyes as her mother pulled through electric snags, and felt the current running straight to her mother's doughy hands.

Her mother used to pet her and say, "You have lovely hair, honey. Take good care of it. Take care of what you have. You're a beautiful girl."

Her mother's life had not been easy. She'd had so much

thankless work with nobody petting her. Betty's father had had an instinct for bad business deals. By the time she was thirteen, he'd cashed in everything they owned for a small orange orchard near Clearwater that never recovered from the frost the year before it was sold. They'd moved from a nice house in Tampa to a ramshackle dump in disrepair. When the orchard failed and couldn't be pawned off on anyone else, Betty's mother went to work in a greasy spoon. Her father, who loved oranges above everything, dropped dead on the buggy porch, a quart of orange sherbet and a wooden spoon in his lap. A couple of weeks before he died, he inscribed her ninth-grade yearbook:

> *Dearest Betty,*
>   *Cultivate the ability to be nice to others, and take things*
> *as they come.*
>
>   *Father*

Her mother was still a young woman but, as far as Betty knew, never had another man. Betty had gone her own long years without men, and just as many long years with them. Now she felt Ronnie slipping away. Every man has a way of growing quiet, but Ronnie, despite his occasional banter and storytelling, has always been the quietest. Sometimes "quiet" becomes an object that you can lead to a specific destination, a wagon pulled by a silent horse. Ronnie is a quiet that can't be led.

As she draws the brush through Rae's hair, light pours in the kitchen window, offering up the chestnut highlights. Betty pulls the brush deftly through the long strands of Rae's brown hair, wishing she had a way to bless her.

Betty no longer envies the lives of the young women that she works with at the hospital. She still banters with them, enjoys their excitement over their cute boyfriends, their babies, their cheap new clothes, but she doesn't envy them. The majority will pass from high youth to chattering plainness without noting the passage.

Betty works the newborn nursery, but occasionally she'll do a shift on the birthing corridor. So many of the women are babes themselves. Poor, mindless as cows, chewing gum and watching game shows, just before giving birth. Sometimes when she's assisting amid the ding, ding, ding of the infernal game show, she'll turn off the TV and say a silent prayer.

Betty puts down the brush and lets her hands fall onto Rae's head, leaving them there a moment in a silent benediction.

"Thank you," Rae says, sliding off the stool. "You're very gentle."

"I liked doing that."

They sit across the counter from each other, sipping coffee, not quite able to look into each other's eyes. Betty picks an orange out of the fruit basket and drives her teeth into its thick, acidic skin before peeling it.

Revolutionaries and Girl Singers

Once Quincy has started to snore in his sleeping bag, Betty makes a vat of popcorn. Rae and Betty sit on big pillows in the TV nook with a couple of bowls of popcorn between them. Ronnie, barefoot in his maroon sweatsuit, sits smoking in his chair. Smoke rises off the face of the TV as they watch the film of her coming into the bank again.

Betty shakes her head. "All they're doing is playing this over and over."

"It's all they have," Ronnie says. "Heck, they don't need any more. Look at us, we're glued to the TV."

Rae drops a handful of popcorn into her mouth, kernel by kernel. She looks back at her father and smiles. He's turned bluish in the television light. Sharp chin, blue haze of smoke. She feels an odd coziness in the room. She is at home with her family. The other girl, the one holding the submachine gun, is the same age as her, is a hostage, even if she claims she's free, out robbing banks for the cause.

"What's she calling herself again?"

"You know, Ronnie."

"I forget."

"Tania," Rae says.

"Right. What's that, Russian?"

Betty shrugs.

"I used to know a woman named Tania."

"I'm sure you did, Ronnie."

"What's that great line of hers? 'Death to the fascist insect that preys upon the life of the people.' Has a real ring to it, don't you think? It would make a nice lyric. I hear a lush arrangement. 'Death to the fascist insect.' What do you think? Barbra Streisand with the Nelson Riddle Orchestra."

"Hush, Ronnie."

"Wouldn't you think that a woman named Tania would be a little bit on the curvaceous side? Have a little bit of meat on her bones, at least?"

"Come on, Ronnie, don't act like an MCP."

"Betty thinks that I'm a male chauvinist pig, Rae. It's not true. Not anymore. Anyway, I've always favored strong women." He extends a hand toward Betty. "Exhibit A. Now this one on the tube, even though she's holding a machine gun, she doesn't exactly project strength, does she?"

"So what's your point, Ronnie?"

"I don't have a point."

Betty and Rae exchange glances.

"You two are ganging up on me," he says, winking at his daughter and blowing a magnificent smoke ring that holds its form for a surprisingly long time in the small room.

"But seriously," Ronnie says, "what do these guys think they're doing? They're supposed to be revolutionaries, but what good are they doing for anyone else?"

Rae props herself up on the sofa. "They've already scored a bunch of food for poor people in Oakland."

"Are you rooting for them, Rae?"

"No. But I'm fascinated."

Betty walks over with the bowl of popcorn and puts it in Ronnie's lap. He takes a handful of popcorn and looks over at the two women smiling at him.

"Hey, somebody take this popcorn, I don't want this popcorn."

"I was just trying to quiet you down, Ronnie."

"There's no quieting me down," Ronnie says, "I'm like a storm. If you're caught in its path, there's nothing to do but wait for it to pass."

Betty turns to Rae. "Did you realize we were waiting on a storm?"

"What I was saying, if you don't mind, is that these 'revolutionaries' always have some crazy leader with delusions of grandeur. They're like big-band leaders I used to play for. They tell you that together you're revolutionizing the music. Then they take all the glory and most of the money. But they're not interested in revolutions, they're interested in controlling people. Turn you into a bunch of junkies if it serves their purpose. Anything to keep you in place. They'd even go out and *score* for you. Make it real easy.

"The big-band leaders usually had a girl singer under their thumb. Maybe she'd lay down for him, and he'd rough her up a little when he wanted. So, this Cinque, what does he have going? He's got a nice cobra design for the bandstand. Very chic presentation. But most of all, he's got the girl singer, he's got Patty Hearst singing for his band."

Deep Dutch

The next morning, the morning after Patty Hearst had herself successfully photographed holding a submachine gun inside the Hibernia National Bank, Ronnie leafs through three morning papers, finding them woefully inadequate—nothing more than a bunch of steamy headlines, GUNSLINGER PATTY HOLDS UP THE WORLD, followed by dull stories rehashed from the evening news. Didn't they realize that the poor woman was trapped, that she might have no choice but to try and shoot her way out?

Rae drops Quincy at the Blue Sea, a day care in Half Moon Bay run by a fat woman named Sky who has the widest assortment of tie-dye muumuus that Rae has ever seen. At the hippie bakery, Sweet and High, she walks in on a conversation about Patty.

"I think it's a masterful touch," says the long-haired counter guy, an old surfer turned speed freak, with a hoop earring and rotted teeth.

He's talking to a barefoot teenager in cutoff jeans who looks like she lives off blood donations, and maybe a little hustling on the side. She makes sucking sounds with her mouth and appears to be looking for a place to spit. "Yeah, so what was so masterful?"

"The bank job. Getting herself photographed with the gun. I mean, it's an instant poster: "Tania, with Machine Gun." I mean, check it out. It's like, roll over Che Guevera. I mean, check it out. They get the money, they get the publicity. Fame and fortune."

Rae looks through the glass case at the sweet rolls, trying to decide whether the speedster is being ironic.

"She's going to find herself in Dutch," the girl says, picking up a plastic bag of day-old glazed donuts, "deep Dutch."

"Who cares about her? She's just the pawn."

The girl shakes her head and goes back to her sucking sounds. She opens a small leather pouch and spills five quarters onto the counter. "You're really wrong about that, you know, there's plenty of people who love her."

The staccato "news" fodder on KCBS fills the bungalow with more Patty. Her father is still in his robe when Rae walks in. A smoking Viceroy hangs from the corner of his mouth.

"Five minutes," he pipes. Within the swirl of smoke, he measures several careful spoons of Folgers into the Mr. Coffee.

Surfers

They leave the bungalow with a thermos of coffee and a couple of cinnamon rolls in a bakery sack. It is a bright, cool morning. The air feels as if it has been washed like the rounded sides of a fruit and left to dry slowly. Aside from a barefoot man in a blue stocking cap and white sweatsuit, running a pair of hounds through the apron of wet sand, the beach is empty.

Her father, zipped into a red parka and sporting a Giants cap, looks less like a jazz musician than a man who's spent his life working the swing shift at Hamm's Brewery.

"How far you feel like walking, Rae?"

"Whatever you like."

"Tell me, 'cause I don't want to get you all tired out."

"I have good walking legs, Dad."

"Good deal. I always think of your generation as being tired. Wake up tired, tired all day, go to bed tired."

She yawns deeply for his benefit. "I'm not quite ready to pass out."

He wants to hold Rae's hand as they go up the beach, but doesn't feel it's for him to take it. He hopes she'll grab his. Rae bends into the wrack of broken shells and seaweed as they step along the wet, glassy sand.

"What are you looking for, honey?"

"I found a bunch of perfect sand dollars on the beach not long ago."

He shakes his head. "You can't find sand dollars anymore."

"You saw them. All those I brought to the house."

"But you bought those. I saw the little price sticker on them."

"What are you talking about?" she says angrily.

He meets Rae's sharp blue eyes, and draws them into a narrow hallway stare, before winking at her. "You have a quick temper."

"When someone's playing with me."

He takes her left hand in his and studies it a moment. The moonstone ring on her wedding finger, he can see, is in a cheap setting. He's curious about the baby rose tattoo, but decides against asking. He thinks of what she said about leaving the boy and is glad nothing's come of it.

"You have small hands like me."

"Well, I'm your daughter aren't I?"

"Yes, madam, you are."

He leads her out onto the stone fishing pier. The waves are breaking nicely on the point. A half-dozen surfers, crouched into black balls in their wetsuits, wait for a serviceable wave. In the time that he and Betty have lived in Half Moon Bay, he's made a point of studying the surfers. He's impressed with their patience, their discipline, how often they sit pat amid furious crosscurrents or ride over the tops of waves that rise up with swashbuckling promise. This is what he likes to watch, even more than the long, sinuous rides they take on their boards: the way they stay poised, alert to each new prospect, yet resist the temptation to spring out in front of waves about to scatter into a muddle of white water.

"I should have taken that up when I was young. You ever go surfing, honey?"

Rae shakes her head.

"Why the hell not? You only live once." He throws his head back in a mighty, but forced, laugh.

Rae had a boyfriend in high school who surfed. Dusty Stevens was her first love, a sweet boy who stuttered and wore a red cotton handkerchief wrapped around his head. For one long season, the year her father left, Rae was a surfer chick who hung out at Kelly's Cove, smoking weed and cigarettes, guzzling beer and Red Mountain wine with the other surfer chicks, but wishing Dusty would come out of the ocean and take her someplace far from this crowd. When he bobbed in finally, out of the white water, he was so shy. She wondered how a boy who'd been wrestling with the sea could walk up the beach, a gleaming survivor, and become skittish. "Hey, Ra . . . Rae," he'd say, glad to see her at the bonfire or sitting on the ocean wall at Kelly's. Sometimes while the other guys mauled their girls, he'd step up and kiss her. But even the kiss would be shy. He reminded her of a boy holding up a shiny apple, trying to decide where to make his first bite. And she'd look at him and want to say, *Right here, Dusty, right here on my lips.* After he kissed her he'd drop back with the guys, and try to keep up a stuttering banter about the conditions of the wind and water. "Gla . . . glassy out there. Real glassy."

Rae feels her eyes going moist and takes a large bite of her cinnamon roll.

"Did I say something that upset you, Rae?" her father asks.

"No."

"Well, forgive me if I did."

Rae forces herself to look at her father, the strange, gnomish character who's swinging his skinny knees together on the rock beside her.

"Tell me something about you," he says, "anything you're comfortable to tell. I'm the last guy in the world to do any prying. You know me."

"I don't know you," she says, and clamps her lips, which are flaked with sugar from the pastry.

He takes her hand and swings his knees together so quickly that she can feel a draft rising from the rock beside her.

"Okay, you don't know me," he says. "But that could be an advantage. We might have a chance to begin a relationship. There were some years when you wouldn't have wanted to know me . . . when it would have been a distinct disadvantage to know me."

He lets go of her hand, and wraps his arms around his knees, drawing them up to his chin so that there is even less of him showing.

"I'm talking about times when the only thing I was concerned with was satisfying my needs, whether they be drugs, or whatever."

Ronnie looks out toward the surfers who are bobbing like buoys in their holding pattern. He compacts himself into a ball and rocks at a furious pace, not like a mystic or a street maniac, but like a man who is trying to exorcise a dreadful memory.

Nature Boy

Rae watches her father without looking his way. He is a small, rocking man, still capable of his share of lunacy. When she was a teenager, her mother used to tell her about Ronnie's wild

days—the way he'd prowl the streets for drugs, how he'd shoot
up anything, go without food or drink for days at a time. The
teeth, her mother said, rotted one by one in his mouth, and the
drugs had a way of separating his body from his mind, so that
he could make it with cheap B-girls, absolute harlots, in public
places. They'd line up single file to get it on with him. Her
mother told all this as a cautionary tale—look what happened to
your father. But these drunken rants had an effect opposite to
what she intended. Rae was emboldened by accounts of her
father's wild behavior. It meant that she had good survival genes,
at least on her father's side. It gave her a certain immunity, like
having a rich dad and knowing that someday you'd inherit it all.
She would never be as wild as he was, never shoot drugs into her
body, or have sex with just anybody. But she'd be wild, her own
wild, wild enough to stay clear of her mother and become her
own person.

Her father is still collapsed into a fetal position, rocking.

"Can I ask you something?" Rae says.

His rocking slows and he snaps to—a man quite used to
leaping from a place outside of the world . . . to right here. She
watches him lift his face, a moon crisscrossed with lines like the
skin of a melon.

"Sure," he says, "anything."

"Would you sing something for me?"

"I don't sing anymore, honey."

Rae looks beyond the surfers to the Farallons, a faint mirage
of sepia islands dusting the horizon. "It's just you and me," she
says, "nobody else will hear. I used to go to bed at night and
wish you were there to sing."

She thinks to tell him that she wants to be a singer. That she's
already done it some, stood up in a little club and had a man ask
her to sing the same song over and over, until song broke out
of her like a rash. She thinks to tell him that the singing is one of
the reasons she's come. But first he has to sing. It seems better to
let him think that she's just a girl satisfied hacking out a living

waiting tables, a working mom with mild aspirations—maybe she'll take her high school equivalency test someday and go to junior college.

She turns to watch a couple of surfers wade in to the beach. Stepping woozily out of the water in their slick wetsuits, they look part animal. Rae is always surprised to see how boyish they are; even the old surfers, guys in their thirties now, appear ageless as they strip off their suits and stand around a bonfire absently kicking sand. Surfers' feet are strange specimens. At one time Rae studied them. It seemed to her that a surfer's experience was inscribed in his feet, because it was with his feet that he did his thinking. Ten beautiful boys would be standing around a fire and she'd look at their feet, and the uneven field of bruise pink, saucer-shaped wounds that covered them. Dings, they called them, that had been rinsed and sanitized by the salt water.

He surprises her with a song. His voice is so calm and present that it scares her. It is a lover's voice, light and breathy, a dusty whisper spilling between speech and song. For a quiet voice at the ocean, it holds up surprisingly well. Rae imagines a roomful of people leaning into her father's song, as if it were a dark hallway he leads them through.

A hundred yards from the stone pier, the surfers, who have no crowd of girls worshiping them this early morning, start a bonfire. Mindful of the sea creatures, even acknowledging them with a nod, Ronnie breaks into a chorus of "Nature Boy." His voice becomes stronger once he's been at it awhile. He sings a quick version of "Witchcraft" and then "Spring Can Really Hang You Up the Most," a tune that he handles with surprising ease even though it modulates all over the lot. He slows the tempo and smiles to Rae. He is as patient as one of the surfers. Waiting. Waiting. She takes a long breath with him, just as he slows through the lovely chromatic finish.

Negative Space

Every morning Betty sits up and considers the empty spot beside her in the bed. For five years she has gone to bed with Ronnie Reboulet and wakened by herself. Since Rae and Quincy have come he has hardly slept at all. She wishes he was beside her, as curled up and distant as he needs to be. She'd like to get up with him as he rises in his pajamas. Red-flannel man, slipping into his leather jacket, a pair of sandals, walking up the beach. She'd like to walk beside him, be a shadow as he steps through his waking night.

Sometimes, masturbating in the middle of the night, she awakens in a flush, and if Ronnie happens to be knotted in sleep beside her, she hushes her body, embarrassed, as if a noisy child had led her to the open door, coming. Once she climbed on top of him while he was sleeping and looked into the whites of his half-opened eyes, as his cock rose and then went soft. She had wanted to use up all that was left of him, to ravish him in the way men satisfied themselves with women, but he was frozen in sleep. The only time the man slept was when she wanted him awake.

At first she thought it must be hard to make love to a woman with a single breast, a lopsided woman with one full breast, the left one nothing but bunched skin, a scar running across her heart. But later, she decided that her missing breast wasn't what bothered him. She was surprised how much more she wanted sex than he did.

When she wakes with a hand pasted to her wet crotch, and the bed is empty, she brings him back in her imagining. She

wraps her arms around Ronnie and leads him into her tiny bedroom, the walls of which are covered with photographs of her
children. She kisses him, pushes him back on the bed. She
unbuckles his belt and pulls his jeans off with a clean jerk on the
hem of each leg, as if she were undressing a sleeping child. But
Ronnie is wide awake in her fantasy. His blue eyes shine up at
her. He throws his arms behind him and smiles. His twin rows of
ultra-white teeth flash a little danger and he has a lump in his
white Jockey shorts that she wants to cover with her hand. But
she'll wait, she tells herself, as long as waiting is as good as this.
His legs are practically hairless. She bends over him and massages
his small feet.

She passes a hand over the rise of his calves. Her hand moves
in small circles up his thighs. She watches his mouth as his lips
come together and twitch into an involuntary smile.

"Talk to me," she says.

"About what?"

"Jazz."

"That's not something to talk about."

"If you played it for me I wouldn't ask."

She lays a hand softly on the bulge in his shorts. "Tell me,"
she says.

"Okay, how about time?"

"Time," she echoes. His favorite subject. She has both hands
on him. She bends over him and takes one of his small, hairless
nipples into her mouth and closes everything around it, her eyes,
her mouth.

"Here's the thing about time—it's as valid when you're not
playing notes, as when you are. It goes on. It flows like a river. If
you don't understand that, a four-bar rest can be a problem. It's
like negative space, the cutout part of an ornamental design. A
mission oak chair, a strip of banister. Without the space it's just a
solid lump of wood."

"Yes," she says, and pulls her nightgown up and slides down
on him.

"Mmmm," he says, but holds on to his line. "I've seen these guys, all the chops in the world, and they don't know where *one* is. They're always anticipating, they've gotten tentative because they've completely lost the beat, which, when you're talking about music, is worse than being deaf and dumb."

After she came in the empty room, a creature swimming through the habitat of her senses, she'd search the room for a sign of Ronnie. Sometimes it seemed he was there, in the negative space.

Inventory

Most mornings she takes inventory, like an old painter confined to bed, sketching everything she's had and lost. She draws Ronnie first, climbing out of bed and gone walking, circling the living room in slippers and pajamas, as if there were a chance he'd return to bed before morning. She zips him into jeans and his creamy leather jacket, the pockets stuffed with cigarettes and matches, tops him with a Giants cap, and sends him where he finally goes, leaning into a low fog at the ocean.

She counts her children just as the Mexicans do. When anyone asks she says, "I have three children, two living and one dead." She hardly knows her living children anymore. The son, John, is a school teacher up in Tillamook, Oregon, where the cheese is made, and her married, childless daughter, Rose, lives in a thankless suburb of Pensacola. Ronnie tells her to have them visit whenever she wants. "Just because my family life is a ruin," he says, "doesn't mean you should go without." But she's made a certain peace with her children. Rose is a Christian type. And

John, it is clear enough to see, is a gay man who prefers a private life.

Betty tries to be a good mother to these children that she birthed at seventeen and nineteen. She tries to remind them that their mother loves them. She sends letters in envelopes that balloon with newspaper clippings. Human interest stories mostly— a woman who had her purse stolen by Bay Area Rapid Transit's automatic doors, at the Concord station; a man in Pacific Heights marketing a set of gold-plated pooper scoopers. These are the kinds of things they might share a laugh about if they were sitting across the breakfast table. She doesn't presume to send anything that coincides with her children's interests. She sends birthday cards with fifty-dollar checks and hand-drawn birthday cakes. Each summer she visits her daughter and son-in-law for a long weekend. She keeps pictures of all three children on her bureau and regularly dusts them. She doesn't blame either of her living ones for their neglect, because it is the dead one to whom she is most faithful, the one she really lives with.

As she counts her possessions, she includes only one breast— the missing one doesn't seem worth tallying like a dead child. She notes a gold ring, a strand of coral in its original Victorian setting, a pair of diamond earrings that Ronnie won on a golf course wager in St. Pete, and some sweet letters and notes he wrote her from their early days. There is a closet full of serviceable clothes, and a few colorful sun dresses, each bought on sale in Tampa but worn rarely now in the cooler Pacific climate. She conjures a pair of nurse's uniforms, and the image of herself standing in one, offering what comfort she can—to women, to babies, to a homely man in Coke-bottle glasses, standing in the nursery beside his hopelessly small preemie. There is nothing more comforting than human touch. She steps from her bed, an accomplished woman who has made far more of herself than anyone expected.

Inferno

On the night of May 17, after the SLA's safe house was blown up in LA, Ronnie and Betty lean toward each other on the sofa, holding hands. Rae sits in front of them on the floor, her legs folded underneath her. The volume on the television is turned low, to a golf-match whisper, as the shootout is replayed and the red and yellow sparks with wings broaden into brushstrokes of fire. The commentators give the score of probable victims, certain that Patty Hearst has been incinerated with the rest of them.

"Patty's not in there," Ronnie says. "I believe she's safe."

He had, of course, no idea that Patty Hearst spent that night in a separate horror, watching the inferno on TV from the Disneyland Hotel.

The morning after the fire, five bodies charred beyond recognition, gas masks melted onto their faces, were removed from the ruins, put into plastic body bags, and delivered to the coroner's office. One female corpse was found eight feet outside the house; the woman seemingly had been trying to crawl to safety. The body of Camilla Hall was found jammed in the crawl space under the floorboards, fused to the remains of her burned kitten. By noon the coroner had made positive identifications from dental records. Only then did Catherine and Randolph Hearst know that their daughter was not among the victims.

The Box

A week later, Rae sits in her father's mohair chair, reading *Newsweek*'s account of the fire. It is already old news. Rae has looked at all the pictures ten times. Patty is somewhere on the lam, while she is safe in her father's house, plopped in his over-stuffed chair—he is much more like an old-time pop, with his very own chair, than she would have guessed. Now he struggles up the basement steps with a sealed box.

"Hey, honey, I want to show you something." The box sits on the kitchen table. Ronnie splits the seam of packing tape with a Swiss army knife. He opens the flaps gingerly. "I had this in a storage place in Tampa. My former life in a single box." He reaches into his shirt pocket for a Viceroy then beckons Rae to sit by him.

Rae looks at the open box but is not really interested to see what's in it. She doesn't begrudge her father his past life, but is afraid that her future is sitting in a box that she'll never get a chance to open. When she got pregnant at sixteen, they told her that she'd be giving up her future. She hadn't imagined it as a box full of experiences.

"This is a minuscule amount of stuff for a pack rat. That's what your mother called me. One box of worldly goods. I used to keep a lot of shit. I'd be on the road all the time playing one-nighters, and if I was doing drugs I might forget what town I was in, where I started the day. It's true. I'd forget where I left my trumpet, where I was s'posed to go. It could get scary. I got into the habit of sticking matchbooks in my pockets. I'd find ashtrays and hotel towels in my valise or my trumpet case, anything with a name or address on it. 'Course, I'd end up with enough shit to confuse myself all over again. Be in Boston, and I'd pull match-books out of my pockets from clubs in Cleveland and Philly, a ballpoint pen from Chicago."

Everybody had a different idea of how Rae should dispose of her baby. The most attractive idea was an adoption agency that specialized in white women giving up their black babies.

"Sometimes I'd find an old piece of buttered toast, wrapped in a napkin in my coat pocket. Musicians have a habit of stashing leftover food. 'Specially the older black guys who couldn't get meals traveling through the south. I met Duke Ellington one year at the Newport Festival. A fastidious man in a thousand-dollar suit. We're backstage talking for a minute, and he pulls a linen handkerchief out of his coat pocket. I'm all caught up with his hands. He has these beautifully manicured fingers, and does this simple sleight of hand, folding back a linen hanky on a cold pork chop, which he starts munching on like it's as natural as a guy walking up the street eating an ice cream cone."

A doctor at the Haight-Ashbury Free Clinic put her on a nutrition program because she wasn't gaining enough weight. He talked to her every time she went in. He wasn't a shrink, or an OB. He did a little of everything. He had a fu manchu mus-tache that looked kind of hip. His name was Rob. A funny name, she thought. Rob. A half here, half not, kind of name. She could tell that he smoked his share of weed. He'd say, tell me what you're worried about. And when she did, he'd nod his head and tell her that no matter what she did, her job was to take very good care of that baby. At the end of the visit, he'd go over the nutrition plan and hand her a big pack of vitamins. And at the door, he'd put his hand on her shoulder. His hand felt good there, both personal and impersonal as if he were her tennis coach. And then he'd put on a voice like Ward Cleaver, the Beaver's father. "Remember," he'd say, "a daily salad is a must," and she'd smile, walking through the green lobby and out onto the buzz of Haight Street, repeating the words to herself: "A daily salad is a must."

"So when I got home from the road your mother would empty all my pockets, turn the damn linings of my slacks and sport coats inside out—I don't know, maybe she was looking for cash, but that was the only thing that didn't fall out. 'Course she wanted to throw all this crap away and we had endless fights about it. But when I'd see the stuff I'd get excited, reading the names off, and trying to remember places I wasn't sure I'd even been.

"We had one of those walk-in closets in that railroad apartment out on Anza, maybe you remember, and I stuffed it full of every piece of memorabilia I could keep hold of. Sometimes, you know, I'd come back from a gig in the middle of the night, and I knew I wasn't going to sleep. And I'd just go in that closet, pull on the string light, and sit for a while looking at all my stuff."

Rae closes her eyes on an image of Quincy in his swaddling blanket. Littlest sack of brown potatoes.

"You all right, Rae?"

"I'm fine."

They sit in silence.

She didn't return to the free clinic after Quincy was born. Her mother got her and the baby on a health plan at Kaiser. She was afraid to go back and show the baby to Rob and say, "Look, I kept him. Isn't he beautiful?"

Her father's voice starts up again. "I can talk a blue streak, can't I? Years go by and I don't do this. And then . . . you just say when you want me to shut up. I'm not used to talking like this. The only people I'm ever with is Betty. She's all of them. We're pretty quiet. Old farts, you know. We don't have so much to say. She knows what I'm liable to say before I think it, and all she has to do is nod to me and I won't bother saying it."

He rummages through the box. "I put this stuff in here quite a while ago. More than five years now. I'd been in the hospital for a few days. When I got out I took care of some business and gathered my stuff. I used to think about this a lot. Storage. Why do people hold on to these things from a former life?"

She'd been living in a commune on Page, near the Panhandle. Her mother brought her home to the big apartment on Jackson, and she spent a week listening to advice on the proper way to nurse the baby, when to wean it, when to start it out on Gerber's stewed green beans. Her mother's voice, harsh with all the smoke and alcohol, tried to offer some tender advice. It was the saddest thing. She made an effort to be nice to her mother. In the early mornings, while Cat slept, she sat in the window seat with Quincy, sweet-talking the baby as she nursed him, counting the container ships sailing through the Gate, long blocks of red or black cutting through the belly of water, its color shifting, according to the light in the sky, between a dull putty and a Turkish blue.

She's becoming a sucker for her father's voice, his story voice as well as his singing. She loves the patience in his voice, in which the world is trimmed to a simple ribbon of hushed speech.

"Want to see a picture?" he says.

"Sure." She thinks for a minute that it will be a picture of her as a baby. But rummaging in the box, he pulls out an old record. "That's me in my gunslinging days."

She laughs. "I've never seen this one. That's you?"

The cover shows a young man in cowboy getup, hat and boots and rawhide vest, dangling a trumpet from his finger like a six-shooter. *Way Out West with Ronnie Reboulet.*

He pulls another album out of the box. It shows a baby-faced young man investigating the valves of his trumpet, as a blond with thick red lips lays her head in his lap. The title, *Ronnie Reboulet Plays for Lovers*, is etched across the cover's soft blue ground.

"I wasn't too bad-looking back then."

"You were beautiful."

"And you were barely born. What else do I have in here?"

After two weeks with her mother she took the baby home to her room on Page Street. Darnell had helped her paint and fix up the room. He planned to stay with her and the baby, but she'd already learned not to expect much from Darnell. He liked to crash at his mother's house, or shack up with rock and roll girls that had a few grams of coke packed into their tight jeans.

Rae rubs her eyes. She wants to climb out of herself. She looks at her father, still holding the old ten-inch records.

"When did you make those records, Dad?"

"These records? I don't know. A few years after I left Stan Kenton. I was pretty much strung out by then. Started chippieing in the Kenton band, but I went whole hog as soon as I got back to California. I'd go light once in a while for a couple of weeks, but heroin . . . heroin fit me well. That old horse needed a rider and I was the one. That's where I was when I cut these records."

Rae nods and looks down at her folded hands.

"You've never been in trouble, have you, honey? You don't look like a girl who's ever been in trouble."

"Not with drugs, or anything. Probably smoked a little too much weed at times, but nothing really bad. I've had other trouble, though," she says with a sigh.

"Yes." He nods with sympathy. "I'm sure you have."

Stardust

"That's about as far as we should go," Ronnie says, interlocking the flaps of the box.

"What else do you have in there?"

"That's enough for one day."

"You might as well go through it, Dad."

Ronnie flips open the box and pulls out a black case. "Look here." He unbuckles the case. "A little mildewed." He holds up the body of a silver trumpet and fingers the three valves for a moment.

"Can you play something?"

"Yeah, that's the sixty-four-thousand-dollar question."

Ronnie pulls a gold mouthpiece from a red velvet slipcase and holds it daintily between his thumb and first finger as if it were a canapé. He buzzes his lips a few times, then raises the mouthpiece and makes a series of crisp duck calls, followed by a long singular wail.

"I didn't know you could do so much with just a mouthpiece."

He doesn't say anything, but attaches the gold mouthpiece to the silver body and, before putting the thing to his lips, shakes some phantom spit from the horn. Mouth opened, filled with man-made choppers, strange things that seem closer to metal than bone, he tries to force a weighty roar through the horn, but nothing more than a tinny sound sputters out. There is no sense to it. His lips don't know these monster teeth. How did he end up with somebody else's buckteeth in his mouth? He tries to hold a middle A with a makeshift embouchure, picturing a wave of oscillating curves untangling into a straight line, a man muttering as he drags his wooden leg up a crooked staircase. He blows a couple of phrases from "Stardust" in a clear legato, but it is like fighting a war to make the notes sound like they've each issued from the same bell, and not from a half-dozen runaway horns in a junior high band class.

He holds out a note in an even vibrato, until it shoots off at a sharp angle like a shanked golf shot. He shakes his head and cradles the horn in his lap.

"You make such beautiful sound."

He shakes his head.

Rae studies her father. He looks down at the floor, at the pale green shag carpet. The trumpet is in his right hand. He says nothing, but suddenly lifts the horn and splutters a flurry of fast, nasty notes that break like a rash over the room. He lays the horn in his lap again and reaches into his shirt pocket for a Viceroy. He inhales deeply and winks at her.

"Sorry, I think getting the horn out is a little emotional for me."

She watches him open the horn's spit valve and shake a few drippings onto the shag rug. He pulls the mouthpiece from the horn and wraps it carefully in a handkerchief before dropping it into his shirt pocket.

Rae takes a deep breath. It strikes her that it might be a decent time to divert his attention. "You want to hear something funny?"

"Hmmm?"

"I've decided what I'm going to be when I grow up."

"What's that?"

"A singer. I've been doing a little singing. Singing around. Nothing big, a club down on Haight and Stanyan called Relaxing with Evone."

"Funny name for a club."

"Yeah, it is. And I sang once at Minnie's Can Do on Fillmore."

"Another funny name."

"Yeah, but that's a pretty popular place, Dad."

"How would I know? So, you're going to make a career singing at places with funny names?" He lights a cigarette from the end of the last and takes a long drag. "A singer, what a crazy thing to want to be. That's great," he says, open-faced with enthusiasm, "how come you didn't tell me? What kind of singing?"

"J A Z Z," she says, slowly, so that she can feel the word buzz as it comes out of her mouth.

Say It Slowly

Not too many days after the SLA house was incinerated, Quincy started asking questions about it. Rae had tried to keep the whole business from Quincy, but he had sat on the fat woman's lap at the Blue Sea watching the house explode, over and over again. He heard it discussed on talk shows. "Why did they blow up those people, Mama? Why did they?" he asked. He wanted to know what happened to people's bodies when they burned up in fires, whether only people with brown skin got burned in fires. He worried that maybe his daddy was in there and got burned alive.

"Not your daddy," Rae said, and she wrapped her arms around Quincy. She closed her eyes and tried to picture the fear spiraling through him, and saw it as a coiled shell, pocked with barnacles that she would have to break off, one by one.

She bent to kiss his ear. "Sweet boy. Sweet boy. Your daddy's fine. He doesn't know any of those poor people. He's fine."

He said something to her that she wasn't able to hear so she crouched low to look into his face. She still couldn't understand him. She held him by the shoulders. "Say it slowly."

"I wanna see my daddy." He said it so clearly that she realized she'd already heard him say it three times.

"I know you do, sweet boy," she said, her own coil of fear beginning to churn. "I know you do."

Narcissus

The day she took a cab over with the new baby, she was greeted by Scooter and Lilah. Shaggy-haired Scooter spent a lot of time in his room reading Chaucer, with dirty wax earplugs stuffed in his ears. He'd go days without talking to anyone, but when Rae walked in with Quincy, he flipped his glasses up onto his head and examined the infant. "Hi, baby," he said. Lilah, the only girl Rae knew with more freckles on her face than herself, had tears in her eyes, and gave Rae a fresh-baked zucchini bread and a ragged but colorful bunch of hollyhocks, in a green, gas-station vase.

Rae could hear a Jimi Hendrix record as she climbed the stairs to her room. She imagined Darnell was inside tripping. The room smelled of weed, but Darnell must have stepped out. The baby's bureau was littered with paraphernalia: a razor and a dusting of powder sat on a smeared coke mirror, beside a pack of wheatstraw Zig-Zags and the Twinings Prince of Wales tin that Darnell kept his stash in.

"This is your new home," she said to the baby.

Jimi was blowing the national anthem. That was Darnell's favorite. He'd rigged the stereo to play it over and over. "I'm just a patriotic dude." The bathroom door was open. Rae could see Darnell standing in front of the mirror. She'd never known anybody who spent so much time at the mirror. Darnell had a problem with it: he couldn't look into the mirror without making a face. Whenever she stood beside him in the bathroom, she kidded him about it. "Can't you just look natural, Darnell? Can't you be yourself?" But even when he tried, he couldn't keep himself from mugging. Sometimes he'd puff out his lips like a man who'd hatched a bright idea, or he'd shift his head sideways in a street man's pose of indifference, or use his baby finger to cover the dark mole on the bridge of his nose, but most often he narrowed his eyes into daggers making like he was a bad dude. He could never just be regular Darnell looking into the mirror; he had to spend half of his time inventing new poses. Rae waited until he came out of the bathroom to show him the baby.

"Let me see my boy," Darnell said. "Where you been keeping him?"

She knew not to say anything. She just handed Quincy to Darnell, who looked frightened to hold the baby. Rae had to show him how to support Quincy's head. Darnell looked down at the baby and said, "Isn't he handsome?" As she looked at Quincy in his father's arms, she saw that the baby's skin was almost as dark as Darnell's. Didn't she count for anything? Darnell could do his father thing for fifteen minutes, and go off forever. But the boy would always be *his* boy, would always be brown like him.

Looking for Junior

Ronnie parks the Alfa in a bus zone out front of Buzzards Bottle Shop on the corner of Fillmore and Geary. As a kid he loved this corner. He only saw it from the back of a green streetcar, his feet propped on the empty seats in front of him. Some days after school, when neither of his folks were around, he'd flee the desolate Richmond district with a two-cent ride to town, shoving five plugs of five-a-penny gum in his mouth and watching Geary Street go by, all the way from his stop near the ocean to the City of Paris, the grand department store on the east side of Union Square.

The streetcar seemed supremely powerful, tethered to its humming overhead cables. Sometimes Ronnie held out his arms and imagined the electric spunk shooting through him as they lurched past the avenues of solid houses and flats, the new houses going up in sandlots sprouting Jack-and-the-beanstalk weeds and soft, spiky carpets of ice plant. The streetcar shot past barren blocks, with few people or automobiles, until it hit the inner avenues, dotted with markets and service shops and taverns.

Ronnie smacked gum like a tough in one of the back seats, and the other passengers stayed clear of him. He chattered to himself, or pretended that he was talking to his brother, Natty, who would never go with him to town. Ronnie loved the foggy afternoons when the streetcar tunneled out of the thick stuff, near the crest at Masonic, and then rumbled through the colored neighborhood. Fillmore was the most enchanted corner, with all its thick cables, crisscrossed and humming, stretched every which way above the telephone poles and streetcars. It had to be the center of the world, with so many people dressed finely, especially the men, who looked like they were always partying, stepping with a mouthful of chatter between the twin poles of Rosy Bowl Barber Heaven.

The last time he parked at the corner of Geary and Fillmore, he was out prowling for dope. He hadn't played for weeks. So many of his teeth had gone wobbly with rot, he started to freak about putting the horn to his mouth. He'd been staying with a woman named Roxie on Potrero Hill. She was in pretty bad shape herself and Ronnie had come to the Fillmore to score for both of them.

Six years and a little change later, he walks into Buzzards Bottle Shop and sets two cans of Coca-Cola and a pint of Rémy Martin down on the counter. He asks the proprietor, a large man with a white, pencil-thin mustache, if he knows the whereabouts of Junior Reese.

The man gives Ronnie a good looking-over, and says, "Junior Reese, Juney Reese. You a friend of his?"

"Used to be."

"Used to be is a long time ago."

"You're right. I played music with him."

In the early forties, Junior had played trumpet with everybody. Earl Hines, Billy Eckstine, Dizzy, and Bud. He wrote a couple of bop heads that Bird loved to play—"Chewing the Suet" and "Guinea Pie." Then he lost his lip and who knows what else.

"I don't believe Juney Reese be playing a whole lot of music of late. He stays in a room up on Buchanan. Bush and Buchanan."

Japanese Birdsong

Ronnie hadn't seen Junior for a good ten years. The little trumpet man had come whistling through a rock garden in Japantown. Ronnie had just hit up in the public bathroom and was nodding on a granite bench, zipped tight in a leather jacket the color of sand. He had on a pair of wrinkled slacks and torn socks. He'd kicked off his Italian loafers and they lay somewhere in the bushes. People walked by speaking Japanese. They didn't bother with him, a helpless junkie.

Ronnie heard the whistling—a bright, staccato chirp—before he saw Junior. The jaunty head of "Chewing the Suet" flew into every Japanese apartment on Bush Street, and was followed by Junior's full voice. "Reb, is that you, Reb?"

He opened his eyes wide. Cherry blossoms were in bloom. Junior came stepping in a pair of yellow sneakers, size five and a half, holding a flowering pink branch in one hand and a large book in the other. He had on a black-and-white checked cap and an old brown suit left over from the big band days.

"Happy Washington's Birthday, Reb. I'm going to visit a lady with this, gonna seduce her with cherry blossoms. Whatya think of that, Reb? Gonna make her feel good, all up and down, with these blooms.

"You know what this book is? You don't know? This is the *Cyclopedia of Jazz*, man. Lookit here. I'm in this book. Old Juney. You're here too. Did you know that? We could find you in here. Contrary to popular opinion, you do exist. And it's not like they put everyone in here. But lookit here. Page two-sixteen. Two times, I got my pitcher on this page. Before I go by and see that lady, I'm taking this cyclopedia to show my doctor. I told him 'bout it. Disbelievin' motherfucker.

"Here I am—Junior Reese, sitting right next to Dizzy in Earl Hines's band. Fatha's band. Band of angels, man. Bird. Sassy, sitting up there facing Fatha on the back to back, piano. Lookit here. Bird, he's got his shades on, 'bout to fall off his chair, nodding. He's axing for it, shooting up right before they take the pitcher. Worse off than you, Reb. Don't I look something? Dapper. Very expensive suit.

"And this pitcher, this is me, Junior Reese, standing between Prez and Lucky Thompson. Pair of tenor heavyweights. Beauteous innovators. And here's Monk. Thelonious. Young motherfucker. We're all young, back then. Fifty-second Street. Nineteen and forty-three. This is before your time, hunh, Reb? You be playing in some baby school band shooting off spitballs at the saxophones. This is before your time, Reb."

Ronnie had salt on his tongue, an ache under his ribs, his mouth was dry, his nose running. He thought to rub it on the sleeve of his leather jacket, but not with somebody standing in front of him. Even if nobody was there but the Japanese men and ladies, going to the hardware store. He wondered what it would be like to stand up off his bench. Had the blood in his legs turned to stone? He got up and went walking, past the pond shaped like a toy boat, with the wishing pennies and the pair of orange carp swimming around. The whistling began again: "Chewing the Suet." He turned to see Juney Reese sitting on the stone bench. Grey cheeks drawn, lips puckered like an angel in a storybook, giving the song a stately balance as it feathered out of the bridge.

Comebacks

He finds Junior in a small, drafty room with yellowed strips of terry cloth stuffed in the window cracks. The old trumpeter has a lovely patch of white hair, and big red gums in his mouth that don't look like they even have a memory of teeth. Junior offers a cup of tea but Ronnie shakes his head and hoists the pint of Rémy Martin to his old friend.

"Cognac, I'll wash my mouth with that." Junior unscrews the bottle top and sucks at it like a thirsty boy drawing water from a garden hose. He looks very old, but he's only in his mid-fifties. Age is a strange thing around here. Bird was an old man when he died at thirty-four.

Junior takes a biscuit from a green candy dish and dips it in his tea, then gums it into damp meal and swishes it around his mouth.

"Reb, you care to share some of my dinner with me?"

"No, thanks. Funny thing, two old trumpet players, and neither one of us has his own teeth."

"I've heard of funnier things than that."

"I bet. So how come you never started playing again, Juney?"

"Simple reason for that."

"What's that?"

"I was never so good in the first place. I had a feel for the music and a tuneful tone, but I wasn't no great shakes."

"What do you think about me starting up again?"

"I ain't ever thought about it. Might be something you could do, might not."

It wasn't exactly the benediction he was looking for.

"Your old Jew manager been after you? They're big on blood from a turnip."

"Murray?"

"That big ole Jew."

"Murray."

"Yeah, that's him. Tell him to give me some money. Tell him I taught you how to play. He the one that put you up to this?"

Ronnie takes a long sip from his Coke. "No, I haven't been in touch with him for a few years."

"Tell that old Jew that I'm ready to make my comeback."

Ronnie laughs. "When's the last time you played, Junior?"

"Twenty years. And that's my point. Tell that Jew mother-fucker that it's going to take a big, fat motherfucking advance, get me to change my lifestyle thing."

Junior goes off into a high-pitched cackle, with his tongue planted in his red gums—zee zee zee zee zee—then picks up another biscuit and starts the long process of creaming it back into meal.

Say Hey

Rae wasn't going to take any shit from Darnell. You had to be firm or he'd steal little things away from you, and keep on taking until you busted him. Once she realized that Darnell was a coward, she called him on everything, and he almost always backed down. Maybe he was just too pretty, with his large green eyes and cocoa brown skin, with his wide, white-tooth smile. His mother had held on to him too closely and, even now, at twenty-three, he stayed at her house in a hideaway terrace off Lyon Street.

At first, Rae had liked going with Darnell to his mother's little row cottage. It was a neighborhood of older, courtly black folks who spent a lot of time tending the potted plants on their porches. When Darnell's mother wasn't there they'd make love in his boyhood bedroom, the sharp smell of collards pasted to all the walls in the place.

Sometimes, in that baby-boy room with all of Darnell's old baseball stuff lying around, she wondered how she landed with a boy, who might always remain a boy. An enormous poster of Willie Mays was tacked to the wall opposite Darnell's bed. Willie, looking nonchalant, was making a basket catch in center-field. The words SAY HEY were printed in enormous orange letters under the picture. That was Willie's nickname, according to Darnell. Say Hey. Once, after making love, she winked at Willie Mays and mumbled, "Say Hey."

Darnell's mother cooked for him when she wasn't working at the hospital, and he'd run back to her house every chance he got, as if a daily serving of her buttered greens was his birthright. He'd sit with his feet up at the kitchen table, begging for another bowl of okra, or black-eyed peas and pig snouts, or a shrimp and crayfish gumbo.

Darnell knew how to flatter his mother. "You such a good cook, Mama, God gonna come down from heaven just for a taste of your okra."

"I don't want God messing with my okra. And Darnell Roper," she said, filling his bowl, "in polite society folks do not eat with their feet up on the table."

Darnell tries to sound indignant on the phone. "Where have you been with my boy? I could get your ass for kidnapping."

But he is all bluff, working the situation for whatever advantage he can get.

"Called your mama three or four times. But she so drunk she doesn't even know where *she's* at. Two months since I've seen my boy."

Rae smacked her gum into the phone. "It's not like you'd been coming around or anything. Only time you get interested is when something goes away."

"Yeah, well I'm not going to let you do this again. Where you been hiding?"

"I haven't been hiding."

There was a pause on the line. "Yeah, so where you staying?"

"With my father."

"Your father! 'Ronnie the famous'! What the hell hole did he crawl out of?"

"Shut up, Darnell."

She asks him to meet at a tiny bakery named Elaine's, out in the Avenues.

"Way out there," he says, "that wouldn't be convenient for me. I'm temporarily without a car."

"Darnell, you've never had a car."

"What do you know, girl? Plenty of ladies gives me their cars to drive. But right now I'm temporarily without, and I don't happen to have enough pocket change for a taxi."

"If you really want to see your boy, I think you can get yourself out to the Avenues."

"You could come and get me."

"I'm not going to do that. All you got to do is take the Thirty-eight Geary out front of your mother's house."

Darnell tries another tack. "What do you want to do going way out there to this bakery? There's nothing out there but a bunch of ole white people and a tribe of Chinamen. They've turned it into goddamn, motherfucking Chinatown Numero Dos, out there."

"Take it or leave it, Darnell."

"You some kind of bitch, Rae. Yeah, so tell me one thing. This bakery, you think they got some kind of righteous chocolate cake . . . some fudge brownie kind of shit . . . you know what I mean . . . out there?"

"I couldn't say, Darnell. You're going to have to take your chances."

Acid Love

Rae met him at the Stones concert at Altamont. She'd driven out from the city with some high school friends, but lost them in the massive crowd in the pasture. People roamed around for hours as a half-dozen warm-up bands played. Darnell was roaming too, but Rae wouldn't meet him until the music was done.

She took a tab of acid from a skinny man dressed like Uncle Sam, who circulated through the crowd with a red frisbee dotted with blue and white tabs the size of saccharin grains. "Just one," he said, "just one, my dear. Only one per customer. Just one. One will be sufficient."

She came on to the stuff just as Mick Jagger took the stage. He raised his hands and said, "Let's see how quiet we can be," and managed to turn the crowd into a single organism. The silence was a miracle like a sung note, sustained beyond the limits of breath. It went on so long that it grew its own waves of vibrato, and a man in the crowd let loose with a huge celebratory whoop. Mick Jagger looked long and lean like Uncle Sam, but she was sitting so far away she couldn't see any stars and stripes.

From that distance, it was all a peaceable kingdom, with joints flickering like fireflies in the warm night. She shared a blanket with two women who were very fond of each other. They broke into deep kisses, from time to time, in which one seemed like she was going to swallow the other. Two hundred and fifty thousand people were whispering to one another, but Rae could hear everything they said. She felt like she was eavesdropping on the intimacies of an entire city. Somebody touched her, touched her very gently, but she didn't see the hand or who it belonged to. The music showed them how they belonged to one another. The entire human race could make love at once and nobody would be left out. The music was so familiar that she felt like they were living in the Bible with God's voice singing to them. She had no idea that a man was getting his head smashed in by the Hell's Angels, three hundred yards ahead of her.

Afterward, people jammed the road, hitching rides to their cars, stutter-stepping from the centerline to the shoulders, inventing personal imitations of Mick Jagger. Darnell, impersonating a suave man, wore horn-rimmed frames with no lenses. Skinny as a speed freak in a beautifully long pair of jeans that belled just above his sandals, he cha-chad up the shoulder. Later he'd say, "I picked you out of the crowd because you were the most beautiful girl I'd ever seen. But I could have had anybody."

He took her hand as he danced up the road and showed her the best way to cha-cha-cha under the circumstances. After a while they slowed to a stop and looked at each other. He smiled at her with remarkable tenderness. They were fellow pilgrims.

Darnell led her down a slope to a brown field and they made love before telling each other their names. She was fifteen years old and had made love to two different surfer boys that by then had blended into a single boy in her memory. One was at the beach, the other in the backseat of a '63 Impala. Both boys were artless. She'd insisted they wear rubbers. This brown boy was older and seemed to know what he was doing. She never wanted to quit kissing him. The acid made her mouth and jaw the seat of all her sensation. She offered to suck him, but he only wanted to work his penis inside her vagina.

The road was still jammed with reveling pilgrims. She and Darnell walked arm in arm like longtime lovers.

Eight Ball

Darnell struts into the bakery with a little package in his hands, grinning like a trickster under his denim cap, his gangly arms doing a roo-too-too sway, back and forth, as he catches Quincy's eyes and the boy chortles in delight.

Rae had tried to imagine a place too constrained for a heavy scene. Open the door to Elaine's and you're standing amid the four tiny tables covered with Provençal cloths and facing a shelf of Devon Motto Ware teapots—SOW A CHARACTER, REAP A DESTINY—and a bakery case filled with lemon poppy-seed cakes, fruit kalachis, rhubarb pie, and scones.

As Darnell steps in the door, he fills the place with randy

energy. The white matrons at the other tables are distracted by the domestic curiosity about to unfold. Rae's concentration is divided. Darnell kisses her cheek, and the white women lean closer to one another.

Darnell puts the package down and is at Rae's ear, whispering, "I don't have any money."

"That's all right, they don't have any chocolate cake."

He stabs his tongue inside her ear, and she wants to slug him but only jerks her head away so as not to titillate the matrons. He tries to catch her eyes but she stares at his sweet spot, the dark mole on the bridge of his nose.

"What's in there?" Quincy asks of the package sitting in front of him on the small table.

"You wanna know what's in there?" Darnell teases.

"Yeah. That for me?"

"Open it up."

Quincy rips the wrapping and the square box open, and pulls out a shiny black eight ball. He turns the ball over and over in his hands. "That for me?"

"Yeah, that's for you. You know what that is? That's an eight ball. You ask it questions, any kind of question you have about the future and it will give you the answer. Say you wanna know, 'Am I going to be rich and famous when I grow up?' Go ahead, ask it that. Go on."

Quincy looks at the black ball like it's a cat that might jump at him at any moment, and mumbles, "Am-I-goin'-be-rich . . . ?"

"That's right." Darnell takes the ball from the boy. "Let's look at the answer. See, it's there. Those little white letters in the triangle. It's magic, Quince."

"What's it say? What's it say? What does it?"

"Says, 'Concentrate and try again.' You got to think real hard about that question and ask again."

After he has concentrated and asked the question again, Quincy hands the eight ball to his father. "What's it say?"

"Says, 'Don't rely on it.' Which means you probably aren't

going to be rich. If you were a little white boy, you might get a different answer. But you gotta practice with this ball, Quince."

Quincy moves his lips as if he is trying to form a question. He is caught by both the black shininess of the ball and the bubbling pool of white letters offering answers he can't read.

Darnell turns toward Rae. "How about what they did to the SLA, Ray-zee?"

"Don't call me that."

"All right." Darnell nods his head four or five times to an imaginary beat. "Don't you follow the news, Rae?"

"I follow it."

"You think they would have blown that house if the thing wasn't run by a black dude? Say they had some white guy, instead of Cinque, I bet they'd call him charismatic, or some shit."

"I don't want to talk about this, Darnell."

"Why not?"

She nods toward Quincy, who's pushed aside the double-size slice of carrot cake to have more space to concentrate on the eight ball.

"You planning on babying the boy, planning to keep things from him?"

"He's four years old, Darnell."

"I know how old he is. I'm the boy's father." Darnell smiles at his son. "What else do they have here?"

Rae stands and takes a step toward the counter. "How about a slice of rhubarb pie and coffee?"

"Sounds good."

She plans to make this visit brief. She won't ask Darnell a single question about himself, and it would never occur to him to ask about her. The object, she reminds herself, is to give Quincy a chance to see his dad. For Darnell these little visits will be the sum of it. He no more wants to be a father in a daily way than he wants to work an hourly job, or cook his own supper. Rae watches them from the counter, her black boy and his black daddy snuggled together, laughing. Even if she got Quincy up every morning of his life, fed him three squares, bathed him, read him stories, took him to his sports, picked out his clothes until he didn't want that anymore, sat with him every night as he did his homework, saved up money to send him off to college, she could never have the same black-boy-and-daddy closeness he has with Darnell.

Now Darnell pulls a baseball out of his jacket pocket. "This is a very special ball, Quince, very special."

Quincy reaches out for the ball. "Why is it?"

" 'Cause it's signed by a great ballplayer, one of the greatest— Willie McCovey."

"Can I hold it?"

"Sure, it's for you. This and the eight ball are the birthday presents I would have laid on you if I had known where you were. But your mama took you somewhere that I didn't know where you were. Look here, that's where he signed his name. Willie McCovey."

Quincy turns the ball over, rubbing his little fingers over the red signature.

"You got to take good care of that ball, Quince. You can't play with this one. It's worth a lot of money. You got to put it in a special place."

Darnell flashes Rae one of his ain't-I-something smiles. "You're looking good, girl. Your mama's a beautiful woman, did you know that, Quince? A very beautiful woman, despite all her freckles." Darnell forces a laugh.

Rae senses the women from the other tables watching. She wants to turn to each of them and say, "Fuck you, and fuck you, and fuck you, and fuck you."

Darnell brings his head close to Quincy. "The Giants went and did something stupid. They traded Willie McCovey to another team. They do a lot of stupid things. First they traded Willie Mays, now Mac. So he doesn't play here anymore. He's playing ball down in San Diego. You know where that is, Quince?

That's right up next to Mexico. So old Willie, he smacks a homer then goes out and buys a bunch of enchiladas. Thing I was thinking is that next time those San Diegos come to town, you and me should go out to the ballpark and say hello. You can come too, Rae. You ever been to a baseball game, girl?"

Rae shakes her head.

"How about your father, 'Ronnie the Famous,' he like baseball?"

"I don't know."

"You don't know. Well, ask him. Maybe we could all go to a ball game together. I'd like to meet this joker. Ronnie Reb-o-let. Did you know your granddaddy's famous, Quince? Frankly, I thought the man was dead." He turns toward his son. "But isn't that something, Quince, your mama doesn't even know what her daddy likes. Do you know what *your* daddy likes?"

Quincy shrugs. "I wanna go see baseball."

Darnell nods. "Sure you do. I like you, you're my best boy."

As Darnell digs into the rhubarb pie, Quincy puts aside the baseball and looks at his own reflection in the shiny black plastic of the eight ball.

Listen to the Beat

Ronnie leaves the bartender a healthy tip and carries two Cokes to the piano.

"What do you want to sing? I'll lay down a little something for you, honey. A few basic chords."

"I don't know. . . . 'My Funny Valentine'?"

"Sure, that be fine." He spreads his fingers over the keys, trying to guess where she'll sing it.

His daughter stands, one hand on the piano, with the face of a dreamy child. He keeps vamping, waiting for her. A four-bar intro becomes eight. He'll vamp all day if he has to, even though he's never been much of a piano player. His hands are stiff, but he'll be able to play for a while. His head fills with bad musician jokes. Why did the singer stand in the hallway? Because she couldn't find the key and she didn't know where to come in. How many female singers does it take to sing "My Funny Valentine"? Apparently all of them.

Rae pictures a handful of singers poised beside the piano, sophisticated ladies with long, beautiful throats. One night she sat with Wallace, making a fuss over a photo book of singers. Wallace said, "Don't get yourself all messed up behind a few posed pictures. These ladies, they know what to do when they see a camera. You gotta think about them in their home environment, you know what I'm saying. Take Sassy, she be walking around her place in panties and a black brassiere, have a nice fat highball in her hand. But, sure as shit, she's after singing some beautiful songs down the bottom of that deep river she has for a voice. You wanna be intimidated, darling, you worry about the way these girls sing, not how they dress up for the photographer."

She asks Wallace how he knew what Sarah Vaughan wore at home.

"I know these things, girl. I've been there."

Rae has a knot of spent Chiclets in her mouth that she'd rather not have, but she can't imagine how to get rid of it. She slides the gum into a corner of her mouth and looks past her father, across the empty room. An old, ruddy couple is sitting shoulder to shoulder at the bar, the woman a regular storyteller, the man nodding, both of them smoking and swilling their beers at a superhuman pace, as if life were running out. Were her parents like this?

Ronnie looks up at his daughter, all grown up with breasts, in a fuchsia-colored blouse. He tries to imagine the quality of her voice. Husky, he guesses, for a girl who doesn't smoke. He wonders if she'll ever get started.

It is three in the afternoon and the tavern, situated on a bluff at the beach near Pescadero, is dark as a morgue. Rae tries to concentrate on the song, but she can't. She looks over at her father. "How about 'Follow Me'?"

"That be fine." Ronnie drops down a half-step, a couple more, somewhere close to his high-pitched, man-child range. "How's that, honey?"

Rae is locked in a zone and doesn't acknowledge his question. He keeps laying down lush, lollipop chords—if he were pitching a baseball, anybody who'd ever swung a bat would clobber it. But she jumps in awkwardly before he can curl to the end of a four-bar stretch.

> When the evening grows dark
> and you're lost in the park . . .

And she's off to the races. Her voice is fine, a little thinner than he'd imagined, but it has a lilt that gives it some personality and makes you think she's singing just to you.

> Darling, don't be climbing up trees
> when all you need, is to follow me.

He was following her, all right. He might enjoy listening to her, and rolling along underneath, if he didn't have to scramble to keep up.

After the song, Ronnie takes his daughter's hand. "You have a lovely sound, Rae. But you need to relax. We're on a very slow train together, just enjoying the scenery. Getting to know each other. Getting to know the countryside."

He embarrasses himself with this talk, as if he were trying to hustle some chick when all he wants is to get his daughter to follow the time of a song. "Listen to the beat," is all he has to say.

Rae sings a half-dozen tunes and each of them races along indifferent to the tempo. For a while he tries to jail her in a rigid

four-four frame, accenting the ones and the threes like a square
pianist practicing with the metronome, but she still won't subscribe to the beat.

Blind Encouragement

"You can sing, honey," is all he says, as they stand in the parking
lot above the dunes. Damning with faint praise?

"You really think so?"

"Sure," he says. Faint praise can damn only those who will be
damned. "You want to pay attention to the beat. You had me
hopping around the piano a little bit. You know I never played
much piano in the first place. There was a crummy upright in
the house growing up. And now I've got as rusty as the Tin
Man. But you sounded good, Rae. No kidding. You have a
lovely voice."

Her face breaks into a wide, girlish smile and then she gets
busy, wrapping her gum in foil, putting on her sweater, pulling
it off again, and tying it around her waist so that it dances behind
her like a flapping skirt. She rearranges herself with the funky
fastidiousness of a teenager. Ronnie smiles at her. Poor girl. She
is too young to be a mother and too old to run away from her
child.

Rae takes her father's arm and leads him on a stately march
along the edge of the water, her small, red-nailed feet sucked,
step by step, into the wet sand, as he tramps beside her in black
tennies, kicking through the sea wrack and white foam.

"When did you start singing, Rae?"

Rae shrugs and offers him a stick of Doublemint, and rolls
two sticks into her own mouth.

"I was always singing. But Mama's boyfriend, Dr. Earlanson, got me going one night when the three of us were sitting around after dinner."

"What's the story with the boyfriend?"

"Dr. Earlanson?" Rae's not interested in deceiving her father, but she wants to dispense her knowledge slowly. "Dr. Earlanson is nice enough. He's a widower with grown kids. Been good to Mama, as far as I can tell. Mama used to pretend to be proud of Dr. E. She'd go around saying, 'He's not just a doctor, he's an *internist*.' It always sounded like something dirty to me, describing her bald-headed old boyfriend as an internist.

"One night Dr. E. made a leg of lamb for the three of us and I had some wine and started singing songs I was surprised I knew. Songs from your records, mostly. I listened to your records a lot after you left. I had a little phonograph in my room and fell asleep to you singing. Mama and Dr. E. were singing a debauched version of 'Laura.' And Dr. E. said, 'How about you, can you sing, Rae?' I just opened my mouth and belted out 'Sweet Lorraine.' I tried to phrase like you. Then I sang 'Isn't It Romantic?' and 'I Fall in Love Too Easily.' Dr. E. said, 'Bravo! Bravo!' He was all excited, shouting, 'You can sing, you can sing!' "

Ronnie smiles at his daughter. The problem, he realizes, is that she really can't sing. He thinks she knows it, but he can't be sure. Has she come to him to fix it? There's no fixing that. He's given the blind encouragement he can give.

He links his arm in hers. "So how's your mother?"

"She's okay."

"Yeah?"

"Well, she's still putting away a quart of Gilbeys every day. She drinks it with grapefruit juice now. She's on a health kick. I don't see her too much. Dr. E. doesn't practice anymore, but stays with her all the time now. Neither of them spends a lot of time walking straight lines."

Ronnie closes his eyes on the picture. "I'm sorry, honey."

He looks past her toward a large wave as it builds its steep arch, drawing enough force from the undertow to move a good-size mountain. He watches it rise, like a distinguished elder standing up from his chair, and let fly its incontrovertible power, collapsing once again into jewels of white water.

Ballfield

At first sight, the wedge of grass and dirt infield remind Ronnie how the field looked to him as a boy. Seals Stadium. He always wanted to go to the empty rows at the top and stand up on a seat, but his father forced them along, like the law, to their numbered row and seats. Natty tugged his father's hand, looked down at his feet, either anxious to get to his seat or needing to pee again. "I got to go sissy, Daddy." Ronnie pulled away, staring down at the field as if it were the ocean, a beautiful man-made sea. From every vantage, a different wedge of bright grass beamed, dreamy as a row of melons split open at a fruit stand.

Now he looks down at Quincy, whose thumb is in his mouth. The boy shuffles down the row beside his mom.

"Isn't that beautiful, Quincy? Look at that field. That's the diamond."

"Where's the baseballers?" Quincy asks.

Ronnie shrugs. "Maybe they're resting before the game."

"Did you think we brought you to see the empty field, Quince?" Rae asks.

Betty leads them to their seats behind third base. She smiles at Ronnie. "I never knew you had any interest in baseball."

"I don't."

The four of them sit quietly in a row. Apples in a tree. They don't know the players. They are like country people in the big city, happy to allow themselves to turn blank as they size up the buildings and watch the city slickers rush by.

In the third inning the wind begins to blow in from the bay, and dust swirls from the infield into the stands. Rae knocks her knees together furiously and Betty spreads a blanket over her and Quincy.

Quincy, wearing a new Giants cap, is twirling a web of cotton candy around a miniature baseball bat. Each of the adults tries to point out something to Quincy on the field, but the boy's focus is more local.

"Who's that man with money?" he says, pointing to a large black man with a metal box strapped around his neck and a sheaf of dollar bills fanned between his middle fingers. "Who is he?"

"That's the hot dog man," Betty says.

"What's he doing?"

"He's selling hot dogs."

"Why does he?"

"Because people are hungry for hot dogs."

"You want a hot dog, Quincy?" Ronnie asks.

"Okay."

"When I was a boy, you couldn't miss the hot-dog man. He'd come roaring through the stands with this great big voice: A LOAF OF BREAD . . . A POUND OF MEAT . . . AND ALL THE MUSTARD YOU CAN EAT—HOT DOGGIES!"

The visiting team, the Cincinnati Reds, is scoring runs at will. The quiet crowd of Giants' fans seems a sad lot, obliged to spend the night in this cold, dirt-flying purgatory. As the Reds score their sixth and seventh runs, a man in the row behind says, "There goes those Reds, there goes that Big Red Machine."

An inning later, the top of the fifth as he reckons it, Ronnie goes off to pick up a Giants' souvenir jacket for Quincy, whose tiny stub teeth are chattering in the Candlestick wind. There's a crowd at the souvenir stand. Ronnie finds himself walking the ramp to the upper deck. Whole sections are empty. He takes a seat in the highest row and stretches his legs across the seats in front of him. He has all of section 21 to himself, with the lovely smell of roasted peanuts that has wafted to the upper deck. The ball game is so far away, in the chill night lit up like day, that it seems like a clever design you can arrange whatever way you like.

Betty swaddles Quincy in the big red blanket. Ronnie has been gone a couple of innings, and now Rae has wandered off looking for him. Neither she nor Quincy is watching the game. They protect themselves quietly from the swirling wind and wait, without really waiting, the way animals stand in a field, free of hope or sorrow, their backs to the driving rain. At middle age, she often feels like a solitary animal: a cow on a hillside, momentarily finished grazing, full as these things go, and yet perfectly empty. She is glad to have Quincy with her.

By the ninth inning the smallish crowd has dwindled to a few pockets of the rowdy and inert. The Giants are behind by six runs. Quincy has fallen asleep. Betty can hear his sizzling breath, steady as a heartbeat. Ronnie walks sleepy-eyed down the steps to their seats, without a souvenir jacket for Quincy, or a memory of having set off for one.

"I went upstairs to have a look around," Ronnie says. "Quiet up there."

"I bet."

"How's everybody?"

"Just fine."

"Where's Rae?"

"Off looking for you."

"But I wasn't lost."

"I didn't think so," Betty says. She looks around and notices Rae, climbing down the steep rows toward them.

On the field, the last of the Cincinnati Reds congratulate one another before running off.

The Caves

Because he doesn't want anybody to hear him, Ronnie starts blowing the trumpet in old caves and tunnels he knows around the city. He likes to play by the ocean and hide himself in sand dunes at Baker Beach and bluffs near Fort Funston. His favorite cave is among the ruins of Sutro Baths. He'd gone swimming there as a teenager. Sometimes he'd sit in the stands watching the pretty girls. Pretty girls with their grandmothers, is the way he remembers it. Sometimes the girls smiled up at him.

Once a girl, bouncing up and down at the edge of a springboard, smiled his way before curling into a perfect dive. She kept her eyes fixed on him, from the moment she broke the surface, as if he'd been the thing that tugged her up. She didn't take her eyes off him as, panting, she climbed a ladder out of the pool and, dripping wet, kept climbing up into the stands to sit beside him. He'd said nothing to her and remained speechless while she pulled off her white bathing cap and a bundle of chestnut hair, dry and lustrous, tumbled out. He kept silent as she took one of his hands and held it in her own manicured and shapely hand. It was only after the girl's heavyset grandmother climbed into the stands that he mouthed the word *sorry*, as if he were truly responsible for pulling the girl out of her element and having the grandmother ascend in her flower dress, cursing in German, both at him and at the girl he'd never seen before. *Sorry, sorry, sorry,* was all he could manage as the girl was dragged away, and the small crowd in the stands roared with laughter at the ease with which young love could bloom and spoil in a quarter of an hour.

Ronnie strolls past a sign stenciled sixty years earlier on a wall turned to mossy ruin. WALK AT ALL TIMES!

The cave has a damp, silky sand floor. Ronnie stands in his black Converse All Stars, his feet spread wide, a little man with a low center of gravity. He looks out through the curved mouth of the cave and pulls his lips around his big choppers.

The high school band teacher made them learn how to spell *embouchure*. Boys tried to make the word sound funny. How's your *embouchure* treating you? Seen any good-looking *embouchures* lately? Hey, I got something to stick into her *embouchure*. The word was French for "mouth of a river."

He flutters his lips and buzzes a few loose-as-taffy octaves; he leapfrogs through a field of arpeggios, his ears opening wider than they have in years, as he makes *mouth of a river, mouth of a river, mouth of a river* his mantra of choice.

The great Mississippi River wasn't a wild river anymore. He'd seen an article about it in *Reader's Digest*. The river met up with the Army Corps of Engineers. They constructed a series of locks and dams to ensure that the Mississippi had a channel at least nine feet deep all the way down. Ronnie Reboulet may not be wild anymore, not since meeting up with a Tampa dentist who fashioned a set of false teeth he can barely get his lips around.

But he does. He imagines a sound, round as the bell of his horn, like the face of a fat man who stands in a field, all afternoon, eating plump Santa Rosa plums. He imagines the man smacking into each fruit so that the juice running down his cheeks drips as slowly as syrup off his chin. In the close setting of the cave, the sound is less a round of echoes than a wonderful, smothering ripeness.

Ronnie lips his way through Clifford Brown's "Joy Spring," just to hear the beauty of it, but every time he tries to bundle triplets the notes slip. Even in his prime, he shied away from Clifford's virtuoso pieces. The man could play. If his monster chops weren't enough to send other trumpeters packing, then his tone, which was as radiant as a sunlit beach house, could do the trick. Ronnie's playing was always limited. His strength was to know how his limits made him appear like other men. He'd been practically artless. That's why they'd loved him. Week after week, in his prime, Ronnie played to full houses. He'd take a sweet and lazy walk through the music that anyone could follow, but then light a fire with his resourcefulness, a two-sticks-together fire through the music, clearing a path for the others.

Back in '57, he played a whole month at the Blackhawk. The Ronnie Reboulet Quartet. Nobody had a gig like that at the Blackhawk, not Miles, not Mingus, not even Bird. Four solid weeks. He got some grief. A couple of the jazz rags said his whiteness and good looks were the real reason for his success. He tried not to pay attention to any of the Great White Hope nonsense. He wasn't out to save anybody, especially not some cracker-headed whities. Screw 'em.

Every night the house swelled with people. There was practically a rumble at the bar for stools. Five hundred dollars a week, just for him. Murray was still managing him back then, and he took care of the other musicians. Ronnie never cared for the business part of running a band; he wasn't so crazy about the rehearsing part, either. But once in awhile everything came together for a joyous and disciplined gig.

Ronnie had a good connection, in those days, who made discreet home deliveries. Things ran like clockwork. He led three rehearsals a week and the band got so tight it could nail anything. He'd get to the gig a half-hour early most nights. That made Murray happy. He liked to make Murray happy. Ronnie would come with his coat and slacks on a hanger every night, fresh from the cleaners. There'd already be a big crowd outside, and the girls would howl when they saw him step out of the cab with his trumpet and hanger of clothes. After he changed and combed some fresh Vitalis through his hair, he'd sit down on a chair and sip from a bottle of Coke. Sometimes Murray brought a few girls in to meet him. He kept his hands to himself, but

these girls always tried to find a way to touch him. They wanted
him to sign things for them, their little autograph books, a piece
of their clothing. Murray knew what he was doing. Fifteen minutes with those girls, their hands all over him, and he was ready
to get out front with his trumpet and blow.

Ronnie tries a more congenial tune, Kenny Dorham's lovely
"Blue Bossa," with its basket of sweet samba notes, each phrase a
warm *bolillos* broken open and buttered. That is a song for a man
like him. He swings his bantam rosiness through a couple of
choruses until his lips and jaw get very sore, and the middle of
his face feels like it's been twisted by a pair of forging tongs.

Ronnie pulls the horn away from his mouth before he's able
to finish the head. He is not unhappy. He stands in the cave,
shivering with clear excitement, listening to the notes he would
have played.

Waves are smacking rocks twenty-five feet in front of him.
Slowly, he packs his horn. With eyes blinking, and his mouth
contorted into a cubist fruit basket, he steps happily out of the
cave and into the bright afternoon.

His Song

That afternoon Ronnie comes into the little house singing. He
scats through the A section of "Joy Spring" and then walks his
light, shaky voice through a chorus of "Star Eyes."

Betty is sipping a cup of Kona brew at the kitchen table. It's
easy to see how he drove the girls mad. His song is the way you
dream of a man being—intimate, but free of affect. In five years,
this is the first she's heard him sing. By the time they'd moved to
the Bay Area, she'd done everything imaginable to get Ronnie

to sing. At the point of giving it up, she found a shiny, sunset orange Alfa in a used-car lot in Daly City. It was her father's color and would become her man's car. She figured that she might never hear him sing but that, surely, one day, driving with the top down in the sunset Alfa, he'd not be able to stop himself from singing.

For a long time she wanted something she could take from Ronnie, but she'd never known a man with so few possessions or so little unguarded self to appropriate. There was no hope of taking his heart, or the songs that he no longer sang. No point in making off with his teeth, or his golf clubs, or the trumpet he hadn't played for years. She found herself giving him things so that there might be something to take away, but that proved as hopeless an idea as holding on to one of his songs in a paper sack.

She smiles up at him, she has little choice, the man is singing. It's also true—he has made her happy.

The Queen's Visit

Three months after she bought the Alfa, he accompanied her to see the queen. The best they could hope for was a brief sighting as the limo drove by. Ronnie was especially courtly that day. He booked them a nice motel room on Sacramento and Van Ness, close enough to the British Consulate to keep themselves fresh.

Betty was christened Elizabeth in 1929, three years to the day after the future queen, and was married on the day of the coronation. She insisted on it, and gave herself up, on her wedding night, to a crude man who hadn't even trimmed his nails. She spent half the night awake, musing about the new queen, wondering if Elizabeth might be thinking of a common girl like her, free to go wherever she pleased.

The *Chronicle* printed a timetable of the queen's visit. At one-fifteen her plane arrived, at two o'clock she'd appear at a reception at the British Consulate, and so on. They checked into the motel by eleven. The windows were open to the bright, breezy day. She loved a motel that left its windows open. The sweet, greasy smell of donuts wafted up to their room from the massive bakery across the street. Ronnie sat out on the terrace smoking. She watched him through the window. He was a man she actually loved. Around noon she coaxed him inside the small room and asked him to make love to her. They talked in whispers, everything in whispers.

She spoke so softly she was surprised he heard. "When are you going to sing me a song?"

"Isn't this singing?"

Afterward, propped up on a pillow, he lit a cigarette. She peeked at him from her pillow and pretended that he was a Frenchman in a movie.

They were awakened, a little before two, by a fleet of helicopters circling above the motel. Betty leaped from the bed and shouted, "IT'S THE QUEEN! IT'S THE QUEEN!"

Betty didn't bother to put on her black pumps, but she beat them against the dash of the Alfa, like a high school girl, as Ronnie aimed the car out of the motel's underground garage and soared up the one-way on Jackson Street trying to catch the motorcade. On Laguna, he sailed down a couple of steep hills past Broadway, where, to the west, they could see a row of yellow police sawhorses stretched across Vallejo. He nosed north one block to Green and followed it across Fillmore, then cozied up to a fire hydrant. They ran—Betty still barefoot, holding a pump in each hand like a pair of stiff gloves. A small crowd, complete with Irish protesters, was allowed to gather after the last of the limos streamed into the consulate.

Betty was disappointed to have seen nothing of the queen or her attendants, nothing really but the air moving. As soon as the crowd was allowed to exhale, the police started to move people back.

Ronnie said, "Don't worry, she's got to come out of there sometime. She's got a schedule to keep."

They tried to guess which way she'd come and huffed the majestic hill to Broadway, where they met a black bus driver who'd pulled over his Gray Line bus. He had a troop of passengers at his side, mostly old white people, fidgeting and peering down the deep-drop hills, past the sidehill ramble of Cow Hollow and the red-and-white sparkle of tiled roofs in the Marina, all the way to the bridge, the final marker, stretching a rosy orange, not unlike Ronnie's Alfa, across the sharp, blue streak of water.

The driver, a white-mustached gentleman with a robust, reddish-brown complexion, nodded his head like he was keeping the beat. "Yes, sir, I think this is the way she be coming. Turning right up here. No, ma'am, I don't have any official proof. I've never had official proof of anything."

Ronnie nodded toward the bus driver. "This may be the best recommendation we get."

The driver pursed his lips. He looked like he should add a cigar to complete his image of well-being. "I got a feeling, is all. These people, they think I'm lying to them. They think I'm out here trying to steal their queen. And they're serious about that. Serious as a heart attack." He shrugged like a bothered papa, and looked across the heads of his old folks. "What did I tell you?" he said to a little man in a beret who'd tilted his head back with a fresh question. "In my opinion this is the best place on the earth, at this particular point in time, to get a look at your queen. But I'm not holding you to this spot. You're free to explore. I intend to stand right here and look her in the eye."

Ronnie looked like a benevolent hood in his leather jacket, open over a black shirt and a black-and-white-striped tie that he'd knotted, one-handed, while driving through traffic. He was still a beauty.

A crowd began to build at their corner. Ronnie smiled at Betty. He stood still as a post. "I played for the king and queen of Denmark once when I was in Copenhagen."

"You never told me that."

"In a quintet with Dexter Gordon. We were honored guests at the Royal Palace. Dex and I were pretty loaded. There was a fancy spread, but I didn't eat anything. I sang 'Making Whoopee' as an encore for the king. The queen came up and hung medallions around our necks. She called me 'Monsieur Reboulet.' "

Two helicopters skittered into the local sky to join the one that had been hovering over the consulate. Somebody shouted, "Here she comes!" Even the old folks began angling intensely for position at the curb. It was as if the air had changed—the line of limos made its way up the hill like a whoosh of cool off the bay. Betty turned to see the bus driver, his hands clasped together like a man who'd done his work. He smiled to her and bowed his head as if he were the event's proud impresario.

The first limo rolled by but there was no queen, nothing more than a pair of royal cousins offering their innocuous smiles. And then the second one went by with a great old fellow who looked to be all by himself. A woman with a strange nest of caramel-colored hair was jumping up and down on the curb. "Maybe they got her on the far side, maybe they got her on the far side of the car!"

Betty held her ground and, as the third limo rolled forward, the queen's bright and doughy face filled the window. She looked out clearly through a sea of astonished faces to find Betty, who was no more amazed to meet the eyes under the vermilion pillbox than the queen was to see her, poised as a stoic soul at a reunion, nodding her assent to the queen's royal wave.

After the car rolled by, Betty continued to stand on her spot, recalling the hat, the pearl earrings, the searching eyes. The crowd broke up into loud chatter, congratulating one another for their prescience, recounting the intimate exchange they'd had with the queen. Betty noticed the woman in the caramel hair doing a little pirouette away from the curb, and the lovely bus driver was actually smoking a cigar as he rounded up his troops. Betty overheard the driver say, "I looked her right in the eye, and it was a good experience for the both of us."

Ronnie didn't ask after her. He backed away to smoke and let Betty have the moment to herself. The street had emptied by the time she was willing to leave her spot. The old folks filed down the block to their bus. Ronnie stood against a building and waited. When she was ready they walked arm in arm down the steep hill to Green Street. The Alfa, parked in front of a hydrant, had been towed away

"It doesn't matter," she said. "I'll buy you another, Monsieur Reboulet."

"Merci, Madame."

Later, they moseyed into the world's largest donut bakery. Pink and white wallpaper ran from floor to ceiling—a pattern of cream pastries far more delicate than the actual fare. They sat at the counter with common people in common overcoats, talking as quietly as they could about the queen. A half-dozen glazed old-fashioneds were stacked nearby on a stainless steel platter.

Ships

Ronnie makes good on a promise to Rae. He takes her and Quincy to pay a visit to Cat, after supper on the fourth of July. She lives in the same Jackson Street building, edging toward decay, in which he left them. Cat had always wanted to live in Pacific Heights—she liked the notion of residing among the rich. Maybe she thought it would rub off on her. Ronnie rented the apartment from a realtor named Sheila Graves who followed him around town from club to club, whenever he was playing. Sometimes Sheila would come looking for him in the barbershop, during the afternoon, and take him driving through Forest Hill or Pacific Heights to show off a new listing.

Sheila was a plump, jaunty woman with streaked blond hair braided in a French twist. She wore lush floral dresses from I. Magnin and looked a little like a madam off to tea at the Stanford Court Hotel. She'd waltz right through a black barbershop like the Rosy Bowl, to the back poolroom where Ronnie and a couple of gents might be nodding on a long, padded bench, after geezing together, and pluck him out of there like a half-rotted fruit she was determined to get her mouth around.

Soon enough they'd be driving up and down hills, with the top down on her black Mercedes. She had the good sense not to talk to him until he initiated conversation. He liked the feel of her quiet presence beside him, the delicate talc smell of her perfume. Sometimes they made love in one of the houses she was showing. Sheila always managed to keep her dress on. He'd lay her down on a Persian carpet or across a sofa as long as a limo.

She had a wonderful body, full of folds. He felt like he was riding up and down a series of rolling hills. "Making love to you," he told her once, "is like balling the state of California." When they'd finished, the room smelled like she'd dusted it with her damp self, and he'd open his eyes on the yards and yards of flowers on her dress. Sheila liked to smoke long, black Shermans and would wait, with a cigarette hanging from her mouth, for him to light it.

She managed the Jackson Street building for an absentee landlord, and took Ronnie up to the apartment one day. There wasn't a stick of furniture, just a mile of hardwood floors, a heap of shattered glass from the French door, and a view of the Golden Gate.

She offered it to him cheap—$350 a month and a quick screw

on the bare floor. But nothing she did could keep him hard. "You're not as frisky as you used to be," she said, and waited impatiently for him to light her cigarette.

Ronnie went back to the empty apartment the next morning, swept up the pile of glass, and Murphy-oiled the wood floors. There was a window seat in the living room and he sat there for a silent hour looking at the Golden Gate. He wanted to keep the place empty, spare, throw a couple of mattresses on the floor, a few big pillows, and scrap the rest of it, the way musicians he'd known had left the crap they couldn't deal with in their shitty apartments before blowing town or moving in with a willing girl who already had her mattress on the floor. But he couldn't do that to Cat and Rae, so they got a truck and moved the whole kit and caboodle.

Cat, of course, wanted to fill the place. In the year and a half he lived there, she'd turned the apartment into a greenhouse of hanging ferns and spider plants. Ronnie had nothing against plants, he just didn't want to live among them. Every time the steam heat hissed he could feel the plants growing thicker around him. A cluster of jade plants and tiny succulents covered the window seat. Cat walked around the apartment in a stylish smock with deep pockets. His wife was left-handed. She kept a plant mister in her right pocket and a pint of Wolfschmidt in her left.

"Ronnie?" Cat says to him at the door. She lays a cold hand on each side of his face. It is the saddest moment of his life, seeing her standing in the doorway—an ancient, hollow-eyed woman, not even fifty. He fights against remembering her as the beautiful young model he'd gone nuts for in 1952. He tries to meet her as she is now—a poor, sickly woman standing in her doorway, a face filled with earnest curiosity until she loses concentration and her hands fly up to her head and flutter about, working to smooth down her hair. Her hands do more shaking than anything. She slaps one hand atop the other until they're fused on her head in the natural posture of a madwoman, her thin white arms forming the shape of an egg.

Cat stares at Ronnie, daring him to draw a bitter conclusion. It isn't until after he's left that he realizes how horrifying he must have looked to her: a wreck of a little man, with scores of new creases on his face and a mouthful of counterfeit teeth.

Cat pulls her hands off her head. "You don't look so bad, Ronnie," she says.

He grins. "Are you damning with faint praise?"

"No, I'm just damning. I thought you'd be dead, Ronnie."

"See what I mean?"

She smiles at him and he nods back. He feels a little glow . . . everything might be all right with her.

Rae destroys the tableau. "Can we come in, Mother?"

"Of course, Rae, come on in here. Hello, Quincy," Cat says, and bends to kiss the top of the boy's head. "It's just such a surprise. . . . Things are in a little *disarray*."

"We told you when we were coming."

"You told me, of course you told me. Did I say you didn't tell me? I never said that." She turns to Ronnie and takes his arm. "I'd tell you to excuse the mess, but you don't have much choice, do you?" Cat's laughter turns into a cackle.

"Come meet my friend Dr. Earlanson," she says, forcing a charm-school smile.

She kicks at a gray cat as she leads the little group up the long hallway, stacked bunker-style with enough newspapers, it seems, to tell the daily history of the twentieth century.

"I bet you've been following Patty Hearst," Ronnie says.

"Like she was my own daughter, Ronnie."

Dr. Earlanson is a loud fellow whom the years have tempered. Ronnie guesses that the doctor is an old military man—he wears his hair in a butch and, though he has the aspect of a classic alcoholic, he carries it off with a bully dignity. The doctor's habit is to wrinkle his forehead as he listens, to demonstrate his abiding concern. The man has five horizontal lines carved across his forehead that resemble music staff lines, and Ronnie imagines a roving note, a shifting Cyclops eye of sound, modulating across the doctor's forehead.

The level of disaster in the living room is staggering. Ronnie squeezes his daughter's hand. This is what she wanted him to see. There is no other way to convey the horror. Dirty glasses and bottles everywhere, cans of tuna, chunks of plaster blasted out of the wall by thrown objects, torn furniture, piles of hairpins and rollers, the disassembled guts of a toilet, phonograph records separated from their jackets. A huge Zenith television set—tuned to *Newsroom*—its picture smeared with egg, is crowned with a twisted rabbit-ear antenna and a family size jar of Tiger Balm, missing its lid. Ronnie scans the room for potted plants, but spots only a single, twisted succulent, dried to death in a Folgers coffee tin, atop a peeling radiator.

"What can I get you to drink?" the doctor asks Ronnie, as if they were snug in the library of his mansion.

"I'm fine, thanks."

Cat cackles, "Ronnie's a clean-living citizen now, didn't you know, honey? He doesn't even play music anymore. I bet he's going to church these days. Your mother raised you a Catholic, didn't she?"

"She tried."

Rae lets go of Quincy's hand and gapes at the sight of her parents, weathered into a pair of gargoyles.

Her mother turns on her, cackling. "What's the matter with you, kid? Cat got your tongue?"

Rae shakes her head. She turns to watch Quincy step gingerly around the wreckage of the living room.

Cat smiles at Ronnie. "And now you have your daughter back."

"Yes."

"You were always lucky."

"Was I?"

"Always."

Dr. Earlanson tries to interject his face into the conversation. His forehead ripples with concern. "I think we should go up to the roof," he says, "and see if we can get a peek at the fireworks. Wouldn't that be something? Nice, clear night. Mild up there. Very mild tonight."

Cat will not be mollified. "You disappear for years. Completely abandon your daughter and she comes right back to you!"

Quincy steps slowly across the room carrying a large hunk of plaster.

"Can I keep this, Mama?"

"Put it down," Rae whispers.

"Whose is it, Mama?"

"I don't know. Put it down, sweetie."

He shakes his head and squeezes the piece of plaster tightly in his small hands before dropping it to the floor and watching it shatter.

By the time they get to the roof, the fireworks show at Crissy Field is almost over. Rae explains to Quincy that thousands of people are watching the show. Some are sitting on a grassy field, some on the hoods of their cars, parked in the Marina, others, like them, are on rooftops.

Quincy doesn't care who's watching, he's upset that he cannot see all the fire in the sky. Finally Ronnie hoists him onto his shoulder and the boy says, "I saw it, blue and red sparkers in the sky."

It has always surprised Rae how difficult it is to explain the unseen to a child. She finds herself going to great lengths to prove the existence of things of which she is skeptical. Such as her phantom father. Is he really there, holding his grandson up to see the full sky? Her father and son fused together on the roof, reacting to the same "red sparkers" in the sky.

Lamps have come on in all the buildings, bright pockets of light warming the rooms of people you imagine you know, but don't know at all. The five of them are standing under the sky. In the night, the bay is like a dark rope that the big ships pull themselves along.

Every time a new blast of fireworks fans across the northern sky, Quincy hollers, "Wow, did you see that one, did you see that one, did you see that one, Mama?"

Rae smiles whenever Quincy opens his mouth. Ronnie has been watching her for weeks, months now, for a sign of her departure. It is like keeping vigil with suicides—you know that sooner or later they are going to do it. No matter how dedicated you are to thwarting them, their determination is supreme. Even if you marshall all your wit, they will be more canny. It is what they live for. He knows it in himself. Nobody could stop him now. He only hopes he's wrong about Rae. He looks north, through the heart of the spreading fireworks, toward the bay.

Once his mother had taken him and Natty by streetcar to the Marina to see the bridge as it was being constructed. They were small boys and had to walk a long way to get a good view. She told them it was something they'd remember their entire lives. She described it to them before they could see it: huge pylons standing out of the water; miles of cables stretched toward the empty sky. It was 1933, or 1934. He and his brother were four or five years old. They didn't know what a bridge was. Natty was afraid to be out, far from home, among so many big things. He cleaved to his mother's side like a puppy. Ronnie swung his mother's other arm. When the bay came into view, he was more interested in the ships than the bridge and kept asking questions. Who was driving those ships? What kind of people were on there? Were they pirates? Did they all wear beards? Where did they go? He stood beside his mother, Natty on the other side of her, swallowed in her greatcoat.

"What do they know?" he asked his mother.

"Who?"

"Ships . . . those ships . . . what do those ships know?"

His mother began laughing about what ships did or did not

know. It was the funniest thing she'd ever heard. They laughed together—his mother who rarely laughed, and he, and even Natty—they stood holding hands, facing north past the hanging pylons and the ships in the bay.

He thinks of them—his lost ones—as the final throb of fireworks, a mouth-swallowing-mouth of patriotic sparkle, dissolves into the blue-black sky.

Gone

Ronnie sits behind the leather-wrapped wheel of the Alfa, a man driving toward the end of his life. He recognizes himself as a man in a photograph who, in the clearest bell of sobriety, has left everything behind.

He's driven south on 101 toward Murray Weiss's place in Carmel Valley. Murray, his old friend and manager, made a bundle as a record producer, an A&R who left jazz for rock and roll at the right moment in the sixties. Murray is also the biggest Jew that Ronnie's ever known, a towering man who used to shop for his clothes beside outsize athletes and bus drivers at Rochester Big and Tall.

Murray, a couple of years older, became his first guardian in the big world. They grew up together in the Avenues. Ronnie was the little fellow full of talent, but Murray became a man first. By his early twenties, during the postwar housing boom, he made a good living, buying small houses that needed work, having them rehabbed, and turning them over for a nice profit. He treated people well, paid his workers on time, and strolled through the world in his crisp gabardine shirts and tweed coats like one of the chosen.

Sometimes when they sat at a table together, Ronnie stared at the thick hairs curling out of the back of Murray's huge hands. Each of the digits had its own ring, even the pinkies. The rings didn't look like anything special. Eight school rings. How many schools had the guy gone to? As far as Ronnie knew, Murray barely graduated from high school.

He got Murray's Carmel Valley number and address from the operator in Monterey, wrote it on a slip of paper, and dropped it in a basket of warm tortilla chips. He had the number memorized before the chips cooled. Murray used to be able to put away fifteen tacos in a sitting. Ronnie was tempted to call him and say, "Hey, buddy, I've got a dozen big ones sitting on a platter at Zepadas, but nobody to eat 'em."

It had been six years since he'd seen Murray. People changed. People that used to be glad to see you, weren't so happy anymore when you showed up. The first time he was in Europe his life exploded in a hundred ways. He'd think of friends back home as a static clan, people who went on doing what they had always done. That was his necessary fiction.

He was gone less than a year that first time. He played packed clubs in Paris, sat in Sidney Bechet's hotel room with its peeling blue-striped wallpaper, as the great soprano player circled the room in sneakers, brewing an oh-so-slow pot of drip coffee. He drove a troubled MG 110 miles an hour through Holland and Germany. But there were days, even before he got busted in Brindisi, when he felt frightfully separated from the familiar, strung out in some medieval town, betrayed by a whore that he thought was just another girl in love with mascara.

Sometimes he'd be destroyed by less dramatic events and become a little boy missing his mother and his dead brother. He'd get blue, go sleepless, be paralyzed by the simple loneliness of being twenty-three and far from anybody that cared for him beyond a single night.

He'd sit wrapped in a blanket all day, in a tiny hotel room or in his Italian prison cell, conjuring up the houses of old friends and the routes he'd take to get to them if he were home and had a tankful of gas. His only solace was imagining everybody in their places, landed in their favorite chairs, lying alone in the beds they'd loved him in, saying his name softly as if it were a prayer, wishing he'd return to them.

Later, he was shocked to realize that nothing had remained static. While he was gone, people had dropped dead, or moved, or found someone else to sleep with, and if they'd thought of him at all, it was a stylized version of his old self they'd imagined, a person he'd never been that had nothing to do with the man he'd become.

By now there have been so many separations. He can't count the women he's loved, if love is being fond enough of people to imagine giving up the rest of the world to be alone with them. Each woman had been a song that he'd wanted to grow old singing.

He had begun to think he'd stay with Betty. She was the song he'd grow old singing, the rare one who'd made her peace. He loved the way she took care of herself. He once watched her spread a cotton blanket for herself at the beach. She lay down with a book and a thermos of coffee. She had an actual smile on her face, and if he hadn't come along there may not have been anyone to see the smile. He hated to disturb her. Perhaps what he most loves about Betty is how well she can do without him. But who else can be so welcoming? He imagines he will always return to her, if she'll have him.

Angel

Instead of calling Murray, he drives out to Carmel Valley with a dozen beef tacos wrapped in tinfoil and shows up on the doorstep of Murray's big-timbered ranch house on Saddle Mountain Road, expecting to be recognized as a walking nightmare.

Twenty-five years before, on a warm October afternoon, Murray had found him in a pair of dungarees and a sleeveless undershirt, shooting pool in a joint on Grant Avenue, across the street from the Tivoli. It was a warm, clear day and the bartender had thrown the front door open, giving the clouds of cigar and cigarette smoke a yellow luminance. He was straight-line sober that day, not a drug in his body, sipping Bass Ale like a gentleman and taking a few bucks off a sailor whose pool game had gone to hell. Then Murray, decked out in a giant silk coat and smacking three sticks of Juicy Fruit, marched into the place with a package under his arm and started bothering him.

"You've got to do a better job looking after yourself, Ronnie."

He was stretched out over a difficult shot. "Get out of here, Murray. Don't disturb me when I'm concentrating."

Murray pushed his way past the sailor. "You look like a fucking scavenger, Reb. What are you doing—collecting garbage for the city and county of San Francisco?"

"I'm about to nail the five ball, Murray."

"What the fuck, you think I'm bullshitting, Ron?"

"It occurred to me."

"Something big's come up. You've got to be ready at all times."

He put down his stick. "You got some gum, Murray?"

"I don't have any gum besides what I'm chewing. You have a sport coat with you, Ronnie?"

"What do you think?"

"Well, it's a good thing you have me looking after you."

"Don't bother me—get out of here, Murray."

The sailor, an Irish fellow with a pair of bushy brows that would cover his face before they buried him, tried to sneak out of the game. "Hey," he said, "it's all right, you can go."

"Don't put your money away, skipper."

Murray said, "Do you know what the fuck I'm here for? Do you?"

"No!"

"Charlie Parker's in town."

"Scram, Murray."

"And he's looking for a trumpet player."

Ronnie turned back to the table and sank the five ball.

"Got every trumpeter in town over there."

"Then he doesn't need me."

"Let's go."

"No, I don't know where my trumpet is."

"You left it with me."

"I don't feel so good, Murray. My chops are all messed up. I don't know Bird's tunes. I couldn't keep up with the tempo. I'm not going." He glanced at the table. "Eight ball, right pocket."

Murray grabbed him by the undershirt, before he had a chance to take the shot, and called him an imbecile. Murray was always in his face like that.

"Lay off the merchandise," Ronnie said.

Murray steered him out of the joint. "Why do you talk like a punk, Ronnie? *Merchandise.* Look here, I could take you down to Roos Brothers, buy you some new *shmattes,* but you'd lose everything in two days. Leave them over some girls's house. What's the use? So I stopped over the next-to-new." He pulls a reddish-brown sport coat, with a few too many creases, out of a bag. "Try this on. It's just your size. It only cost five dollars. You can pay me later. Try it on. Come on, try it on, come on!"

Murray was too excitable back then. He had a gut full of ulcers. Ronnie pictured a stomach of raging neon.

Murray manhandled him into his Buick.

"I gotta pee, Murray."

"Pee on yourself, for all I care, pee on yourself."

So there he stood, bladder full to bursting, inside the front door of the Blackhawk, staring, almost blind, into the dark club after coming in from the sunny afternoon. He could have gone swimming in the rumpled brown coat that Murray had bought him. He went off to pee and thought of ditching Murray, ditching the place. But when he came out of the can, Charlie Parker was calling his name. "Is Ronnie Reboulet out there . . . Monsieur Ronnie Reboulet . . ."

I've Got a Place

He stands at Murray's beautiful carved door and lets the knocker, a thick ring of brass, drop against the wood. Murray answers with a cigar in his mouth. He's wearing an enormous silk kimono and a pair of sixty-nine-cent flip-flops.

"Ronnie," he says, and throws his arms around the little man at the door. "Come in here. What the hell? Come in. Could drop a guy a card, you lousy bastard. Somebody'd said you were kicking around California. Cat probably. I try and stay in touch with Cat. Send her a little something, you know. No big deal. You see Rae?"

"Sure, she's been staying with me."

"Regular family man, hunh?"

"Don't push it, Mur."

"Ahhh, get your ass in here."

The proportions of the place are just right for Murray—the burnished redwood pillars are a good twenty feet tall. Murray's come a long way from high school. He'd been a poor, oversize Jew, in a day when the only Jews you knew were puny. He played a mediocre tenor sax in band and kids picked on him mercilessly. His saving grace was his buoyant nature. He was either oblivious to the disdain directed toward him, or so successfully apart from it that he regarded his tormenters with a smirking indifference.

Some days after school they'd sit in Murray's family's apartment on 34th and Geary and listen to the same six Count Basie 78s over and over again. The place smelled of lentils and kasha. Jewish food, Ronnie thought, old-time Jewish food. There were glass candy dishes filled with sunflower seeds which he and Murray cracked open with the efficiency of chipmunks. The routine was simple—Murray, the possessor of countless "facts" about the world, flipped the records and provided a running commentary on the red-light district in New Orleans, or the slave auctions of Kentucky, or the Jewish gangsters of Chicago. They'd spit shells into paper bags, and Ronnie would stand in honor of each of Buck Clayton's regal trumpet solos, pressing imaginary valves, while Murray, wearing one of his father's beat-up homburgs, pretended it was a porkpie and tilted his sax like Lester Young, every time Prez soloed.

Now Murray, returned from dressing, stands before him, tall and surprisingly lean, in a pair of weathered corduroy slacks and a beautifully woven russet sweater.

"You got yourself a regular Hearst Castle, Mur."

"What the hell, Reb? It doesn't buy you happiness. I have an empty house here. The wife left, but I don't remember when. I got enough room to stash Patty so they'd never find her."

"She's not your type, Murray."

Murray shrugs.

"I brought you a heap of tacos from Zepadas."

"You're breaking my heart, Reb. But I can't eat like that anymore. They got me watching my cholesterol, my blood pressure, my blood sugar. They got me watching everything. The world's become a salt-free zone. I haven't tasted anything in years. What the hell, this is what it means to be alive."

Murray leads Ronnie into the library and watches him take it all in. The mahogany-hued leather sofa. The overstuffed chairs. The high wall of bookshelves stocked with hardcovers which the old trumpeter seems to be counting, one by one.

"You read all these books, Mur?"

"I read the spines, Reb. I'm a voracious reader of spines. Hey, you look good, Ronnie."

"You don't have to bullshit me, man. But I'm clean. People have been after me to get clean for the last twenty-five years. So here I am—a clean wreck."

"Congratulations."

"I'm drug-free, cavity-free, and practically penniless."

"They tell me everything comes at a price."

Murray considers his friend. He looks like something that's walked out of the earth, a tough weed that's dusted itself off and thrown on its old leather jacket. Murray has spent years of his life loving this creature, wanting nothing more than to be in his company. He loved to watch the ease with which Ronnie could make the world relax its rules, the way he'd take a simple song and make it simpler, let the pure lyric take a walk down the street, coaxing it along when that's what it needed.

Ronnie could outline a ballad that you'd heard a thousand times and deliver it fresh without pyrotechnics or radical surgery. Drinkers in a chatty club would grow quiet. For the fractured moment before the club swelled back into sociability, everyone listened to Ronnie's song.

The man was maddening, of course. Not in the manner of the typically selfish, who spend much of their time trying to figure how they can beat you out of what you have. When he was with you, Ronnie was loyal, he just had a way of disappearing. He'd be playing a packed club and disappear, head back to the john after a solo and scoot out a back door. Nobody would see him for three days. He'd walk to the store for smokes and you'd find him a half-day later, if you were lucky, sitting at the ocean with his legs crossed, like a man doing yoga, but having chain-smoked his way through three packs of Viceroys. He'd camp out in the Arboretum, fly to Rome, drive to Santa Barbara in an MG Midget he had for a ten-minute test drive, disappear into the Fillmore with a coed, looking to get high, run off to the wine country with a fat-assed society matron and come back a week later with a beatnik chick he'd met in the mud baths in Calistoga.

Ronnie lights a cigarette and looks across at Murray. "Mind?"

"I'd join you, but I'm . . ."

"You're preserving yourself. That's good. Me . . . I don't really have much to preserve. You know, everybody told me I'd be dead by twenty-five. Maybe thirty. I sort of counted on it myself. Then they said forty. Here I am pushing fifty. It's down-right scary. Can you imagine me in a home for the aged, Murray?"

"What the hell? Me and you both, Reb."

"I see us ending up in different digs, Murray."

"Yeah, so what do you need, Reb?"

"I don't need anything."

"Nothing?"

"No, I just came to see you. To see a friend."

Murray smiles and takes a stiff-legged walk to the far side of the room and passes a rumble of gas. "Pardon me. I eat every-thing they tell me to eat, measure out the portions, but I still can't stop farting."

"Go with it, Murray."

Murray strolls back to the center of the room. "You playing any music, Reb?"

"No."

"Why the hell not?"

"How long you been out of the business, Murray?"

"Long enough to know better."

"Me too."

"I don't believe you, Reb. You have a trumpet?"

"Haven't played in years."

"You have a horn?"

"In the car."

"So you need a place to go, is all. I've got a place for you."

The Routine

The cabin is nearly hidden in a stand of pines on the south shore of Tahoe. Ronnie doesn't leave the cabin during the first two weeks, except to take short jogs beside the highway and down along the lake. He plays long tones and scales, and works on articulation exercises for as long as he can bear. "Got to keep up with your tongues and slurs," Junior Reese used to say. He chops wood, builds big fires, paces the cabin, corner to corner, closes his eyes as he sings snippets of songs, trying to coax forgotten lyrics into the room. Some days the cabin fills with breathy lyrics, each song tied to the tail of the song before, a hapless caravan weaving its way through the main room.

He picks up his groceries in Meeks Bay and keeps a pot of chili going most of the time, pounds of yellow onions peeled and sliced, and sautéed into their caramelized selves. He goes through enough thawed burger and ground lamb to consider adding meat to the list of undesirable hazards he's given up.

Soon enough he realizes that he is living for his lips and his mouth, his tongue, his dentures and stickum, his breathing. It is not about music, but problem-solving. He has a terrible time forming a firm yet flexible embouchure around the false teeth. At first, his lips are downright spastic, flapping loose and drooling spittle, the teeth wedged in their place, an alien organ that his trumpet-playing lips want to reject.

One day he finds himself forcing notes. His lips have knotted and he's desperate to get the notes out. Fury drives through his lips. In a snap, they go from easy flutter to reckless force, and he can feel the small heart of a blister forming on his lower lip. And yet he is unwilling to back off, like a man so frantic with a stuck zipper that he yanks the damn thing until he rips it free, managing to snare the baby folds of his limp penis in the zipper's teeth. And, like that, he knows he's grown a two-week blister. It will be two weeks minimum before he'll be able to pick up the horn again. He lays the trumpet on the oak library table and wonders if he'd be able to take a heavy hammer to it. If he clamped it to the table, he could level the bell and smack the fuck out of the valves and tubing, flattening the horn into a one-dimensional object.

Mono Man

Instead, he buys a map in Meeks Bay and goes driving. He heads south on 89, over Luther Pass and Monitor Pass, down 395 to Mono Lake—the vast crater lake that has been drained to near dying by Southern California's impossible thirst. He parks himself for a week at the Mono Tula Motel, a dusty strip of empty kitchenettes. The tiny office has a hand-lettered sign that reads, perversely: WATERBED ROOMS AVAILABLE.

Ronnie gets a squeaky bed with a chenille bedspread for nine dollars a night. During the warm, late July days, he walks the rim of the dying lake, hardly seeing anyone but the occasional backpacker come to witness a ghost lake. Ronnie is not sure what holds him here. Why spend a week of days staring at a dried-out lake? What's to gain from kicking your boots through dust, and chips of granite, and more dust, as every wrinkle in your head is ironed out by the emptiness of the place? But by the time he heads west, one night, into Yosemite, he's singing in the car. "What's New?" "Lush Life." "Stella by Starlight."

At Yosemite, Ronnie stays in a simple tent cabin. Slowly, without purpose, he hikes through the valley and on trails that loop the falls. After his time at Mono Lake, he craves water. If he could operate as a miniaturist, it seems to him, he might have a chance with nature. In the evenings, he lights small fires and lets himself feel his lip quietly healing.

Thatcher

Ronnie has a book of poems with him, a little pocket book that had been tucked away in his trumpet case, next to the valve oil. Poems by a fellow named Thatcher, a large, raccoon-eyed character who'd come into jazz clubs in the fifties and want to read his poems. He had something of a following. A poet in a shirt with leather laces open at the throat, his hairy chest heaved with passion whenever he read a poem or emoted some feeling for the music. The guy was a cross between an undertaker and a hipster.

A woman Ronnie took to bed one night told him that there was nothing sexier than watching Thatcher blow smoke through his nostrils. He thought to ask her why she hadn't gone off with

Thatcher instead of him. Somebody told him that Bird used to carry a book of Thatcher's poetry in his sax case, so, once in City Lights, Ronnie picked up this tiny book of love poems by Archibald Thatcher, and it ended up in his trumpet case.

He'd said four or five words to Thatcher, twenty years before, in a club on the Lombard strip. They'd nodded in a friendly way to each other for years, but Thatcher came up one night after a set and told Ronnie something daft about his playing: "You are like a natural stream digressing through the hub of nature," or some such nonsense, and he answered Thatcher in the chilly way that Bird sometimes handled his anonymous admirers: "So are you, brother, so are you."

Once back at Murray's cabin, Ronnie copies out a poem of Thatcher's, every few days, on a clean sheet of paper, folds it into an envelope, and sends it without a message to Betty. He never claims that they are his poems, but he makes no effort to identify the poet.

For several weeks, Betty responds with brave letters in which she tells scraps of news about Rae and Quincy. "When are you coming back?" she asks. "When can I see you? Tell me, please. And tell me who this wonderful poet is who surprises me so often?"

Retooling

Betty ate nothing but creamed herring on Armenian flat bread, and spinach salads with dates and walnuts, in the first weeks after Ronnie drove away. She bought a floppy red straw hat and sewed an elastic strap to it so that it didn't fly off as she walked along the ocean trying to reinvent herself as a wise and eccentric

older woman. She spent fifty dollars on a trunkload of white
hydrangeas, pure as snow, and planted them around the front of
the house. She stocked the house with a basketful of vegetable
and herb soaps from Body and Soul: avocado, cucumber,
lavender, and sweet pepper. She bought stationery that featured
cutouts from Matisse's *Jazz* series running down the margins of
each sheet. And, in an effort to gain balance in her musical taste,
she joined a classical record club. When the promotional ship-
ment of twelve records arrived, she tacked a collage of album
covers to the wall, and did her best to rejoice to Brahms and
Mahler as the sober faces of Bruno Walter, Arthur Rubinstein,
and Otto Klemperer stared down at her.

English Muffins

Something had gone off in Rae, a small madness, as if a part of
her brain had been shuttered. Shortly after Ronnie left, Betty
began to find Rae's leavings around the house. It started in a
quiet way with a half-eaten banana, or a sucked-out Santa Rosa
plum left on a radiator cover. Betty smiled to herself with each
discovery—a small animal was loose in the house. Her first
thought was Quincy, but the boy didn't have fruit unless it was
poured into a glass as juice, or floated in sugary syrup.

Soon, Betty discovered in odd corners a number of items that
belonged to Rae: barrettes and lipstick canisters, open jars of
cold cream. The more personal the leavings the further they
ventured into Betty's private space, until she awoke several
mornings to the faint odor of Rae's smeared and knotted tam-
pons fermenting on her bedside table.

One morning they were both up early. Rae sat at the kitchen

counter, engrossed in a newspaper story speculating on the whereabouts of Patty Hearst. Betty padded around the kitchen tidying up. She wanted to say something to Rae, to pet her, to tell her that everything would be all right, but the shared silence seemed the best idea. The sizzle of Quincy's snore sounded a little like a radiator coming from his corner of the big room. Betty dropped two English muffins into the toaster and listened to the quiet ticking as they browned. Rae never looked up from the paper, and only nodded when Betty placed a plate of buttered muffins in front of her.

Welcome to the Lost Art

Ronnie adds five minutes to his practice each day, trying to build his lip strength and general endurance. He needs to regain his feel for backing off, like a man making love knows to bring it down a notch before losing it, knows when he can return to that golden zone of hard fucking that can go on half the night. He needs his thermostat as much as his chops, or one night of fly trumpeting will bust him up again.

In the old days, he and Cat used to do their daily exercises with Moss Mathews on Channel 2. Moss was the first TV aerobics man that Ronnie ever saw. "Welcome," he said, "to the lost art of body building."

In the middle of the day, Ronnie'd get down on the carpet with Cat and Moss. The beautiful thing about Moss was that he was always on. Back in those days, the only shows on Channel 2 were Moss Mathews's and *Roller Derby*.

He and Cat might drink and shoot drugs all night, but they always did their exercises the next day. Ronnie knew a bunch of junkies, in the late fifties, who went on health kicks, guys absolutely obsessed with their bodies, stone-cold fiends who actually believed that by lifting weights and jogging, by swilling a tall gas-station glass of carrot juice, they were counteracting any damage the drugs did.

Moss had a nice manner. "Welcome to the lost art of body building," he'd say, "where moderation is the key." And then he'd get you doing your tummy stretchers and your thigh lifts, get you scooting along the carpet for two minutes of his patented "bum busters." Timing was everything. "Two minutes on each exercise," Moss said, "no more, no less."

When Moss wasn't leading exercises, in his stretchy white sweatsuit, he was selling things. Food scales and isometric-exercise booklets, Blasto Energy Bars and grapefruit knives. Now, Ronnie opens his practice each morning with two minutes of easy trumpet buzzing, and tells himself, "Welcome to the lost art."

August 19, 1974

Dearest R.,

Thank you for the new poem about the friendly porcu-pines. I read it to Quincy. He thought it was pretty funny. I wish I had a better way of saying this but, truth to tell, the poem did not satisfy me. None of the poems have satisfied me. There you have it. Every time I tear open an envelope, I hope to hear from you.

xxxxx Betty

Ronnie reads the note three or four times, then slips it into Thatcher's book beside the love poem he had planned to copy next. He wedges the thin poetry book into a shelf between a couple of Murray's oversize photo books. Murray has a thing for glacial landscapes. *I'm sending you off to Siberia, Thatcher,* he thinks, as he tries to forget the note the poet carries off with him.

Sitting In

Ronnie begins driving down Highway 89 to Southshore in the evenings. He finds a palatable salad bar at Ronson's and spends a little time each night at the dollar blackjack table. He fancies it a part of his conditioning—to stay relaxed and alert among addicts, swilling at least one Coca-Cola and lime for each tumbler of cheap bar bourbon that he nurses as if it were an estimable sipping whiskey. He walks away from the table as soon as he is either ten dollars up or ten down.

Some nights he wanders into the Cherry Room at Ronson's to listen to a young pianist, a talented hippie boy named Artie Rhodes, who wears his long brown hair coiled in a chignon. The first night he heard the way the kid's florid right hand jibed with the crisp changes he laid down with his left, Ronnie was at the point of crying. How in the world did he find so pure a sound on the strip? Every other lounge features silver-lamé torch singers, or disco lip-syncers, or suburban rock and roll bands with two guitars and a synthesizer stamping out a music product with an ugly, programmed beat.

Ronnie brings his trumpet in its zippered sack on the fourth or fifth night. Truth is he's developed some feel in his lips as he's slowly built their strength. Notes still crack on him, occasionally, shoot ringing out of the bell and collapse at the knees, but he can play. He talks to himself like he'd chatter with a frightened girl to make her feel at ease; he pretends it's his good old lips talking to the teeth he was born with, saying, *All right, I'm not going to hurt you now, sweet ones, come to papa, now, I haven't come to hurt you.*

Ronnie stands at the back of the lounge, aching to play but a little frightened. The piano player is half his age. Ronnie orders a tequila neat with a twist of lime, quaffs it, and orders another. Between sets he approaches young Rhodes.

"It's just me," the piano player says, "there's no bass and drums."

"I can see that. You sound real good. I thought maybe we could manage a little interplay."

Rhodes smiles as he looks into the used-up face of the small man. The guy's upper lip, a fossilized specimen worthy of slight curiosity, has a trumpet player's half moon carved into it.

"That kind of thing's not done here."

"I imagine not. I've played quite a bit."

"What do you have . . . a trumpet there?"

"That's right, and I sing some."

"You sing, too, huh?" Rhodes forces a bloodless little laugh that, were it liquid, would barely cover the bottom of a glass. "And what did you say your name is?"

"Ronnie Reboulet."

"Yeah, sure, Ronnie Reboulet. Isn't he dead, buddy?"

"Missing in action."

Rhodes takes a deliberate look at the stranger and shakes his head. "All due respect, Ronnie Reboulet was a very good-looking fella."

Ronnie is impassive. "So I've heard."

"Yeah, like he's really going to resurrect on the strip in Tahoe."

"Had to wash up somewhere."

Rhodes looks out at the tables. "Well, there's hardly anybody here, anyway."

"Not your usual crowd?"

Rhodes glares at Ronnie. He can't decide whether to try to lose the old fellow, or to string him along. "May I buy you a drink, Mr. Reboulet?"

"Allow me."

"Thanks, but I need a stroll before the next set."

"Mind if I join you?"

"All right."

Ronnie follows Rhodes out of the casino into the warm evening.

"Let me see your horn."

Ronnie unzips the case, and the bell of his trumpet flashes under the lights outside Ronson's.

"Silver, hunh. Play something for me."

"I'll play for you inside."

"You want a little smoke?" the pianist asks.

"Sure."

They saunter across the parking lot to a baby-blue Corvair and sit in the warm car with the windows rolled up. Rhodes pulls a joint the size of a chunky cigarillo out of the glove compartment and they smoke it halfway down without speaking a word.

Artie Rhodes takes a long look at his companion. "Who are you, anyway?"

"I already told you who I am." He wants to ask this baby-faced punk who he thinks he is wearing his hair in a chignon. Mozart? But he says nothing.

Back inside Ronson's, Artie Rhodes signals him up to the bandstand. "What do you want, a ballad? A little waltz? You want something to run with?"

"Well, I am a little rusty. How about an accommodating head like 'Blue Bossa'?"

Artie Rhodes nods, and lays down a suave Latin beat. Ronnie walks tentatively through the theme. The trumpet is a thin man strolling up a trail with a trusty stick. He stumbles here, goes up the wrong fork there, and has to back his way down. No fancy steps yet, no switchbacks. Just a walking man telling a warm story with enough quick, pop laughs to punctuate the tale so that any dumb fool, wondering if he's pissed away his life, feels he has a compatriot on the stage, walking a deceptively simple trumpet line up the trail.

A Fan

Artie Rhodes recognizes the sound immediately. The wrecked little man is actually Ronnie Reboulet, laying down one lovely, unadorned line after another. Rhodes plays with his mouth open. He loses his place a couple of times in the first form and has to let go of the top line for a few measures, until he finds his way back into the chords.

Back in the sixties, in high school, he had a few of Ronnie's records. He'd play them late at night in his basement bedroom, propped against three pillows on his bed, pretending to sip brandy but actually guzzling Coke, as Ronnie Reboulet glided through a dozen ballads. Sometimes the guys he played with sat around his room listening to records. A couple of them thought that Ronnie's trumpet sound was too clean, his singing too fey, that he sounded like a faggot. Artie Rhodes wasn't impressed with the analysis. He'd light a roach, suck it till it sparked his lip, boost the volume, exhale, and say, "Who's the faggot?"

Rhodes is hypnotized by Ronnie Reboulet. The trumpeter stands absolutely still while he plays, like they say Charlie Parker did. He doesn't twitch or even tap his foot to the beat, but you can see the music sally through him like an electrical charge, the way a symphony conductor swells down to his cummerbund with the sound of a hundred musicians. The voice punched through Ronnie's horn is so plain and honest that everybody in the room looks up to see who it is that's talking to them, even in this ridiculous room, with the constant jangle of coins and the slot machine belching forth an occasional rumble of quarters.

There is a healthy burst of applause, at least for the Cherry Room. Artie Rhodes swings his legs over the piano bench and joins the clapping, until he picks up a "Be Cool" glance from Ronnie Reboulet.

Rhodes bobs his head, trying to affect an acceptable indifference. "Care to play another?"

"Sure. How about 'Solitude'?"

"Oh, man, that be bitching," Rhodes says, remembering Ronnie's famous recording of the tune with Hampton Hawes.

Facing the piano, Rhodes offers a simple four-bar intro and then holds his breath through the assured beauty of Ronnie's opening phrase:

DA BA DO-BA-DO   DA BA DA.

Rhodes is enraptured by the sound. The tone is fuller than he remembers from the recordings. The little man seems able to produce his sound from canyons of various depth, as if his body were an open gorge.

The room has grown quieter than it's been at any time during the gig. The crowd of insurance men and dry cleaners with their chatty companions in fat-zippered, peach and boysenberry leisure suits actually seems to notice that something extraordinary is happening. Until Ronnie walks in off the street, and dazes them with the possibility that they're still alive, solitude is a state that has eluded these folks.

Rhodes has such an overwhelming desire to lay out and listen to Ronnie take the song apart that he needs to keep reminding himself that he's the one doing the comping. He can't afford to get caught up in Ronnie's glory run. He's heard of sidemen that have fucked themselves like this. They might be making a symphony gig, a little orchestra in a pit to accompany the ballet, and they go off their nut watching the dancers, and they miss their cues and forget to keep playing. But he wants to stay with the music. There's nothing he wants more. He closes his eyes. Fingers spread, he has far more work in the left hand than the right. The piano is an open road he cobbles as the bright horn soars above it. The two of them are heading the same way.

Later, Artie Rhodes sits up in his bed with a young woman named Julie, a cigarette girl at Harrahs that he treats like a sister. Her long fingers explore the perfect knob of his chignon.

"Who does this for you? It's so cool."

"Nobody does it."

"You mean you do it?"

She uncoils the bundle of hair at the back of his neck and helps it fall out of its knotted clump. She plays with his hair awhile, then lifts his right hand, kisses it, kisses each of his melody fingers, and places the hand on one breast, then the other, saying, "What's the matter? What's the matter?"

Rhodes tries to explain a miracle. "You ever had a visitation? It was like a visitation. A saint coming to you. I'm not saying the guy is a saint. The thing is, he came to me, like a bum walking in off the street. I should have had him kicked out of the place. A situation like that . . . everything points to having him kicked out of the place. Of course, I didn't believe he was who he said he was . . . but I believed something."

The Miracle

Ronnie doesn't show for the next couple of nights. He wants to take things slowly. The world will add him back without blinking. He fasts for two days, taking long, slow drinks of hot water and chicken broth. He isn't sure why he puts himself on this regimen, or even how long it will last. But he doesn't argue with it. There's something enjoyable about cures when you aren't sick, like throwing money in the bank and having the amount stamped into a crisp bankbook, or the perverse pleasure of being frisked when you are actually clean.

Artie Rhodes has trouble concentrating on his playing. He spends too much energy looking out at the audience. It's nothing but pikers. Besides the insurance guys, you also have the red-nosed five-and-dime store owners, the matrons jangling quarters, dolled up in bouffants from the sixties. Rather than someone who's seen a miracle, he feels like a guy who's seen a ghost and is searching for a corroborating witness.

On the third night, when the miracle walks back into the lounge, wearing his hair slicked back and, of all things divine, a string tie with a lovely knob of turquoise, just below his Adam's apple, Artie Rhodes wants to call out into the room, *There he is, there he is,* but bends to the keyboard, instead, and pours himself into a sprightly "Tea for Two," a waltz to make the room go 'round.

Big Ole Cadillac

Wedged between Quincy and Dr. Earlanson in the pew, Rae listens to the minister talk about her mother's generous heart. Rae can't stop looking over her shoulder. Two days before, she'd talked with Murray, and there he is, a gentleman of genuine stature, sitting three rows behind her. But where's her father? She keeps expecting him to walk into the church like Joe DiMaggio at Marilyn's funeral, a white silk scarf wrapped around his neck, a hush spreading over the crowd. But there is no crowd in the church. Poor Dr. E. dabs at his eyes with his coat sleeve, and Betty, impeccable in a black suit, tries to distract Quincy, every time his restlessness kicks in. What would Rae do without Betty, a woman so different from her mother?

Her mother had been a beauty, a woman with a thousand friends who liked nothing more than to have a good time, to dress up and go out dancing, to blast records until the neighbors knocked, to sing along with Peggy Lee and Anita O'Day. She'd been a working model, but her ambition was casual, and gave way to the first party to come her way. Her life with a famous, disappearing husband was spent in an alcoholic haze. She was a brief, warm wind that had finally blown itself out.

As the minister says a few final words, Rae lets go of Quincy's hand and stands up. She isn't exactly sure why she stands but it feels good to hold herself apart from the others. She has witnessed more of her mother's adult life than anyone else.

Early on, her mother ceased being her mother and became her rowdy, out of control, big sister Cat. She hadn't been much of a mother. It wasn't something that had occurred to her. Rae spent a lot of time watching. Watching that all the simple things got done—dinner made, rent paid, milk bought, school forms signed. It was almost worse when her father was there. Then she had to watch them both, that they didn't hurt the cats, or the appliances, or each other. She needed to protect herself from the sweep of their moods and know when they needed an especially wide berth, or when she could tell one of them that the second notice from PG&E had come, and if they didn't pay it soon the lights would go off.

Rae looks at Quincy, playing a quiet game, his fat fingers swallowed up in Betty's hands. It has hardly occurred to Rae to be anything but a mother. She's tried to do her best by the boy.

When she was little her mother sometimes handed her Pyrex Jell-O cups filled with chocolate chips and they'd stand together outside the house. Her mother wore jaunty hats and chewed gum. She was very beautiful. While Rae nibbled the chocolate chips, one careful bite after another, her mother watched the cars sail by and said, "How do you do? How do you do?" when she saw big ones. Was she really expecting Mr. Ronnie Reboulet to drive up, after a long absence, and whisk her away? Cat would smile her big-tooth smile to Rae, and say, "How would you like to go for a ride in a bright, yellow Studebaker like that? How would you like to go for a ride in a big ole Cadillac?"

The Smell of Eucalyptus

Three days after her mother's funeral, Rae takes Quincy to the zoo. Time still has the peculiar, suspended quality of a holiday. Nothing new can start quite yet. She forks over five dollars for a plastic yellow zoo key that Quincy wants. He turns it in a few yellow boxes, activating the nasal voice of a man who describes the feeding habits of the rhino, and the fact that pygmy hippos can turn russet potatoes into juice faster than their full-grown cousins. Quincy doesn't like the man's voice any more than she does and slips the key into his pants pocket.

He claims that he wants to see the elephants, and that's all. They find a bench near the family of Asian elephants and sit for hours. He sits with his eight ball on his lap. From time to time, she goes off to get him something, peanuts or cotton candy. "Stay here," she says. She backs away and watches her little boy alone on the bench.

When the path between him and the elephants is clear, Quincy looks straight toward the grey, dusty ears of the mama and her baby boy. When people block his view, he shakes the eight ball and waits for the elusive white answer that he can't read to bubble up.

One time, rather than getting directly in line for an orange soda, Rae walks past a huddle of gloomy zebras. They don't seem much cheered by the tangy fragrance from the nearby eucalyptus trees. Rae loves the smell of eucalyptus. Usually when she returns to a site from her childhood, the scale of everything seems dwarfed in comparison with her memory of it. But these majestic trees are much taller than she remembers. Can they really have gained such stature in a dozen years?

When Rae returns, Quincy is sitting right where she left him, straight-necked, looking directly at the pachyderms, the sticky eight ball settled in his lap. He doesn't seem as happy to see her as to have his orange soda.

"Quince, I have a friend I'd like you to meet."

"Does he have four legs? Does he?"

"Nope, not the last time I looked."

Cat Remembered

Ronnie sits all afternoon in Murray's Stickley chair, with the made-over red leather seat, trying to conjure an image of young Cat. Catherine. She had a beautiful, pouty mouth and an opinion about everything. The rest of the world was made up of dull, humdrum particles that had been stored too long in a bottle, while Cat was formed from atoms with the character of Mexican jumping beans. When her anger swelled, he learned to stand aside and watch her as if she were a neighbor ringing the doorbell with one immense complaint after another.

He tries again to picture Cat with her high cheekbones and high breasts and long white neck that he loved to drive his teeth into. She was tall and leggy. She reminded people of a dark-haired Lauren Bacall. She had so much style, she could throw on rags and look like she'd dressed beautifully.

Sitting in Murray's cabin, two hundred and fifty yards from Lake Tahoe, Ronnie has trouble calling up an image of Cat's face from the last twenty years. The image of her young isn't what he wants anymore. She'd aged poorly, like him. But nobody remains frozen in youth, unless they die young. When they wrote about his demise, the stories always featured some beautiful photo of him at nineteen or twenty-one. What was the point? Even if he'd lived "right" he would have aged.

Ronnie conjures a memory of Cat without a face. It was the first time he'd talked with her in years; a lifetime ago, but only a matter of months. He'd wanted to let her know he was back in the Bay Area, even though he'd been back for nearly a year. He'd tried to write her, but was unable to get the letter done.

Surprisingly nervous, he sat on his high stool in the starter's shack. All the golfers were out on the course. His legs crossed, he lit a Viceroy. Cat answered after the third ring. He held the phone for a couple of silent beats after she picked it up.

"Hello . . . hello . . ."

He exhaled a slow, steady stream of smoke.

"Hey, asshole," she said, "shit, why don't you, or get off the pot."

"It's me, Cat—Ronnie."

Cat was quiet, except for her breathing, the cadenced wheeze of a heavy drinker and smoker.

"Sorry to startle you," he said.

"Nothing startles me, Ronnie. Where are you?" she said finally, breathless, and quite a bit loaded, he guessed, on Four Roses, or Wolfschmidt.

"How are you, Cat?"

"Fuck you, Ronnie. Fuck you."

He thought of hanging up. But what did he expect? He hunkered down quietly with the phone.

"Ex-cuse me," she said, enunciating each syllable with the peculiar orthodoxy of a drunk, "I was a lit-tle star-tled to hear from you. What was it you said? How am I? How am I? Hey, Ron-nie?"

He lit another cigarette and crushed the empty pack. "Yeah?"

"You ever heard of time, Ron-nie?" she screamed.

He held the phone a little off his ear, willing to ride a moment with her familiar logic.

"Time, Ronnie. Too much of it has gone by for you to ask me how I am. You don't get to ask that. And if you ask me how Rae is, I'll tell you to go fuck yourself, so don't ask that either." Then she turned plaintive, almost tender, and said, "Where are you, Ronnie?"

"I'm staying close by—down the peninsula."

"Where?"

"Half Moon Bay."

"Nice down there?"

"It's okay."

"Pretty nice?"

"Sure," he relented.

"Half Moon Bay. I'm writing that down, Ronnie."

Ronnie felt time fold up. She was writing down where he was. What did she plan to do? Climb into her old yellow Buick, or whatever piece of crap she now had for collecting parking tickets, and drive down to fetch him, as if he were still her husband, stranded somewhere in the middle of the night, after a gig? Lost, or loaded, or in jail. He reminded himself to remain respectful.

"I didn't mean to bother you, Cat. I just wanted to let you know I was . . . I'm back in the Bay Area, and I wanted to make sure that you were still getting the money orders."

"You and your lousy money orders. Since you go to all the trouble of sending them, you might make them worth something."

"I wish they could be more money. . . ."

"Of all the things to wish for," she said, and started laughing, a rolling, hideous laugh that he listened to for half a minute before hanging up.

Quiet as a Morgue

Wallace greets them in his bathrobe. He opens wide the door to his house.

"How do you do, son?"

"Fine, thank you," Quincy says, overwhelmed by the majesty of the large black man whose door he's just walked through.

"You're a very well-mannered young man," Wallace says, and smiles at Rae. "Can I get you something cold to drink, young Quincy, Rae? Ginger ale, ice water, Coca-Cola, rum and Coke?"

Ever since her father left in early July, Rae has been racing to catch up to herself, and the look of Wallace's red velvet sofa is so appealing that she wants to throw herself down on it and close her eyes.

Wallace carries a tray from the kitchen with Cokes in tall, frosted glasses, and a bowl of chips with salsa. "So where you been keeping yourself, Rae?"

"Quincy and I have been having a little adventure." She turns to smile at the boy, who takes small slurps from his Coke, but doesn't smile back. He has the eight ball in his lap and will pick it up any moment to ask a few silent questions.

"We've been staying with my father down in Half Moon Bay, but he just up and left with his trumpet. He hasn't played in five or six years. I don't know, I guess the family thing was a little much for him."

"Hmmm," Wallace offers.

She looks at the deep, leathery creases in Wallace's moon face. He is a good man. Only months ago she thought she was in love with him. The idea was absurd. The man is from another world, he grew up in an atmosphere of hushed civility. He was taught not to fear the dead as much as those who walked the streets, who still had tricks up their sleeves, even when they came to pay their respects to the dead. Instead of carrying on the family business, Wallace went to medical school. But something bad happened there that he would never tell her about. He studied pathology. He learned how to dissect and preserve bodily organs. One time she saw him cut through a huge sirloin steak with a pair of scissors, and she was unable to eat it, even after it had been beautifully broiled.

Wallace is studying his recent manicure.

"You look lovely, Rae. To what do I owe the honor of your visit?"

"I just wanted to see you, Wallace."

"Is that right? Well, thank you. So, what are you planning to do, darling?"

"I don't know."

As Rae fidgets, Wallace looks into her face and tries to hold her eyes, but she is off in a dozen rooms of her imagination.

"Look at me," he says quietly, but with force.

Wallace holds her gaze for a moment. The room has been quiet since Quincy stopped bubbling air through the straw in his ginger ale. Now it grows quieter. *Quiet as a morgue,* Rae thinks, and wants to stand up, or say something funny, or just look past Wallace. But his dark eyes hold her as persuasively as a hand around her throat. It is as if the owner of the house has anticipated, then ambushed the intruder. He will not let go. Finally, he demurs, dropping his eyes back to his beautifully kept hands.

After Rae exhales a slow trail of breath, just enough to blow out a single taper, she notices Quincy, knotted in the white letters of his eight ball, little boy as ancient man, deciphering hieroglyphics.

Wallace breaks the formal silence. "He seems like a very nice boy."

"He is a sweetheart."

"I can tell that he's a nice boy. You should be proud of what you've done. You should be proud of that."

"I'm not proud."

"You ought to be." Wallace takes her by the arm and walks her across the room. "Look here, we must play wisely with the cards that we are dealt."

Spare me the lecture, Wallace, she wants to say, but she says nothing.

"Myself?" he says. "I've never raised a child, and much as I wanted to when I was a younger man—I really thought I'd have a brood of them, you understand, and people would call me Daddy Wallace, and I'd become a stout old man with a shiny black head, like my daddy and granddaddy, and there'd be all kinds of children running around—but it wasn't meant to be."

"I'm scared, Wallace."

"Everybody's scared, darling."

"I'm afraid of what I'm going to do."

"What? You going to jump off the Golden Gate Bridge? You going to become another statistic? I think they're up to six or seven hundred leapers by now. Jumping off the bridge is a hard way to distinguish yourself, darling."

"I'm not looking to distinguish myself."

"Well, you should be, in a positive sense."

"I can't go on with the boy."

"Why not?"

"I don't have anything to give him," Rae says, and begins to cry.

"You are giving him what he needs."

"But what about me?"

"You?" Wallace looks at her uncertainly. "What *you* need is another matter. That's something I'm not prepared to answer. I'm not qualified to answer that, you understand? We're talking about the vagaries of satisfaction. I don't have a clue what you need . . . what it is your satisfaction depends on. I try to concern myself with concrete details. I have enough trouble keeping up with the concretes. Pardon me." Wallace opens a large, burgundy handkerchief, turns aside, and fires a deep, phlegmy cough into the center of it.

"So what do you propose to do with this fine boy, eat him? You going to leave him wait on a church step? He's too big to shove inside a little wicker basket like a Moses-child. You going to turn him into a big-ole-foundling boy?"

"I came here to ask you . . ."

"I know what you came to ask," Wallace says, assuming, even in his bathrobe, the formal posture of a funeral director who has to deny yet another request for the deluxe package on credit. He tightens the tie of his robe and inhales through his wide nostrils.

"I understand your circumstance, and am flattered by the trust you place in me. I mean that, I am sincerely flattered. But, at this moment in time, I know what's within my capabilities and what is beyond. I can't take a boy from his mother—I don't care if he's black and his mama's white—and raise him like he's mine. You understand? But in saying that, I want you to know that I place no judgment. I am not, nor will I ever be, your judge."

Rae cannot look again at Wallace. She wonders what it would be like to run out of the door, straight across Turk Street, and hop on a trolley, heading down Fillmore, before Wallace can get his pants on, but she doesn't wonder for long. She collects Quincy and his eight ball, and tells him to thank the nice gentleman for his hospitality.

Naming a Leader

By the beginning of December, Ronnie and Artie Rhodes, the young piano player from Ronson's, have formed a quartet with a black bass player named Buster Shipley, who is gigging with a money band at Harrahs, and a blond, blue-eyed drummer named Skippy Peterson, who's a friend of Rhodes's from Los Angeles. They practice most afternoons at Murray's cabin, jammed together in the main room with Shipley's bass fiddle, Peterson's drum kit, and Rhodes's electric piano. The keyboard lives in that room for weeks at a time. Ronnie spends a lot of time cursing it for being an ugly little box that sounds like fried tin. Some mornings he marches around the electric piano, his trumpet blaring at it, as if he could knock it off its pencil legs with the force of his disdain.

Ronnie asks Artie Rhodes to lead the band, despite the fact that Artie is a pothead who rolls doobies with his right hand as he comps with his left, giggles through his solos, and asks for munchies after every other tune. If they ever get themselves together, they'll play in a club with an actual piano, eighty-eight keys that don't have to be plugged into the wall, and the bartender will be instructed to set out peanut butter sandwiches and a tall glass of milk for their prodigy.

Artie balks at the offer; he is still in awe of Ronnie. "I'm sorry, but I think I got to be adamant about this," he says, and takes a long hit off a stogie wrapped in wheatstraw, "I'm just not advanced enough to lead a band that's got Ronnie Reboulet in it."

"Cut the shit, Artie."

"No, I'm serious. People are going to say, 'Hey, who's that asshole on the piano, thinks he should lead this band?' "

One day before the others arrive, Ronnie sits the pianist down at the kitchen counter and passes him a plate of buttered toast. Artie Rhodes looks at the toast.

"What do you want, jelly?"

"What is it?" Rhodes asks, looking suspiciously at the plate.

"What do you mean, what is it? How many of those fatties have you smoked since noon? It's toast, Artie. Buttered toast."

"Why do you want me to eat toast?"

"Because I want your mouth to be stuffed when I talk to you."

Artie nibbles at the corners of a slice of toast.

"You sure you don't want jelly, Artie? Listen, it's not an honor leading a band, it's a job. And you're the man for it. Me, I'm wrestling with the trumpet. I have a mouthful of false teeth. I can hardly read music. Much as I hate to say this, *I need you, Artie.* We ever start playing some actual music, I'll become the nominal leader. That means the guy whose name is on the band. But we're a long way from that."

Ronnie looks at Rhodes and then down at his empty plate.

"Good fella, you even ate the crust, Artie."

Quartet on Fire

It doesn't take long for the band to get too big for Murray's cabin, to grow restless like a baby in the womb. A couple of months is all. Ronnie is sorry that it takes a fire to wake him to the fact.

The afternoon of the fire, Skippy gets them off on a lively "Night in Tunisia." Instead of driving the thing with a subtle Latin-Arabic feel—lots of cymbal, tom-tom, rims, and the occasional brightening of a cowbell—he bashes out a very fast beat on the snare with the fat ends of his sticks, like a rock and roller, the constant bash of the bass drum making the framed pictures on the wall look like they are exercising. Ronnie does his best to keep up, without trying any fancy Dizzy stuff, although the old hipster always hovers over his song. Ronnie wasn't able to make high notes like Diz, even in his prime. Still, he flies through the changes, his teeth nearly coming unfixed from his gums, the damn drummer driving them all wrong, but still driving him. Ronnie takes a breath as vast as a body of water, drops his cigarette into Murray's open-whale's-mouth ashtray, and closes his eyes.

When the break arrives, Skippy curls his feet off the pedals and holds on to his sticks for a blessed moment, as Ronnie drives straight into the vacuum, which is like the empty shaft of an elevator that will kill you if you don't soar above it with bright sound. Artie Rhodes hollers. Buster says, "Uh huh." Skippy twirls his sticks in the air, waiting an eternity to pound his way back in.

Nobody notices the lit cigarette fly out of the whale's mouth.

It drives a burning hole into the sofa. Flames shoot from the middle cushion. Everybody wakes from the dream at once. Ronnie is standing close, his back to it. He turns to see the golden flames stand up on their hind legs, and rips off his shirt to swat at them. Skippy races over with a yard of traveling carpet from under his bass drum, but instead of beating down the flames, tosses the carpet on top like he is feeding a bonfire. Buster yells, "Help," to no one in particular, and hugs his bass in the corner. It is Artie Rhodes who saves the day. He waddles over from the stove with a large cast iron kettle full of fatty sausage water and all but douses the flame, the steam making them cough, as Ronnie beats the damn thing to death with bathroom towels.

Outside the cabin, Buster Shipley shivers in a cotton turtleneck. "Got a little toasty in there."

Rhodes lights a fresh joint. "We were smoking." He sucks in a bellyful and passes it to Buster.

Skippy shakes off the joint. He pulls a pair of drumsticks from his back pocket and does a little ra-ta-ta on the frame of the ruined sofa.

Standing beside the sofa in the snow, Ronnie remembers the fire he and Cat once had in a mattress, the burning head of a cigarette boring a hole right between them in the bed. When she drank, Cat could be a frightening sight with cigarettes, a cavalier goddess who made sweeping gestures with her smoking hand. That night Cat was clearheaded and poured her glass of bedtime water straight down the drain of the widening hole. They also carried the burned thing outside, once it had been doused.

He and Cat stood on either side of the mattress, keeping it propped up, not wanting it to fall to the street. It was their bed, and still in decent shape. If they let it fall they'd have to abandon it. The hole was really quite small. They said nothing. They stood there, in the cool evening, and smoked a couple of cigarettes. After a while, they carried the mattress back upstairs and slept on it, more or less, for the next five years.

Dirt

She met Dirt at the restaurant in Moss Beach. He'd come in
most afternoons and order coffee and a slice of fruit pie. He
drove up on a big Harley so, in a sense, she'd hear him coming
before she knew he was there. Dressed in chains and leather,
Dirt didn't look like the kind of guy you wanted to cozy up to
and say, "Care to have a scoop of vanilla ice cream melted over
your hot pie?" That was the boss, Rodney's, pet phrase. He tried
to get all the girls to use it. He hired only big-breasted girls. He
said, "Call me Rod," and told them that they should try to *titillate* the customers if they wanted bigger tips. Everything out of
Rod's mouth was dirty. Weirdos came into the restaurant,
middle-aged guys, with binoculars hanging around their necks,
who'd been out peeping from the cliffs at nudie beaches in
Pacifica.

Three or four weeks after Dirt started coming around, Rae
found herself looking into his eyes, which were soft and brown
and rather lovely, and asking if he would like a scoop of ice
cream on his pie. She put the question to him straight.

Later, she rode off on the back of Dirt's Harley, a fast ride
down to Half Moon Bay to see if Betty would watch Quincy
for the evening. They drove up to the city. Dirt took her to a
Mexican restaurant called Mi Boca on 24th Street and South Van
Ness. There weren't many customers. A mother and her fat son,
who seemed to run the place, were sitting together on cracked
vinyl kitchen chairs, watching a soccer match. When they saw
Rae and Dirt walk in, the mother hurried to the kitchen. The fat
young man came to their table with a couple of frayed menus.

The man nodded to Dirt. "Hi, Randy."

"Hey, Pablo," Dirt said.

Rae stared at Dirt, trying to guess how old he was. He had a thick mustache and bad teeth, but his eyes really were lovely. He laid his hands on the table. Rae was surprised to see how nicely cared-for they were. Despite his name, Dirt had a certain fastidiousness about him. On his right pinky, he wore a thick ring that had once been a piece of silverware. He seemed like a guy who probably looked twenty-five when he was sixteen.

"Randy?" she asked.

"Randolph," he corrected. "Most people call me Dirt. But Pablo and I go way back."

"Do you eat here a lot?"

"I live here."

After dinner, they walked up 24th Street to a Mexican bakery where Dirt plucked dry cookies the size of saucers, one by one, with a pair of tongs, and dropped them into a paper sack. Rae held the sack as they scooted over on the big bike to Dirt's apartment on Treat.

She was a little scared, walking behind him up the dark steps. He stopped midway up. "Don't worry, I'm not going to ravish you."

It was a strange thing to say, but it calmed her.

She liked his apartment, a railroad-style two-bedroom chockfull of refinished oak and stained-glass lamps. A collection of mirrors in carved frames hung from the wall opposite a piece of decorative stitch work that caught Rae's eye: *The days are long, the years are short.*

"Where did you get all this stuff?"

"I'm a collector," he said.

He had her sit on a Victorian daybed and brought over a beautiful tray, a strip of Chinese silk framed in oak and glass. "My grandmother used to serve cocktails on this." It was hard to think of Dirt as anybody's grandson. He opened a brass case, engraved as a scarab, and spilled a couple grams of coke onto the tray. "There's plenty where that came from," he said, dividing the powder into feathery lines with a vintage Boy Scout's knife.

Sunny Side Up

Ronnie chooses the day big snow is coming to leave. He stops to have chains put on in the town of Markleeville, and carries his trumpet in its case up the street to a diner. It's been weeks since he's eaten a cooked meal. He puts the trumpet down on the counter and scoots onto a stool across from the Indian fry cook, who wears her hair in a tight, thin braid like a weighted chain down her back. Eight Christmas stockings are strung high above shelves stacked with five-gallon bottles of sweet pickle chips and giant cans of fruit cocktail. Each stocking has a five-dollar bill pinned to it. Ronnie reads the names on the stockings, hoping that five bucks is not the extent of their Christmas bonus.

He studies the cook. She's not exactly a pretty woman, with her pocked complexion and oversize features. But he watches how gracefully she shepherds a dozen breakfasts through the grill: flipping over-easy eggs, slathering butter on hunks of sourdough and flopping them belly-down, laying hamburger buns to steam atop mounds of hash browns, mixing buttermilk batter, dropping an iron press on the thick, sputtering slices of bacon.

When men walk in—and the only creatures that seem to walk in are men—they pay the fry cook their respects. "Sarah," they say. And she greets them each by name, "Hey, Bobby. . . . Hey, Henry. . . . Hey, Cliff. . . . Hey, Kenny." It's an efficient business. Ronnie figures she's one of those Indians who doesn't waste words. Who could blame her? She pours your coffee, lays out the menu, gives you two minutes to mull it over, and turns your way. Ronnie can hardly take his eyes off her. She's a beauty. He looks up and finds her name on a Christmas stocking. When she brings his plate, he offers his own name.

"Ronnie," she says, and turns back to her flock of breakfasts. "I've known some guys named Ronnie, I just as soon forget."

He watches her scrape gritty crust into the grill's bunghole.

"Didn't mean to offend you, Ronnie," she says, topping his coffee.

"No problem. Say, I'm curious, when's the last time you apologized to someone?"

"About the last time I burnt somebody's hotcakes. Never twice in a day." She shuffles a short stack onto a plate and passes it to a guy down the line. "You play the trumpet?"

"Yes, I do."

"You any good?"

"Used to be."

"If you were once, you can be again."

"Think so?"

"Yes."

A big-bearded gent, looking like somebody left over from the gold rush, walks in, past the ding-dong of the open door, and says, "Sarah, when are you going to come over to my house and cook for me?"

Sarah turns back to the grill. "You call that a house, Wally?"

"You don't know where I live, Sarah."

"Don't underestimate me, Wally."

"You can come over to my place and cook for me anytime," he says, licking his chops.

"Wally, you wouldn't know what to do with a woman like me."

Ronnie, nibbling his bacon, wonders if *he'd* know. As he spins off the stool, ready to go, he says "Sarah" just loud enough to be heard over the hiss of the grill, and watches as she slides a pair of sunny-side-up eggs into the center of a white plate.

Fire and Ice

Despite the oncoming blizzard, it is not particularly cold. He feels uncommonly robust. A sign, heading out of town, says seven miles to Grover Hot Springs and Ronnie decides to go exploring. With chains wrapped around its wheels, the Alfa is a strange creature, a proud dog forced to walk through town with a muzzle. It drags its chains, humbly enough, through the early dusting of snow in town, and the several miles of switchbacks, into deeper snow.

The hot springs, it turns out, is a state park, closed for the season, but there is nobody to stop Ronnie from having a little walk around. The other vehicle in the parking lot, a hippie van with Texas plates and windows dusted with snow, looks as if it has been abandoned for the season.

Ronnie walks furtively up a trail that weaves through scrub pines to the springs. He can see three distinct pools, each an odd-shaped black hole, aproned with snow, large enough to swallow a pickup truck or two. Three active craters of the moon. Snow and steam. Steam and snow. Ronnie approaches the closest of the pools and drops to his stomach like a boy in the snow. He reaches a hand in. The water is no warmer than a hot bath. He stands and strips off his clothes, folding them with sharp creases, the way he'd learned in the army. Naked, he shoots a long arch of pee that steams yellow in the snow. The flurries, which had been scattering with no more purpose than a maiden flight of gnats, are now forming distinct flakes that fall to fixed spots of earth.

At first Ronnie is afraid to step into the pool—not that the water will burn him, but that once in he may not be able to get out. What if the pool has no bottom and the sinking never ends? He slips in slowly and is calmed by the bubbling water and the burst of unseen minerals. The water rises to the bottom of his neck. He laughs at the idea of his Adam's apple bobbing. A man could cleanse himself like this and die satisfied, no matter how he'd lived his life. Snow is falling. Ronnie hears a flutter of birds rippling in the far pool, as he hunkers down into the hot springwater.

The Fugitive's Bath

He opens his eyes to snow flakes that have grown to the size of a large man's fingernails, and sings a few lost lines of a show tune, until he hears the flutter of crisp laughter and forces himself to see two young women, through a veil of snow, steaming in another pool. He suspects that they are as naked as he, and have been watching him for some time.

"Hey, there," he says.

The women laugh again, perhaps at the absurdity of a conversation between steaming bodies in the falling snow.

"You have a nice voice," one of the women says.

"Thank you. It's not much of voice, really."

"It's enough."

He remembers the hippie van in the parking lot. "Are you girls the ones from Texas?" The talking woman is Asian, the other looks like the face from a magazine.

"Not Texas," says the Asian one, who has a surprisingly throaty voice.

"Then that's not your van?"

"I didn't say that."

"I see."

"Are you just passing through?" the Asian woman wonders.

"No, I live in this hole," he says, and runs two fingers, like a skater, over the top of the water. "Just kidding."

The three break into nervous laughter. Ronnie studies the white girl, who doesn't say anything. Her hair is cut shorter than in most of the pictures, but he knows her. From thirty-five yards away, he knows her. He can see, through falling snow, directly into her eyes. They are not the darting eyes of an animal, nor the bedroom eyes of a girl on her back. Her eyes are calm and watchful, certainly the appropriate response for the eyes of a fugitive. And yet they hardly seem like the eyes of a girl who could hold a big gun steady during a bank robbery.

"Doesn't your friend say anything?"

"No, she doesn't talk much," the Asian woman says.

"I guess that's what happens when everybody's looking for you."

"Yes."

"Well," Ronnie says, "I wish you luck, whatever it is you're doing. Now, I've got to ask you ladies a favor. I need to get out of this hole and on my way. And the thing is, I'm kind of bashful. Would you mind turning your backs? I'm not much to look at, anyway." Ronnie boosts himself out of the pool and wipes dry with his undershirt. His pants up, he turns back toward the women.

"Good luck to you both."

"Thank you," the white woman says. The voice is so familiar.

"Take care of her," he says to the other woman, as if he were asking her to look after his own daughter.

Sugar?

The snow swirls in all directions. Even though traffic is stuttering along very slowly, Ronnie concentrates on keeping his eyes on the white centerline. There are distractions everywhere. A steaming, late-model Thunderbird, its front end stacked at the guardrail, seems to grow out of the ground like a totem. State troopers are abundant, flares in their hands, their cars parked in gathering drifts of snow, with the gyrating red lights veiled a muted orange.

Ronnie argues with himself about Patty Hearst. Did he really see her? Even with his eyes pasted to the centerline, he thinks of the two women in the hot spring. Were the troopers heading after them, like a modern posse, when the blizzard materialized?

Once he makes it safely into the foothills, and the radio comes back to life, Ronnie listens for news of Patty and her traveling companion, but there is none. She has transformed herself into a successful fugitive. He has no reason to root for her, but does.

By the time he stops at a diner in Lodi for coffee and a burger, he is almost giddy. He sits under bright lights, beside a fat Chicano at the counter, and watches the man pour a mound of sugar into his coffee. When the man's finished, he swivels toward Ronnie and asks, "Sugar?" Ronnie wants no sugar. He will never tell who he has seen. It is his secret. Nobody would believe him anyway. He buys a bag of donuts on the outskirts of town, and aims the Alfa south through the valley.

Looking for Dirt

One evening after work she bundles Quincy into the car and heads for the city. He wants to know if they are going to see his father.

She takes her son's hand. "I don't know where your daddy is, anymore. He went away somewhere for a while. Your grammy doesn't even know where he is."

Quincy nods his head and hums a quiet song to himself, all the way to the city. After they park on Treat Street, Quincy stands tall beside his mother at the doorstep. There is no answer when she buzzes the doorbell. She squats so that she's able to face her son, eye to eye.

"You like Mexican food, Buddy?"

"Tacos?" he says.

"Yeah, you like them?"

He shrugs. "Kinda crunchy. You like Big Macs, Mama?"

"They're okay."

"Okay, let's get one."

"Not now, honey."

A few minutes later, at Mi Boca, Pablo walks up to their table with a menu and a basket of chips. He smiles to them in a friendly way.

"Do you have any crayons?" she asks, nodding toward Quincy.

Pablo smiles, and in a minute he's back with three stubby crayons and a sheet of butcher paper big enough to cover the table.

She thanks Pablo and says, "You haven't seen Randy, have you?"

He doesn't seem to have heard her.

"You know, Randy. Randolph. Dirt."

Pablo doesn't respond. "You know . . . what you want to order?"

"Two chicken tacos," she says.

Quincy sits crunching thick Mexican chips with his baby teeth. "Who's Randolph Dirt, Mama?"

"Remember the man on the motorcycle?"

Quincy nods. He picks up the red crayon and draws two beautifully crooked wheels with distinct spokes, like branches, that force the wheels into blooming motion.

Little grown-up man, she thinks. Sometimes he seems to know what she is going to do before she does. She wants to give Quincy something but isn't sure what it should be. She takes hold of one of his small brown hands.

"Quince, I'm not saying we're going to do this. In fact, we can't in our present situation. But, say, someday when we have our own place, I think maybe we should get some sort of a pet. What do you think?"

"Yeah," he says, warily.

"What kind would you want?"

He shrugs. "How about we get . . . a grizzly bear," he says, suddenly silly.

"A grizzly bear?!"

"Or, maybe a . . . a skunk. Something that stinks."

"What do you *really* want, Quince?"

"I don't know."

"Come on."

"A dog," he says, and draws a big red animal with circle eyes. He hears two men talking to each other loud in Spanish. Quincy turns his head and sees Pablo sitting down in front of the television. When the street door opens, he watches the man on the motorcycle walk in.

The High Waves

After the New Year, Ronnie and Artie Rhodes become a duet. Rhodes got them a poor-paying gig at his uncle's tavern in LA, and the rhythm section fell away. Buster, a decent-enough bass player, opted to stay in Tahoe with his gig at Harrahs. The drummer, Skippy, a basher bred on rock and roll, crowded too much of the available space for Ronnie's taste and was persuaded to find a more suitable venue for his talents. Ronnie doesn't like the idea of being as exposed as they are without a bass and drums, but he and Rhodes decide to try it as a tasteful duet until they can come up with an adequate rhythm section.

The club had recently changed names from Toners to the High Waves. Ronnie liked the new name. He pictured an upscale watering hole near the beach in Santa Monica, and smiled the first time Rhodes took him by the club, on a crumbling stretch of Figueroa Street in downtown LA. It wasn't really a jazz club, just a smoky joint with a bad piano, a crowd of dedicated rummies, and a few youngsters out slumming. They play Tuesday through Sunday nights. A cardboard photo of Artie is attached to the greasy front window under a carefully lettered sign advertising the Artie Rhodes Duo. There is no mention of the trumpeter, which is fine by Ronnie, who enjoys ribbing the young prodigy.

"Hey, Artie, who's the ghost you're playing duets with, or is that two of you sitting at the keyboard?"

Ronnie's habit is to step outside, between sets, to get away from the noise. He stands in the gentle LA night and smokes three or four Viceroys in a row. Whores and dope fiends and small-time hustlers stroll by in a regular procession. Ronnie kindly declines all offers of products and services. If anybody asks what he's up to, he takes a pull on his cigarette and says, "Just catching my breath."

He can't get enough of the photo of Artie Rhodes in the window. Artie uncoiled his chignon and let his stringy hair hang to his shoulders, as soon as he left Tahoe. His hair is shiny clean for the photo. He's posed at the bad piano, with one of his Maui-Zowie grins, his fingers in the air, ready to pounce on the ivories, THE ARTIE RHODES DUO.

Ronnie has begun to call the tunes—a mix of jazz standards built on the backs of film and show tunes. "Weaver of Dreams," "Green Dolphin Street," "The Days of Wine and Roses." It seems best to keep things simple with this crowd. *Simple and strong.*

One night, after the first set, Artie Rhodes walks up to Ronnie in the back room and puts his hand on the trumpeter's shoulder. "Hey, Reb, you used to sing in the old days, how come you don't ever sing?"

"Because I don't want to sing," Ronnie says, walking across the room.

"But it'd be good for the act."

"Sorry, Artie, I'm afraid that what you see is what you get."

He used to think that when his playing days were over he'd make a go of it as a singer but, given his limited range, he's afraid that he'd be nothing but a stick-figure voice sugared with pathos. It's too soon to become a novelty act.

But later that night, as the crowd thins and the waitresses ease back toward their own reveries, Ronnie holds the mike up to his lips and sings the opening of "Night and Day." He's got nothing to prove, nobody to charm. Take a weak voice and make a picture with it. Say, all you have is a stub of charcoal. Nothing more. No sense trying to get fancy, to go where you can't go. Can you draw a dotted line? Can you find a way to make it go uphill, and down again? Can you shade it so it's nighttime, brighten it up for day? Are you human? Do you have a voice?

When Ronnie brings the song in, he notices that the sparse crowd is with him. So, he can sing for his dinner, if it comes to that. As he backs away from the mike, the crowd hoots in appreciation. It's not a song to hoot for. Artie Rhodes is grinning like a simple child. Cheap dates, Ronnie thinks, the whole bunch of you.

Phoenix

Ronnie takes great pleasure in keeping his name out of it. The High Waves is not the type of place where musicians need to introduce themselves. If a patron inquires after the old trumpeter who closes out most nights with a soulful "I've Grown Accustomed to Your Face," a waitress says, "That's Phoenix." If Ronnie is asked, he says, "Phoenix here." And if he's feeling particularly loquacious, he adds, "But I'm not really from Phoenix . . . north of there . . . a little town north, called Jewel."

The moniker came from Artie Rhodes. One afternoon shortly after they hit LA, they were sitting in a veggie cafe in Hermosa Beach. Artie had a terrible case of the munchies. He'd already polished off a pair of soy burgers and was stuffing the live foliage of a "passionate" garden salad into his mouth, crunching croutons in a grotesque jam of spinach and romaine. Ronnie imagined a high-wattage lightbulb tripped in Artie's brain.

"You're like that bird that got all burned up in the desert fire, and then rose from the ashes."

"What bird?"

"I thought of it in Tahoe, Reb. You'd just blown the roof off 'Night in Tunisia,' man, you flew through that fucking break. Skippy was back in, going crazy, beating holy fuck out of his drums. Buster and I, we're looking at each other, like, *This is getting a little deep.* Then I check you out, and there's a fire coming from behind your head. I'm frozen at the keyboard, thinking *Who is this mother?* I'm looking at the flames, absolutely paralyzed, trying to remember the name of the bird, when this Phoenix fucker finally flies into my head. I don't know how I ever got to the sausage water in time to put out the fire."

Alfalfa sprouts, wedged between Artie's teeth, waved to the world as he spoke.

"He's like a mythological bird, Reb. That's who you are, Phoenix!"

Ronnie blew smoke in Artie's face.

"I'm telling you. He was this really beautiful bird, with gorgeous plumage. Only bird of his kind seen in the Arabian desert for hundreds of years. And then he burned up, Reb. The sun is what ignited the fire, not some lamer cigarette. Old Phoenix, he did some serious fanning with his beauty wings, and eventually he rose, he rose right up and went flying."

Ashes

Her mother once said that she wanted to be cremated. Rae didn't really believe her. "Hey, I've got enough alcohol trapped in the crevices of my body, all they've got to do is light a match." At the time, it was a grotesque, but funny, comment. Certainly her mother, like every other flaming narcissist, would have preferred a headstone atop a small hill, with a lush view of eternity. Rae was disappointed with the blue urn that her mother's ashes came in. Who would want their remains poured into a cheap vessel the color of a hospital scrub suit?

For weeks she'd kept the urn at the bottom of her day pack. She strolled with the pack up the beach and hung it on hooks at work, amused at the thought of her mother poised amid the grease and steam of the industrial kitchen. She wore the pack with her mother's remains, blasting through town on the back of a big Harley, and tossed it on the floor of a small room in the Mission district, as a man named Dirt made love to her.

Now she drives with it into the city and parks in the municipal lot on Vallejo, next to Keystone Korner and the police station. She strolls past a produce market mobbed with Chinese women in heavy coats, picking through oversize cabbages.

Rae pushes through the swinging doors at Cafe Roma and steps to the bar to order an espresso. She likes the way the Italians banter here. Some are playing pool, others pinball. A few of the young men would like to touch her, a few would prefer that she not be there. Nobody says a word to her. She sips her espresso, with her mother on her back. For the shortest moment, a middle-aged man stands beside her at the bar, sugars his espresso, then pours it down as if it were medicine.

She walks down Vallejo, across Columbus Avenue, past the Cafe Trieste to the Schlock Shop on Grant. There isn't a suitable urn in the place, but she buys herself a hard-brimmed black hat that makes her feel like Zorro. She wishes she could buy one for Quincy, but they don't have one his size. She picks out a straw hat for him, a cabbage farmer's hat, from the looks of it. It starts to rain after Rae slips, through the alley behind City Lights, into Chinatown. She skitters in and out of store awnings, pretending to look at the baskets of souvenirs and practical junk. Are the long-fingered plastic back scratchers and gilded chopsticks also aimed at her eyes? She thinks about going to Sam Wo's on Washington for a plate of chow fun, but buys a steamed pork bun instead, and keeps going up the street.

She thinks about Lawrence Ferlinghetti's poem about the dog strolling up Grant Avenue, nosing into meat and fish markets, picking up the general atmosphere. They'd discussed it in high school English, days after she found out she was pregnant. First, a stoner boy read the poem and then Rae volunteered that the poem made you feel like you were the dog, walking up the crowded street. The teacher said, "Of course, that's the point!" Maybe it was a stupid thing to say. As far as she can remember, that was the last comment that she made in her high school career.

Rae is soaked through, despite her new Zorro hat. She steps into an herbalist's narrow shop, near Sacramento Street. The south wall of the shop is a warren of small wooden drawers, presumably filled with herbs. She thinks of her mother's remains, interned in the cheap container inside her backpack. Has her mother become an herb?

There are shelves on the north wall with many glass containers in which the tall, gnarled roots of ginseng stand like dancing creatures, headless marionettes ready to break out. Square tins, painted in an elaborate filigree of red and black, are stacked along the higher shelves. A row of white urns with single Chinese characters, brushed gestures in an unknowable language, line a lower shelf. A man in a beige sweater-vest is standing behind a glass counter.

"I need a container for my mother's ashes," she says.

"Yes."

"For putting my mother's ashes in."

"Yes, what color you like?"

The man does not seem to understand.

"What color?"

"Red."

He bends down and opens a drawer, then gathers two boxes covered in a blue silk cloth and brings them to the counter. The boxes have mock ivory tooth clasps and, before the clerk opens the boxes, Rae knows that she wants one. He pulls a turquoise urn out of a packing of Chinese newspaper and stands it up on the counter. Beside it, he stacks the brightest red pot she's ever seen. Porcelain.

"That one for my mother," she says.

He nods.

"How much?"

"Twenty-five," he says.

She nods, and smiles at the man's busy fingers as they pack the urn for her.

Union Square is empty, but for pigeons, in the rain. What a strange place it is—she once stood in the bright sunshine and listened to speeches during a Vietnam peace vigil, other times she'd seen cable car bell-ringing contests and fashion shows.

Rae makes a wet zigzag through traffic, and goes directly to the restroom in I. Magnin. She imagines that all the detectives in the store are following her, but there are none in the bathroom. She enters a stall and, pulling the two urns out of her pack, pours her mother's ashes into the deep red porcelain. The red urn is stunning even on the bathroom floor. She sits on the toilet admiring it.

For a while she walks around the store, scouting. She carries the red urn in her hands, conspicuous as a lovely thing should be. She walks along the perfume stations. A beautifully put-together gay man standing behind one of the perfume counters smiles at her.

"Like to try something?"

She points to the Cabochard. "My mother liked to wear that when she was going out."

The clerk bows in recognition. "Yes," he says, "it's very mature. Replete with character. A fragrance for a powerful woman." He hands Rae the atomizer. She sprays it on her left wrist as it wraps around the urn. Enveloped in her mother's floral vapor, she must concentrate to keep from dropping the urn.

"Mature," she says, and looks dreamily into the man's face.

"Are you okay?"

"Oh yeah, my mother . . ."

"I understand."

Rae forces herself to study the clerk's milk mustache until she's regained her balance.

"That's a pretty pot you're holding."

"Thank you."

As she drifts toward women's dresses, it seems to Rae that the store detectives have lost interest in her. They must have figured out that her interest is in *leaving,* not in *taking.* She stops by a small mahogany table that holds a still life of dried pomegranates and browning limes in a flat Indian basket. The effect is a little hollow. The table stands across from a rack of Anne Klein dresses. It needs some help. Her mother once worked as a model, back when California was California, she liked to say. She'd had a wonderful sense of style. The red urn looks lovely on the table, Rae decides, as she slowly backs away from it.

Spiderwebs

A couple of weeks after Ronnie has settled in an old downtown hotel—the Alhambra—he writes Betty to let her know his whereabouts. The Alhambra was once a grand place and still has a beautiful pool in the back, with a couple of acres of palms to remind you that LA was once paradise. He has a suite full of mismatched furniture, high ceilings, with Spanish-style arches, and a plaster job that's remained untouched for fifty years. Sometimes, in the late afternoon, when the sun peeks through the west window, Ronnie lies back on the bed and watches the spiders doing their thread work on the ceiling.

One morning, as he was in the bathroom shaving, he scared the chambermaid out of her wits. He had the hot water going and shave cream layered over his face. He was crooning "Fly Me to the Moon," à la Tony Bennett, when he heard the maid cursing in Spanish. He walked out into the main room of the suite and found her wobbling back and forth on a straight-back chair. She was swinging a dry mop at the spiderwebs. It was hard to get her attention. He hollered, "Leave 'em. Leave 'em, dear. I happen to like spiderwebs." She screamed when she finally turned and saw him, a face full of shave cream. He'd never seen anybody run out of a room so fast.

L.A. Observer

The name Phoenix lasts about six weeks until a kid critic from the *Los Angeles Observer,* a throwaway weekly stuffed with waterbed ads and a mass of personals, starts nosing around. He'd been coming to the club for a couple of weeks. One night he strolls outside between sets, and stands beside Ronnie. He's a short, middleweight muscle guy in a blue blazer, with a blond head zipped close to the scalp. He looks like the captain of the college wrestling team.

"I know who you are," the kid says, not in an asshole way, just saying it because there is no other way around the fact.

"Yeah?"

"How you doing, Ronnie?"

Ronnie holds out his hand. "Pleased to meet you. I'm not exactly the Fugitive, you know."

"Heck, no. Just a helluva trumpet player. I feel lucky every chance I get to hear you. I'm Jimmy Landreth."

"Jimmy."

"I know your sound. There isn't anybody that can play low notes as soft and clear as you."

Ronnie grins. "Ever listened to Miles Davis?"

" 'Course."

Jimmy wants to do a cover story about him for the *LA Observer*. Ronnie turns aside and smiles at the photo of Artie Rhodes. "There's not going to be anybody interested in that story."

"I think you're wrong. You know the *Observer*?"

"It's a bunch of classifieds, isn't it? 'Pretty darling, if you're looking for a sensitive, well-hung, nonsmoker who loves Joni Mitchell . . .' "

"I'm not trying to sell you an ad, Ronnie."

He studies the young man for a moment. A smart kid with muscles. A brainy bodybuilder. As a small man, Ronnie has always been intrigued by men who lift weights; guys who go for the total transformation. Some of them are fruiters, but most of them just want to bulk up to their image of manhood. Magazines used to be filled with Don't-Be-a-Ninety-Pound-Weakling ads. He and his father lifted barbells together, but he never took it seriously. First he had his golf to work at, then the trumpet. By the time the boys in high school were getting greedy for muscles, he was building chops on the horn.

Jimmy Landreth stands tall for a short man. He has a quick eye on the corner and notices people coming up the street before they notice him. If he's nervous, he does a good job keeping it cool.

"You don't look like a reporter, Jimmy."

"Thanks."

Ronnie laughs. "The *Los Angeles Observer*, hunh? That's something like the *Berkeley Barb*. Are you a hippie radical in disguise? Any clean-cut reporter would be out chasing after Patty Hearst. You must be a subversive."

"You can tell me to fuck off, Ronnie, but I'd like to do a story about you."

Ronnie nods, and offers the young man a time and place to meet.

At the Window

When the motorcycle drives up, Betty knows that Rae is gone. She watches the way the girl embraces her son, like she's trying to make a memory for later. Rae goes out the front door with a bulging day pack, but without a word to Betty. Not even "Please, take my child for a while. I need some time." Betty is at one of the front windows watching the plume of exhaust from the motorcycle, and Quincy is at the other. She will always remember the boy standing at the window, standing between the yellow curtain and the glass, saying "Bye Mama, bye Mama, bye Mama," in a high, baby-boy voice barely audible from the other window. The dull, steady cadence of the chant rises over the blast of the motorcycle.

Betty feels as if she has just witnessed a crime, and after the initial *oh my god* she asks, "Who is that man, Quincy? Do you know who that man is?"

Quincy shakes his head. His face is smeared with tears.

"You don't know what that man's name is?"

"Dirt."

"What do you mean?"

"That man's name is Dirt. Randolph Dirt."

"Well, that's sure a strange name."

"Mmmmm hmmmm," he says, dreamily, now that any sign of the motorcycle is gone. Quincy's eyes are fixed on the spot where Randolph Dirt's burning cigarette butt dropped, after he let it fly.

Radish

The Pantry, the grand twenty-four-hour diner that claims not to have closed since its original opening in the thirties, has always been one of his favorite dining places. Straightforward American fare, no hippie alfalfa sprouts allowed. Even the Spanish omelettes are American. Ronnie first ate at the Pantry in the late forties when the Kenton band landed in LA for a couple of weeks. Stan, long and lean in his sharp suit, liked to sit at the counter and chatter with the fry cooks.

Nothing's changed. There's a stainless steel bowl, iced with raw, barely washed celery, carrots, and radishes, sitting on every table. Some nights, after the gig, Ronnie sits at the counter, beside the old ballplayers and rummies, and orders a ribeye steak, medium rare, despite having to slice it into baby bites.

Now, waiting for the kid reporter, he sits in a booth, rolling a crudely trimmed radish in his hands. He wishes he could trust his bought teeth to crunch the radish without incident, but he can't. He imagines the spray of sharp flavor a clean bite through the hard red root offers. Sometimes he'll set a whole radish into his mouth and suck on it for a moment, daring himself to take little nicks at it with his false teeth. But not now. He holds the radish in his left hand. When he walks out of the Pantry, he will put the radish in his pocket and there it will stay for days, wedged against his penknife.

Jimmy Landreth hustles, breathless, into the restaurant, a reporter's notebook in his hands. "Sorry I'm late."

"Sit down," Ronnie says, pushing the stainless steel bowl toward the kid.

Jimmy nods and eases into the chair across from Ronnie. He takes a deep breath and looks into the bowl. "A vegetable garden."

"Just about."

Jimmy picks out a fat radish, rolls it over once, and drives his teeth straight through it.

Do Not Disturb

Ronnie watches the kid pull a tape recorder out of his satchel and set it beside the stainless steel bowl.

"You got fresh batteries?"

"I think they're fine. You ready?"

Ronnie lights a cigarette. "I believe so."

"So, how does it feel to play again?"

"It's okay."

"How do you think you're sounding?"

"I'm not the one to say."

"Most of the people that have heard you since you've been back, don't know who you are."

"Well, just who am I?"

Jimmy bites his lip. "I think we know."

"Do we?"

"Okay, let's back up."

Ronnie laughs. "We haven't even gone forward yet."

"That doesn't seem to be your direction of choice."

Ronnie holds up the bowl with the radishes. "Here, have another nut."

"Why'd you quit playing?"

"Well, I had a bad reaction to some medication. And then my

teeth went weak on me and started to fall out. That took the heart out of things for me in terms of trumpet playing. Without my choppers, everybody pronounced me DOA.

"I didn't exactly have a noble reaction to their pronouncements, like one of those guys who sits up on the table and says, 'Not me, doctor, I am going to walk again!' I didn't say anything like that. When they gave me the sour prognosis, I shrugged. I sure as hell don't want to be mistaken for an inspirational story."

"I'll be careful not to let that happen. It's been more than six years since you've played in public. Isn't that right?"

"I haven't been counting."

"What have you been doing all this time?"

"Staying alive. Playing a little golf. Doing a little hustling."

"I can't picture you playing golf, Ronnie."

"You play, Jimmy?"

"A little."

"That all? You sound awfully modest. A guy develops an ear for modesty like that. I bet you can hit the fuck out of the ball with all that muscle hanging off your arms. You like to wager a little bit, Jimmy?"

"I better not."

"You sure? It might give your story a unique twist. No bull-shitting. 'Course you'd have to give me a few strokes. Strapping young man like you, dried-up old shit like me. Well, in case you change your mind, I'm always up for a game."

"I'll let you know. So, getting back to the music, would you tell me how you got started?"

"I might."

Ronnie tells about picking up a trumpet as a teenager, how he'd hit the practice rooms at school as soon as the janitor opened the building. How the scales and leaping arpeggios eased their way into his muscle memory. At seventeen he joined the army, played in the 298th Army band in Berlin, and nearly got himself kicked out for talking back to the sergeant-drummer because the guy couldn't keep a beat. Went AWOL, finally, and after several weeks of psychiatric observation was given his release, declared "unadaptable to army life." *Unadaptable to all forms of life,* became his motto.

"Then I spent a crazy year touring with Stan Kenton, and got myself hooked on junk. Thing about heroin that pleasured me most is what it took away, not what it gave me. No more clatter of obnoxious people. People don't realize how noisy they are. I could tune them all out, live inside my own quiet tunnel, and make pretty good music. The first time I tried to kick was in LA, right after that tour. I had a motel room in Santa Monica. The tour ended with a concert at the Hollywood Bowl. I didn't want to go back up the coast to my wife, strung out. So I asked a pretty girl that had been following me, the last few stops, if she had the stomach to help me out. She was very kind to me, as I remember. She sponged me and brought me buckets of chipped ice, and got lost whenever that's what I needed. She made sure the 'Do Not Disturb' sign was in place on the door handle. I remember laughing hysterically about the 'Do Not Disturb' sign, laughing to the point that I got terrible hiccoughs and almost choked to death.

"I stayed clean for about five minutes. That was it. I played music up and down the West Coast. Big crowds everywhere I played. Good money. Women following me. I never went after women or drugs. They both came looking for me. That's not entirely true, I spent a lot of time hunting down drugs, but not women. I had to leave entirely if I wanted things to be different. I don't think I would have done it if my teeth hadn't rotted on me. A blessing in disguise. Don't you think, Jimmy?"

Bird for Dog

Betty arranges a leave from the hospital. She wants to do her best for Quincy. She holds him for hours at a time when he is upset, answering sobbing questions about his mother's whereabouts, until he's stilled to sleep, a big, round button in her arms. Waking, the boy wants his father, and she talks three times to Darnell, who sounds like a boy himself and has little interest in coming after his son, "Being, as I am, in the middle of a very complex business deal."

Betty buys a huge roll of white paper and unrolls it on the kitchen floor. She and Quincy get down on their knees with handfuls of markers and begin to make a picture of the world. It's a big project, she tells Quincy. They could spend their lives making the picture. Each day they unroll more paper. Quincy asks questions about Jesus and the "Mother of Heaven." He produces a sturdy population of men and women and monsters. Some of the figures have crosses attached to them and sharp sticks pointing out of their heads. Betty tells the story of Noah's ark, and for days there is nothing but rain and animals.

A week after the motorcycle sped off, Betty drives Quincy to a pet shop in the city to look for birds that make a pretty sound. Quincy isn't sure what sort of a bird he wants. Maybe green, he says. They look at finches. Betty wants a bird that sounds content, if not chirpy with good cheer. But it's hard to hear that quality in a small creature when you are only visiting. The birds make Quincy recoil, they give him the creeps every time they flutter their wings.

"Betty," he asks, plaintively, "could we get a dog? Could we?"

Before she answers, she finds herself thinking, *Dogs, they're a lot of work, they are.* Then she listens again to what he's asked. Could *we?* Could *we?* They've become a unit so quickly. She makes the mistake of looking at Quincy. He stares up at her with moist brown eyes. It's her call, she's the boss, whatever she says goes. She didn't ask for Quincy to come to her, any more than she asked for her son Adam to leave. But now the boy is here. Her foundling. One price you pay for being an orderly adult, Betty knows, is that disorderly persons and projects come your way with disarming regularity. But Quincy is just a boy. She squats to face him at eye level and throws her arm around his shoulder.

"What about a bird, Quincy?" she says, just to give the idea a decent burial.

"A bird would be nice," he says, and pushes out his bottom lip in a pout.

"But a dog . . ."

"Yeah, I really want a dog."

Fame

A week after his radish party with Jimmy Landreth, Ronnie steps out of the Pantry into the early afternoon haze and sees his face staring back at him from a newspaper box on the corner of Olympic and Figueroa. Actually, the Ronnie Reboulet in the picture isn't so much staring as squinting into the January sun, a weathered fella in a string tie. The headline reads JEWEL IN THE ROUGH.

There he is, dozens of him, sitting in a free news rack beside coin boxes filled with fruiter rags and nudie girl let's-get-acquainted sheets. Ronnie doesn't like the company. He stands on the corner for a moment, smiling dumbly at the absurdity of being captured in a box. The story builds a portrait of a small, hardworking man, living a quiet life in a funky suite at the Alhambra. "A jazz great has returned from the dead," Jimmy Landreth writes. "He practices nearly every waking hour. His sound is deep, his sound is wise."

Two days after the *Observer* piece appears, he is swamped with phone calls. The wire services have picked up an item about his being alive and well, and playing better than ever. He gets up early, not having played the night before, and sits up in bed with the paper and a dull pencil, circling winners at Santa Anita. Then the phone starts ringing off the hook. He might as well be a bookie. He moves to the green vinyl chair and sits in his underwear, with the black telephone in his lap, chattering, sipping coffee, and nibbling cold toast from a room service plate of milky scrambled eggs.

The *LA Times* wants to do a feature on his resurrection. He hangs up on a stringer from *Newsweek*, after saying, "Look here, I'm old news, very old news." Herb Caen is on the horn from San Francisco, wondering when he's moving back. "You realize you're city property," says Herb, "we never gave you permission to live among Dodger fans, or fade into a studio stiff, or join the Lighthouse All Stars." Rudy Beeson, the city's jazz apostle, and Herb's *Chronicle* colleague, calls to wish him well and suggests a couple of studios that would be thrilled to record him. An assistant to Jimmy Lyons at the Monterey Jazz Festival wonders how his schedule looks for the third week in September. A young woman from the Bing Crosby pro-am at Pebble Beach is sorry to ask an "indelicate" question—but is he a convicted felon? Ronnie imagines the Crooner snuggled in an office with a cocktail shaker and a picture of himself with the pope. "Tell Bing I did everything they say I did."

In the afternoon, musicians he's known for a hundred years

start calling: Shelly Manne, Hampton Hawes, Art Pepper, Shorty Rogers.

The strangest call came from a scout at *The Tonight Show*.

"Listen, Ronnie, how you doing, buddy? So anyway, Johnny'd like to have you on the show."

"*The Tonight Show?*"

"Yeah, Ron, that's the show he does."

"Thanks, but I haven't exactly aged so well for television."

"Know what you mean. But I bet you clean up well."

"I'll have to think it over."

"Do it, Ron. Look, you're cool. So don't change."

Every time he thinks of putting the DO NOT DISTURB sign on the door, the phone rings, or somebody comes knocking. A waitress from the High Waves sends a bouquet of Peruvian lilies with a card that reads, "I knew you were a great man, the first time I set eyes on you." Late afternoon, a couple of telegrams come:

PROUD OF YOU, REB. DON'T LEAVE BEFORE I GET
THERE.
I BUY OMELETTE ESPANOL MANNA AT PANTRY.
--MURRAY

RONNIE, YOU ARE AN INSPIRATION!
--JEANETTE (THE NINETEENTH HOLE)

Hub

Ronnie is happiest to hear from his old buddy Hub Mosca, the great bass player and the sweetest of men. He hadn't been in touch with Hub since the mid-sixties, when they were both staying in Holland.

"I never knew you played golf," Hub said.

"Yeah, the asshole blew all my covers."

"How did he get you to talk, Reb? Sticks of bamboo under the fingernails?"

"I have a big mouth, Hub."

"That's all right, Reb, you're famous again."

"I wasn't looking for notoriety. I thought this was a shitty little newspaper a few guys picked up for the sex ads."

"They tell me that fame and anonymous sex are kissing cousins in America. So how are your choppers holding?"

"I'm putting the goop on all the time, Hub."

"Don't you know it."

"I should do a few ads for Polident."

"A regular Martha Rae."

"My daughter's name."

"Rae. How's she doing?"

"Good. Grown up and beautiful. Lost. It breaks your heart to know all the years went by."

"Don't you know it? Sometimes it seems like a lousy deal. We're strange beasts, Reb. We're supposed to play music to calm the savage hearts. But who is there . . . who is there to play for us?"

Skunk Train

It was the third day in a row that they'd taken the miniature train ride from Willits to the coast. She was working up her nerve to tell him that she hated it. They walked each morning, in a misty rain, from his father's motel to the train station, which was teeming with chattering tourists all excited about their ride to the ocean on the fabled Skunk Train. She wanted to make a little speech to the tourists. She'd stand up in the middle of the miniature waiting room of the miniature train and twirl a baton, toss it into the recesses of the waiting room until she had their attention. "How you doing, folks. I gotta tell you something— it's a nice little ride through the woods, really is. It would be one thing if it lasted fifteen minutes, but it lasts way longer than that. Way longer."

The coke gives her a lot of funny ideas, but she keeps them to herself. Dirt has enough troubles. Every morning he fights with his father in the motel office and bustles back to their room with a plate of toast for her and says, "Eat it, willya, it makes me nervous you don't eat." Then he spills out a couple lines of coke and, as he horns it, she does her best to cover the toast with a paper napkin.

The Harley is parked in a storage garage with the riding mower. She isn't sure why. "For safekeeping," he says. Either somebody is after him or he imagines that somebody is after him. She isn't sure which is worse.

Dirt's greatest pleasure is to have a total-body "horizon buzz" with the coke, as the train twists out of the redwoods and you get your first sighting of the ocean. "That's my idea of a simultaneous orgasm," he likes to say.

This time he loses a couple of grams to the breeze, after he's spread four giant lines across one of the rear benches, during a mail stop.

"Shit, fuck, shit," he says. Then, "Sorry, excuse my French."

He is a strange man, the way he changes moods.

"Hey, I got something for you," he says, "found it at the motel." He reaches into his pack and hands her a coffee-stained copy of *The Sacramento Bee* with a story about her father.

Come, Comet

It isn't difficult to find the deli on Ocean Avenue in Carmel that she once visited with Ronnie. The wall of tiny mustards is as she remembered it. Betty chooses three small jars of mustard to tuck away in the glove compartment, as souvenirs. She buys a couple of hard rolls, a quarter-pound of prosciutto for herself, and some honey-baked ham for Quincy. The idea of picking up a sandwich for Ronnie crosses her mind. She thinks of building him an enormous poor boy on a soft loaf, with a dozen different meats and cheeses. But, the way she's driving, it will be days till they get to LA. She imagines a giant sandwich stretching across the top of the dashboard, all the way to LA, and Quincy asking, "Why is that sandwich there, Betty, why is it?"

When they get to the beach, Quincy confesses that he didn't want ham, he wanted bologna. He got confused when she named all the meats. But he isn't *real* hungry anyway. She lets Quincy feed a slice of honey-baked ham to the dog. She watches the little beast gasp, nearly choking, as he inhales the flapping slice of reconstituted ham. It is almost enough to take away her appetite. Quincy pats the dog's head. "One good thing about Comet is he really likes ham."

She thinks about the decisive way Quincy chose the dog. They'd walked through a pound called Pets Unlimited. It must have been frightening to the boy—two rows of cages with barking dogs. Quincy kept his eyes on the concrete floor as he walked up the rows. He stopped in front of the one cage where the dog wasn't barking. "I want that one," he said. It was a black terrier mutt with a white diamond marking on its throat. She inquired about the dog's history. They thought that his name might have been Angel. He hadn't barked since he'd been brought in, but there didn't seem to be anything wrong with him. A week later he still hadn't barked.

The afternoon they got home, she told Quincy that he could name the dog anything he wanted. As soon as Betty filled its new dish with Kibbles, the dog raced across the kitchen floor. "He's fast as a comet," Quincy said, "a real comet. Hey, Comet! That's his name—Comet."

Now, momentarily off his leash, the dog, with the taste of honey-baked ham in his mouth, sniffs and wanders his way up the white beach. He's gone far enough. "Comet," Quincy screams, "COME COMET."

The End of Anonymity

Every evening since the cover story in the *Observer*, and the follow-up feature in the *Times*, a line snakes around from the entrance of The High Waves. Even the hotel lobby gets crowded, at times, with fans who want a glimpse of Ronnie.

One night a busload of Japanese tourists pulls up in front of the hotel. Ronnie watches from his front windows as a parade of well-dressed men and women, cameras slung around their necks, climbs out of the bus. A Japanese tour guide stands on the street by the door of the bus, checking off names on a clipboard. Ronnie watches the proceedings with a pained disinterest. Who are these people, speculators from a distant land angling to buy up a depressed quarter of downtown LA? It takes a moment to realize that this procession of orderliness has come to attend him.

Ronnie leaves the back way, past the pool, down the alley,

and in through the back door of The High Waves. The management, since instituting a ten-dollar cover, has freshened up the musicians' dressing room, with flowers, bottles of beer and wine, and a tray of cold cuts. Artie pushes the cold cuts onto paper plates so that he can use the meat tray to divide grams of coke into long wavy lines that look like city streets.

Tonight, as Ronnie walks in, Artie is using a hundred-dollar bill to snort up a city block.

"You ever thought about going into urban planning, Arthur?"

"My man!" Artie says. He turns away from the tray and launches into a spasmodic series of sneezes.

"You're going to burn out your nasal membranes, sonny, if you haven't already."

"Then help me out with some of this stuff, Reb."

Ronnie pulls a crisp dollar from his wallet and rolls it into a tight cone. He's been using for a few weeks now, but the coke doesn't do a whole lot for him. Although he's known a lot of guys that swear by it, he's never quite seen the attraction of cocaine. If that's your thing, why not shoot a little meth? Snort it, and it might persuade you to sit up straight for a moment, freshen your breath. It may turn you into a cocky dude, if you let it. But it also crowds you, it's in your face. Instead of protecting you, like heroin, by giving you space, it changes you into a mental muscle-bound, a guy who's jerked the wrong weights, a curious specimen too easily pleased with the face in the mirror.

Ronnie horns a discreet line for each nostril. *It's two mints,* he thinks, *two mints in one.*

"Have some more, Reb."

"I'm fine, thank you."

Ronnie lights a Viceroy and sits back on a stool. The cigarette assumes a miserable mentholated quality. If you're going to use, Ronnie decides, you may as well use something that you like. He watches Artie race through a spasm of sneezes then go back to work with the tray, slowly turning the city of white powder into a ghost town with nothing left but two or three broken alleys.

Jeanette

He didn't know her at first. Maybe it was that he'd never seen her caked in makeup, or tottering around in high heels. Mostly it was middle-aged women who approached him now. If they gave him enough room, he tried to be kind to them. He signed autographs and pretended to remember them, but he never went away with them. Those days were over.

He knew her name as soon as he saw her, he just couldn't remember how to say it. He was almost mad at her when she said it for him. She stood in front of the bandstand at the center of a semicircle of fans. They were like a section of a church choir standing mute before their director, waiting to be actively inspired. She was the soloist.

"I'm Jeanette," she said.

"I know." He wanted so scold her. "How are you, honey?"

"From the Nineteenth Hole."

"I'm not suffering from amnesia. What are you doing down here with yourself all made up?"

She tried to blush through the makeup. Ronnie nodded to the choir of fans, dismissing them, as it were, and led Jeanette by the arm to his dressing room.

Cold Cream

It has been so long since Ronnie's slept with a woman that the prospect doesn't even frighten him. He and Jeanette walk hand in hand across Figueroa Street to the twenty-four-hour Walgreens. He has a few items to pick up, he tells her, and, with his trumpet encased under his left arm, he tugs a red basket up and down the aisles, tossing in a carton of orange juice, a couple boxes of Kleenex, a jar of cold cream, and a pack of Hollywood Skins.

He'd made love to Jeanette once, the two of them coupling under a static windmill across from the ocean. They'd put down a golf towel for a blanket. Draped over the damp grass, the towel was as close as they would come to having a home. Ronnie had kissed her and cooed in her ears, and she'd told him he could do anything he wanted with her, even as she climbed all over him.

It would have been a funny picture had anybody seen it: the two of them with their knickers down around their knees, one of her hands under his sweater, squeezing his left nipple, asserting her right to hold on to some part of him as they thrashed around on the ground.

Now, at three-thirty in the morning, he walks Jeanette into his suite at the Alhambra. His hotel life has been upgraded with a small refrigerator. He offers Jeanette three brands of Mexican beer, or a chilled martini glass filled with Bombay. He has no vermouth or toothpicks, but he does have green olives.

They are skittery together. Ronnie remembers her awkwardness. He sits her down in front of the bathroom mirror and fingers cold cream over the caked makeup on her cheeks, watching a thin crust rise and the girl's blotchy skin come into the room. She slugs down her gin and wants to kiss him. He doesn't like the taste of gin on her tongue. He doesn't like the taste of her. He wipes her face clean with tissues and hands her a towel to wash up. She unzips his pants and rubs his cock with cold cream until it becomes hard.

"I saw you bought rubbers," she says. "Can't we do it without?"

Hitler's Angel

He really doesn't want any of this and asks her to give him a couple of moments alone in the bathroom. He has a brand-new leather kit for his works, and another, smaller kit for the road. In the old days they used to hide their shit everywhere, in the sockets behind the light switches, dug into the bushes in a Prince Albert tin. No more of that now. He spreads out his equipment: eyedropper, spoon, a length of elastic, a razor, an assortment of needles, matches from the club, and some fine-powdered smack. Nice to see it all laid out, ready for action.

He used to shoot anything, anything available. Short-action Dilaudid, meth, Dolophine. Years ago, he had a pharmacist in San Francisco, an amateur trumpet player, who'd trade his services for lessons. It was a high price to pay for pharmaceuticals. The guy was big on Dolophine, a synthetic morphine. He brought Ronnie a dozen little sealed bottles of the stuff each week, and Ronnie had to make a fuss over how good the guy sounded on the trumpet. Richard Perkins was the man's name. Dr. Perkins, he called him. The man had a shiny trumpet, but no ear, no chops. His idea of heaven was Harry James. Fine. Harry

had a bright, wonderful sound and a sexy wife. He played a solo
and you pictured Betty Grable prancing about in a tight tunic, or
less. Dr. Perkins, on the other hand, had a nasal tone and an
indifference to intonation that bordered on the pathological. It
hurt to hear the man play. One day the doctor came for his
lesson in a nasty mood. He handed over the little bottles of
Dolophine and said, "You know where this stuff comes from,
don't you? German doctors made it up for their main addict,
Adolf Hitler. Named it after him. Think about that sometime
when you're getting high. You and Adolf Hitler."

With that Ronnie tossed Dr. Perkins out of his home and
swore he would never use Dolophine again. There was just a
small problem—twelve little bottles that he couldn't have going
to waste.

Still as a Bonsai

Ronnie cooks the milky mix in his spoon. Once he's shot it into
his arm, he sits on the counter and begins to feel well. A short
nod. Still as a bonsai.

A knock on the door. "Are you okay, Ronnie? Ronnie, are
you okay?"

"Fine. Just fine."

A little later, he walks into the bedroom, where she is sitting
naked on the bed with a blanket around her neck. He smiles at
her. It is nice to smile at her. Last time, after they had rolled
around on the hard ground, he grew morose. He was bruised
and startled, his cock throbbing and chapped for the first time in
years. Jeanette, that's her name. There was a reason for her to tell
him. The sad truth is that he hardly ever thought of her again.

The world intervened. He came home in the middle of the night to discover his daughter, who he hadn't seen for years, sleeping on the floor beside a little black boy who had a halo of sand dollars circling his bushy head.

He feels surprisingly well, sitting in a soft hotel chair across the room from the girl. He smiles over at her again. She stands and the blanket falls away from her, so that she's naked like a big fish in the market. She comes toward him, leading with her two oh-so-white breasts that he wouldn't mind sucking, one after the other, until morning turns bright. But these things never work the way you'd like. One time he wanted to wear her like a cashmere coat. He feels perfectly warm now. Perfectly warm and quiet. She's close to him now, her hands stretched out. He tries not to back away and aims one more smile at her.

"Thing is," he says, "I'm feeling a little fragile now and would rather not be touched. Just a little fragile. Fragile, like a china cup."

The Crack Between the Worlds

They find Ronnie sipping a margarita through a straw, in the tiki lounge by the pool. From a distance, sitting on his high stool, he looks like a guy who comes with the place, decked out in dark glasses, a Hawaiian shirt with a lovely cane pattern, and a tan silk coat. At first, Betty thinks he's talking with someone obscured to her view but sees, as she gets closer, that he is alone, mumbling song lyrics under his breath.

He is alone like one of those creatures on an ocean cruise whose eyes are permanently fixed on the sea and distant sky. It is six months since she's seen him, and it is clear, even from a distance of twenty yards, that he has transformed himself into a man who needs no one.

"Monsieur Reboulet," she calls.

Ronnie swivels toward her and lifts his glasses. "Madame."

He stands, barefoot off his stool, to greet them.

Betty notices a loose pair of fisherman sandals under his stool. Her hands go to her hair.

Ronnie steps toward them. "You're a sight for sore eyes, Betty. And how are you, big boy?" He offers his open hand to the terrier. "Who is this fine fella?"

"That's Comet. That's my dog."

"Comet, I like that. I bet he's really fast."

"Yeah." Quincy clamps on to the dog's short leash and Comet, a faceful of fur, pants uncomfortably.

It is a warm afternoon with a sky rippled in white overcast and smog.

Ronnie has them set up at a table by the pool. Between each long sip of root beer, Quincy sings a little ditty. "Mug woot beer, Mug woot beer, Mug woot beer, Mug . . ." Betty tries to calm herself with a gin and tonic as she watches Ronnie stroll barefoot into the lobby. Will he disappear, just like that, set them up with a single round and vanish?

Ronnie returns, half an hour later, with a bag of sundries.

"Madame," he says, and hands Betty a witty pair of sequined shades that make her feel part aristocrat, part drag queen. He pulls a tube of Sea & Ski and a pair of kid's sunglasses out of his bag and dumps it all, with a couple of magazines, on the glass table beside Betty. "Hey, I brought you some reading material."

The faces of Randolph and Catherine Hearst, framed by the red headline WHERE IS THEIR MISSING DAUGHTER? stare up at Betty from a *Newsweek*. She pushes it under the February *Sunset* and tries to imagine herself sitting in the luscious flagstone patio pictured on its cover.

Quincy, in his new sunglasses, has stationed himself a little bit away from the table with Comet who, given more leash, is down on all fours, resting.

Ronnie takes Betty's hand. "I'd love you guys to stay with me. I have a big suite upstairs. It's more room than I need. I guess I've been waiting for you."

"Can we go swimming in there?" Quincy wonders. "Can we?"

"You know how to swim?"

"No."

"You could learn. I used to go swimming in the ocean when I was your age. It was really cold and the waves would knock me down like I was a runt, which is what I was and still am, and turn me over on the ocean bottom, and spit me out like Jonah onto the wet sand."

"Don't frighten him, Ronnie."

"This is a lot safer here. There aren't any waves like the ocean. That is, unless a big fat guy jumps in."

Ronnie lifts the boy into his arms. "No, you're perfectly safe here. Safe as a baby in his bed. Really."

He walks Quincy over to the pool, hikes his pants over his calves, and sits at the edge, dangling his small white feet in the water. "Oh, it's so warm, Quincy, it's like a bathtub."

Quincy dips in one foot and then the other, squealing with delight.

Betty wants to forget both of them for now. She stretches out her legs and flips open the copy of *Sunset*. Dusk. Somebody once called it the crack between the worlds.

Righteously Beautiful

Dirt became sweeter toward the end. It was like something went off in his head and he wasn't so anxious anymore. First, he ran out of coke. That might have been a big part of it. She'd never known him when he wasn't snorting a couple of grams a day. It was too risky for him to go into the city for more—people *were* after him—so he got his Harley out of the storage garage and disappeared for five days. Later, he told her that he rode up to an Indian reservation near Covelo and sat in a sweat house for three days. His old friend Jimmy Coates, who he used to ride with in the Gypsy Jokers, looked after him.

Dirt came back with gifts for her, a chip of volcanic rock on a silver chain and a whole carrot cake from Covelo's new-age bakery. "Eat, baby," he said, "you got to eat." He pulled his hunting knife out of its sheath and cut two wedges, thick as his muscular arms. "Eat," he said, and shoved hunks of carrot cake into his mouth. She ran a finger over the frosting and gave it a good lick. Dirt also brought a knob of wicked hash that they smoked every evening—it was a lot easier than the carrot cake to get down.

They didn't take any more rides on the Skunk Train. She finally told him that the only part she liked was going to the ocean once the train came into Fort Bragg. Now they drove to the ocean every morning on the Harley. Sometimes they took strange back roads that Dirt knew. One day they bombed from one remote country store to another. "This is like taking a tour of the sacred missions," Dirt said with a laugh. Each store had fifteen or twenty kinds of imported beers, and gardening tools.

"Somebody's gotta service all the marijuana ranchers who've developed an advanced taste in beer."

Every time they parked at scenic overviews along the ocean, Dirt said, "This is righteously beautiful, don't you think?"

"Yeah," she'd say, wistfully. When he was tender like that, turning solicitous questions at the end of his sentences, he reminded her of Quincy.

She once heard of a man who was mean and miserable until the particular pressure from the brain tumor that would kill him changed him into the kindest man alive. Dirt was never mean to her, she'd just hadn't known, until the end, how tender he could be.

One night they went to an old Maurice Chevalier film in the town of Mendocino. It was fun to sit in a big room at the community center with a bunch of hippie artisans and their long-haired kids as the projector crackled and Maurice sang and danced, blabbering about girls . . . girls . . . girls. Dirt even tried an impersonation of Maurice on their way back to the Harley. "You ahh traay belle, mone chair . . . I'm talkin' fuckin' bu-tee-fool, bebe."

Another night they had a picnic with Dirt's father, Wes, on the ocean near Point Arena. The two men seemed like they had made their peace. They had a round loaf of sourdough, a roll of Genoa salami, and a block of jack cheese riddled with hunks of hot pepper. As they worked their knives, Rae ate a little bit of berry yogurt. Wes said, "Got to eat more than that, honey, you'll waste to mush."

Wes was a thin man himself, with a dark black mustache and brown eyes a little more speckled than Dirt's. He wore a metal brace on his left foot that didn't keep him from riding a Harley of his own. His bike had a bumper sticker attached to its baggage hatch. LET GO & LET GOD. He didn't seem like a particularly religious man. His leg had been crushed by a five-hundred-gallon oak barrel at the Sonoma winery where he'd worked for ten years. With the settlement he bought the motel in Willits and two Spanky Clean laundromats in Ukiah.

"Thing is," Wes said, "I never cared for wine."

He guzzled from tall cans of Miller High Life. He was a funny man. He liked Rae and liked to tell her things.

"You know why Miller costs more?" he asked.

"Why?"

"Because they got all this fancy shit on the can."

She smiled at Dirt, who shrugged. He thought his father was a little crazy, but he loved him, even if they argued half the time.

"The thing about this country," Wes said, after passing the hash pipe to his son, "is it's all about remembering and forgetting . . . a little bit about remembering and a lot about forgetting. You know who I blame for it?"

"Who?"

"The media."

Dirt coughed after expelling a lungful of smoke from the hash pipe.

"Take Patty Hearst. For six months we can't forget her for a moment. Now, she may as well be dead and buried for all the remembering we do. That's the media at work."

When the sky turned bruise red, Dirt's father said, "Fuckin' beautiful sunset."

"Fuck, yeah," Dirt said.

Two mornings later, Dirt was killed with a .45 Magnum. A bullet through the head, right outside the Food Villa in Willits. He was loading tall cans of Miller High Life into his saddlebag. He didn't drink the stuff. It was going to be a gift. That was the part that really tore his father up.

The police took one look at him and said, "Drugs."

Billie's Book

For two weeks they carry on quite nicely, without a mention of Rae. Betty has expected the man to ask after his daughter, and the boy to whimper after his mother. When neither of them do, she lets it go. She tries to see the time the three of them have as a discrete adventure, a savored chapter from a book. They spend afternoons by the pool, eat at the Pantry, drive the Alfa up through the canyons and out to Santa Monica and Malibu. One Monday they surprise Quincy with a ride to Anaheim, a little family on parade through Disneyland, as Quincy transforms himself from Davy Crockett to a pirate of the Caribbean with all the cheap paraphernalia that Ronnie buys without prompting.

It is clear to her that Ronnie is using again, and she resolves not to speak of this any more than she'll speak of Rae. The man is a professional junkie and is very adept at taking care of his needs. She is surprised how little, aside from his appetite and sleeping habits, is visibly changed. The only nuisance seems to be his shoes and car keys, both of which he has a hard time keeping track of.

One afternoon, at her bidding, Ronnie takes them to a studio on Wilshire Boulevard. It's been nearly a decade since he's recorded, and Betty is surprised to notice that he has some nerves. The two spectators sit in a glass booth with a plate of fruit, many boxes of Cracker Jack, and a couple of big bottles of Coca-Cola. They watch Ronnie, under a black headset, carry on sweetly with the rhythm section, a trio of black men chatting beside the piano. Occasionally, one of the musicians sticks his head under the grand piano's open hood to refer to a music score. Ronnie doesn't bother with the music. He stands by, immaculate in a pair of new jeans with waxed seams, a hounds tooth vest buttoned over a crisp blue oxford shirt, and a pair of reddish brown cowboy boots that have been buffed to a high shine. Ronnie has a cigarette in his mouth, a can of Coke in one hand, and his trumpet in the other. He turns to wave to them and clown for Quincy.

An engineer ushers the drummer into one booth and the bass player into another. Ronnie hustles over to the big sound room directly across from the booth that she and Quincy are in. She watches Ronnie ease onto a high stool, light another Viceroy, and, after a single drag, drop it into a large glass ashtray in which two or three earlier butts are still smoking. There is a swirl of smoke between him and his window.

The A&R is a man named Axel Cox, who likes to be called A.C. He's followed everywhere he goes by a spaniel named George. A.C. has his arm around Ronnie as he gives final instructions. Ronnie is not a man who likes to be touched in vain. Betty watches him endure the man's meaty arm, and the simpering spaniel at his feet.

Alone in his booth, Ronnie Reboulet counts out the first number. The piano player, a tall, lovely man with a pencil-line mustache, laces a rhapsodic intro that seems like a surface of water held up high, a lake in the mountains supported by the muscular bass and crisp drumming. Ronnie blows the theme of "I Cried for You," clean and tearless, his eyes wide open like a fish in an aquarium, not giving away a clue.

"The best way to create emotion in a song," Ronnie once told her, "is to withhold it, so that the song is out there on its own like an orphan."

"It takes an orphan to know one," she thinks as she watches him in his booth.

Betty wanted to come today because he was recording an album of Billie Holiday songs. She's always adored Billie, and once, driving west along the freeway, Ronnie named Billie Holiday as his favorite singer.

"Why's she your favorite?" Betty asked.

"Because she never raised her voice."

That seemed a curious reason for admiring a singer, or a woman. Despite his love of Billie, Ronnie had trouble with the concept for this session. Was it pure exploitation? Toss one junkie on the back of another, so that you're bound to come up with a winner?

The A&R said, "Picture a cover with a painting of your horn. Real elegant, know what I mean? With a white gardenia blooming out of the bell. *Ronnie Reboulet plays the Billie Holiday Songbook.*"

It was hard to argue with the song list:

> *Fine and Mellow*
> *What a Little Moonlight Can Do*
> *Don't Explain*
> *Good Morning Heartache*
> *This Year's Kisses*
> *Stars Fell on Alabama*
> *God Bless the Child*

At his first meeting with Cox, the A&R had demanded that Ronnie add "Strange Fruit" to his list. "It would be something special," the prick had insisted, "take the whole terrible race business full circle, know what I mean?"

Ronnie shook his head. "I don't think a white man doing a sympathetic song about a black man being lynched and left to hang off a tree, like a strange fruit, is a good idea. And I'm not going to do it."

Betty smiles over at Quincy, who sits quietly in the booth, a marvel of self-possession. He has been granted a headset of his own, and it seems to have led him into a tunnel of imagination where he is able to construct a hundred silent games with his Cracker Jack prizes.

She watches Ronnie through two partitions of glass. He plays beautifully. His solos on each song are inventive, but also have the uncanny character of Billie's moods. "Fine and Mellow" is good-natured and sensual, "This Year's Kisses" rippling with whimsy, "Stars Fell on Alabama" a landscape turned to soulful serenade.

The session is amazingly fluent—the musicians rarely do as many as three takes of a song. Ronnie's bluesy solo on the first take of "Don't Explain" starts as a beautiful ache of bent notes, a human cry. But instead of pushing it deeper, Ronnie pulls it back to safety. Betty stands up out of her chair. She'd wanted something more from him.

"What you see is what you get," he told her once. But in her experience, she has seen far more than what she's got.

Betty continues to stand, in silent protest. She watches Ronnie light a cigarette. He draws in a long trough of smoke and blows it out in a tight stream. She can see he's begun to sniffle. The man has made himself into a junkie again. He looks toward her and smiles and waves a hand.

Betty tries to picture the days and weeks ahead. She imagines driving back up the coast with Quincy and trying to legally adopt him. It might take all of her savings for a white woman, too old for the purpose, to become a little black boy's mama. Betty closes her eyes as the band plays the theme of "Good Morning Heartache." She imagines Quincy standing in front of the bathroom mirror, a mountain range of white shaving soap circling his brown teenaged face. *Peach fuzz,* she thinks. *Peach fuzz.*

It is something she hears in Ronnie's playing that gets her to open her eyes, a tailing off where you wouldn't expect a song's bloom to fade. He is in the middle of his solo on "Heartache." Panic is growing in his eyes. They are open wide enough to see what is gathered behind them. A hundred times in their life together, she has hoped to see him compromised to the point of asking for her help. But she has not imagined this face.

She can see that the poor man's teeth are slipping. Like a well-mannered boy at a formal dinner party, he makes it through a chorus before holding up his arms. Everything comes to a halt. He disappears into the lounge. The asshole A&R looks at his watch. Betty studies the musicians who, now that the music has stopped, have become as relaxed as bamboo in a soft wind.

"Quincy," she whispers, "you stay here."

Betty knocks on the lounge door. Ronnie is sniffling in front of the big mirror. He is shaking a little and his mouth has lost its shape. She notices his ugly dentures sitting on the counter beside the double sink. "You okay?" she whispers. He nods. She wants to touch him, but decides she'd better not. Still, she puts a soft hand on his shoulder. "What do you need?" He points to the teeth.

There are a couple of knocks on the door. Ronnie raises his voice to a soft holler each time: "I'm okay. Be out in a little while."

Betty squeezes a beaded line of Fixadent around the base of the dentures and helps him fit them in. "What else do you need?"

He shuts his eyes and opens them again. "Nothing, thank you," he says in a mumble, barely opening his mouth. "Maybe I should be alone for a few minutes while these set." He looks up at her and winks.

Quincy doesn't seem to have noticed her absence. He has pushed his little prizes to the side and is building a yellow brick road from Cracker Jacks. Two of the musicians are playing cards. The third, stretched out in a languorous pose, is reading the newspaper. Axel Cox paces the studio with the spaniel, George.

Half an hour later, Ronnie emerges from the lounge with a subdued smile on his face. As if to test gravity, Ronnie blows a forceful trumpet fanfare to "God Bless the Child." Betty looks toward Quincy when she makes out the song.

In the middle of Ronnie's solo blood begins to stream down his chin, over his fingers and the horn, onto his sport coat. Betty stands up in the booth. She wants to scream, but stops herself for the sake of the boy. There's blood everywhere, his face is a smear. But he keeps blowing, and the bright voice of the horn walks reassuringly into the room. It's *okay . . . okay . . . okay . . .* It's hard to tell where the blood is coming from. It is as if someone is torturing him with a remote control device. The music keeps coming out of the wounded face.

Ronnie's upper lip is split open so wide, she thinks of a street, the center of which has been excavated for new pipes. "Split like a sausage," he says. He holds a bloody white towel to his mouth as he nods through the bright playback of "What a Little Moonlight Can Do." He won't be able to play again for months.

Cox, his arm around Ronnie, is like the magnanimous host of a party.

"Beautiful music, Double R," he says, "truly beautiful."

"Whatever you say, A.C."

"A great musical event, didn't you think, fellas? We've got it in the can!"

George licks dried blood off Ronnie's loafers until he nudges the dog aside. The musicians gather around, telling Ronnie how well the session went. Cox offers an actual prognosis. "Your lip will be as good as new in a couple of weeks." Ronnie nods. Betty stands apart with Quincy. The A&R talks about how well the record will sell. A trumpet with a blooming gardenia on the cover.

False cheer rises into the room like a gas that you can actually see. The lovely pianist with the pencil-line mustache stands beside Ronnie. He speaks in a mumble that Betty can't make out, and places the tips of his long fingers on Ronnie's shoulder. This is the way that you touch a man who doesn't like to be touched.

She's surprised to see that Ronnie doesn't quite want the party to be over. He holds the bloody towel away from his mouth to tell a story. Blood drips down his chin onto his shirt.

"When I was on the road with Kenton in 1949, Louis Armstrong came out to hear us one night in Chicago. I don't think he cared a whit for our music, but he was in town so he came by to pay his respects. After the gig he's backstage shaking hands. A beautiful man. And one of the horn players asks Satch how he's managed to take care of his lip all these years because, if you ever heard him, he was the most powerful trumpet player there ever was. He could blast open a cage with that horn.

"So the whole horn section gathers around. You have to understand, we were all young and white, a bunch of shiny nickels with our hair slicked back, and Louis was hitting fifty and, as beautiful as he was, his lips were these big, puffed wrecks already all scarred up.

" 'I tell you what I do, I give my lips a bath, " he said, 'soon as I get off the stand, with a fine honey lip salve and some sweet spirits of nitre. And I bathe them once more before I go to bed. Sweet spirits of nitre takes the soreness and worn-out nature out of anything, man. Sure, it stings! You bet it stings. I put it on and then I grab a chair for about five minutes. Next day 'fore I go to work, I put it on again—witch hazel and sweet spirits of nitre, and my lips remain relaxed at all times.'

"We thought he was talking some crazy voodoo stuff—'sweet spirits of nitre'—but the man went on to play another twenty years."

" 'Sweet spirits of nitre,' " the piano player says, producing a deep, clench-toothed laugh—da-da-da-da-daaaaa—reminiscent of Louis.

Ronnie, sniffling, goes back to mopping his lip. "So much for my good looks."

"You'll do, Monsieur Reboulet."

"Madame." Ronnie turns toward the piano player. "John, I'd like you to meet Betty. She's my life."

"Ma'am." He takes her hand and holds it until the room grows quieter.

"And this is my grandson, Quincy."

"How do you do, son?" He nods toward Quincy. "You're a good one, that's easy enough to see. I was watching you. Did you know that? Yes, I was. I'll tell you what, if I'd had my boy here, we'd have had all sorts of trouble, you know what I'm saying. But this one, he's got himself a little secret, a little *brrrrr* of a motor running inside his brain, keeping everything interesting."

Axel Cox shakes everybody's hand at the door. "Couple of weeks, be good as new."

"We'll see, A.C.," Ronnie says, staring right through the A&R and handing him the bloody towel.

Get Ready for the Bicentennial

The train leaves from Oakland at ten in the morning. By noon, Rae has been to the bathroom three times to look at her new henna job in the glass and chrome mirror. It pleases her. The henna job may not give her a particular radiance, but at least it makes her look like a woman with a concept, it gives her an edge. The woman in the mirror is among the living.

If she could afford it, she'd buy a new wardrobe. As it is, everything hangs off her. She has been losing weight, a little at a time, since her mother died. It's not so much that she's uninterested in food, but that every time she has it in her mouth it makes her think of a hundred things she should have done or still needs to do. Chewing, she's decided, is a kind of trigger, so she mostly has berry yogurts and chicken broth.

On the train, Rae's hungry. She's brought nothing with her but a bag of clothes and toiletries. It's a good feeling, hungry. Dirt would get a kick out of her riding the train.

"What the hell are you doing on the train? I thought you hated trains."

"I've done it for you, to think about you. But all of a sudden I'm so hungry."

She wanders into the club car and buys an egg salad sandwich. It comes with potato chips on a red, white, and blue paper plate that, around the rim, says, GET READY FOR THE BICENTENNIAL. Rae wonders what would be the best thing she could do to get ready. Have her hair dyed and frosted in patriotic stripes? At the moment, she doesn't think she can eat her sandwich.

The black man that sold her the sandwich—his name tag

reads CHESS—is making his rounds through the club car, picking up debris from the tables. He stops by her table. He's cute and he knows he's cute. He knows it so well that he's been able to forget it, which makes him as natural-looking and generous a man as Rae has seen for a while. His mother adored him, Rae decides, without taking any credit for his sweet nature. "He was that way the moment he was born."

For some time, Rae has divided the world into two types: those whose mothers naturally adore them, and those whose moms, for any number of reasons, are profoundly distracted. The division, she's decided, is wider than black and white, or rich and poor, in determining the degree of a grown-up child's happiness in the world.

Chess smiles at her. "What's the matter with that sandwich?"

"Nothing's the matter with it."

"Then how come you're not eating it?"

"I kind of lost my appetite."

He stands back from her table and appraises her. "Pardon me for saying it, but you look like you lost your appetite some time ago."

Rae smiles at him. "I'm just getting it back."

"Is that right? Well, good for you, good for you. By the way, I like what you've done with your hair."

"Thank you." She winks at Chess. The man is a pleasure to look at.

He reaches for her plate. "Shall I take this?"

"Yes."

"I'm off when we get to LA. I'd be happy to take you out for a decent meal, if you promise to eat it."

"Maybe next time."

Rae looks out through the big window to a field dotted with farmworkers crouching in the midafternoon sun.

Blue Bossa

The crowds keep coming to The High Waves even during the weeks Ronnie is unable to play the horn, and croons through entire sets. "I'm afraid I'm turning into Perry Como," he tells Betty. He's begun to talk more to the crowd. "When you don't have much left, that's when you become a showman," he says.

The more he plays to the crowd, the more distant he grows. Betty watches his drug habit deepen. His nose is always running. He never can find his shoes, he loses the keys to the Alfa. He disappears for whole days and nights and she has to send Artie or somebody from the club to look for him. Sometimes she feels as if she's witnessing the final weeks and days of a terminally ill relative. People talk to her about "intervention." Why doesn't she get Ronnie into a methadone program, or check him into Synanon? "I'm not a rodeo star," she wants to tell them, "I've never been much at roping bulls."

For his first night back with the trumpet, a month and a half after he split his lip, Ronnie hires a well-known rhythm section to complement him and Artie Rhodes—the bass player Reggie Root, a slender giant in a white tuxedo shirt, and Larry Jarvis, the drummer, a squat, full-faced man who can't keep from grinning. Ronnie looks like the fruit of the harvest, clad in a linen suit the color of a persimmon, with a maize-colored Italian tie. He has on a pair of Bally loafers, buffed to a high, black cherry shine, but no socks. Betty imagines him, barefoot in his carpeted dressing room, deciding he better slip on his shoes before going onstage. She can tell he's high by the way he glides up to the mike. High, but very cool tonight with his trumpet in his left hand. So cool, he wants to talk.

"Good evening. Nice to see you here. Thank you for coming out. As some of you may know, I've been unable to play for the last month. Had a little accident with my lip, which is an occupational hazard for trumpet players. But I've tried to be conscientious about letting my lip heal. Tonight we've got a great band together and I thought I'd do a little experimenting.

"The late, great trumpeter Kenny Dorham wrote a number of fine compositions, including the one we're about to play. I always admired K.D., for his sweetness as a man and as a trumpeter. K.D. had a wonderful way of talking about his tunes. I think the only reason he went to college was to accrue that dignified vocabulary. I picked up mine on the street. About this number, he said, 'It's a mystic original with an authentic feeling of melancholy and buoyancy.' So, here's Kenny Dorham's 'Blue Bossa' . . . 'Blue Bossa.' "

Larry Jarvis, grinning from the start, kicks off a sneaky Latin beat and Ronnie takes a staccato walk through the theme, so simple that people in the crowd begin to hum it. Betty watches him slip off one loafer, and then the other, as he struts through a dozen bright choruses, each one a walking man, heading out of the room and strolling back in again. The theme, it seems to Betty, is as supple as a peasant's body. Ronnie outlines a bit of it each time through. He strips it of its clothes, dresses it slowly, beads it in simple ornaments, lets it trill a gaudy moment like a whistler in the quiet streets at dawn, then draws it back to its bare-bones self. She watches his bare foot tap the beat as he takes out the theme, the crowd whooping its approval.

Genealogy

Ronnie holds a tall glass of whiskey in one hand and grabs the microphone with the other. He looks out at the audience. "Thank you very much, thank you. We're just getting started tonight, but I can already tell that you're a wonderful audience, and I want to thank you for coming out. It feels really good to play again. It really does. I'm not an effusive type of individual. Most people who know me, and I'm sorry to say that there aren't many in that category, would describe me as quiet—quiet in an odd sort of way. But to play again with musicians like this . . . turns me into another kind of man, who wants to dance around and holler and tell people what he feels, how much he loves them, how good it is to have them in his life. So, thank you, everybody, for your support."

Ronnie swills his whiskey in a gulp and then takes a deep breath. "At this time, I'd like to introduce the band." He turns toward Artie Rhodes. "Would you mind giving me a few chords? I want to do something a little special here."

Artie lays down a quiet vamp.

"Thank you. I'm very honored to have on bass tonight, the elegant Reggie Root, who's played with Art Blakey, Dexter Gordon, Lee Morgan, Sonny Clark, Junior Cook, Woody Shaw, Art Pepper, Carmen McCrae, and most recently Hampton Hawes, who learned his craft from the fine piano man Dodo Marmarosa, who . . . made some famous sides with Bird, who played with *everyone*—from Hootie McShann in Kansas City, to Cootie Williams, and the great Fatha Hines . . . *who* learned to make the keys of the piano bite like a trumpet, after playing with

Satchmo, the greatest of them all, who cut *his* chops with Joe Oliver . . . *who* as a teenager heard Buddy Bolden blowing himself toward madness on the steamy streets of New Orleans!

"And on drums we have the charismatic, Larry Jarvis, who's played with Zoot Sims, Shorty Rogers, Red Mitchell, Sonny Criss, Pony Poindexter, Howard Rumsey, Victor Feldman, and my old buddy, the thoughtful Warne Marsh, a native of this town, who before he met up with *his* master, Lennie Tristanto, blew with a band called the Teenagers, led by an old guy named . . . Hoagy Carmichael . . . who'd stopped being a teenager thirty years before, but who in his prime wrote some of the great songs in the repertoire, like 'Stardust,' 'Winter Moon,' 'Heart and Soul,' 'The Nearness of You,' 'Georgia on My Mind,' and the beautiful, 'Skylark.' If you think of the musicians who've played those songs, you understand why I'm carrying on like this. Hoagy also played a little piano with the likes of Bunny Berigan, Eddie Lang, Paul Whiteman, Tommy Dorsey, Clarence Williams, and his beloved Bix.

"All of which is to say, that we have the history of jazz in this room, and I am very grateful to play a small part in it. Now I'd like to introduce our pianist, the lyrical Artie Rhodes, who's played with . . . *me*. I owe Artie a great debt. He's killed me from the first time I heard him. Artie Rhodes, a wonderful young player who will undoubtedly go on to play with his share."

This I Dig of You

"I want you to know that I'm coming toward the end of this speech, which has to be the longest piece of uninterrupted talking that I've done in my life." Ronnie steps back from the mike for a moment and looks down for his shoes and slips them on. He nods toward Betty then steps back to the mike. "And I promise those of you who still think you might have a little future with me, that I'll never do it again. Right now, I want to dedicate our next song, 'This I Dig of You,' a lovely original by Hank Mobley, to the most important person in my life, the beautiful and soulful, Betty Millard."

Betty feels her cheeks nearly fatten with blushing. She smiles up at Ronnie, who blows her a kiss before turning to count off the song. It is hard for Betty to sit still with all that she feels. It would be nice to play an instrument now, to have another way of saying that she, too, is happy.

Ronnie takes the lilting head at an easy tempo. It is a bright, leap-frogging joyful melody that sounds to Betty like a child's song, the way it hops up the fat rungs of a ladder. It wouldn't take much now to persuade her to stand up and shimmy in front of the little stage, but she won't do it unless someone else stands first. She's past caring what people think, but it doesn't seem right to cause a ruckus in a room where everyone is held by the music.

As Ronnie launches into his solo, he raises his trumpet aloft, so that the bell is aimed above him. The room has gone quiet. It is a song of pleasure, Betty decides, but pleasure with just enough gravity to make it smack. Ronnie runs three, four, five choruses, and is still going, the trumpet pitched to the gods. Sometimes Betty tries to follow his place in the song and she thinks she can hear him running through the bridge or driving around the bend, along with Larry Jarvis's big drum kicks, to the top of the form. He lowers his horn so that it is aimed directly at her. It is a single song, she knows, with a hundred variations. Right now he is singing the song for her. For her. It *is* a song of pleasure. "This I dig of you."

You Sonuvabitch

Around midnight, as the band is about to open its final set,
Ronnie notices a familiar form stroll into the club. She has done
something to her hair, turned it the color of roan. Like a horse,
he thinks. Betty has already gone back to the hotel to relieve the
sitter. By now Quincy is snoring away in the big bed with Betty.

It makes him nervous to see her out there with her short
horse hair. He checks that he has his shoes on. It's always good
policy to begin a set with your shoes. He wants to sing something bluesy. He turns to Artie, " 'Black Coffee.' "

> I'm feelin' mighty lonesome,
> haven't slept a wink,
> I walk the floor and watch the door and
> in between I drink—black coffee,
> Love's a hand-me down broom—
> I'll never know a Sunday
> in this weekday room.

"Good evening, ladies and gentlemen. It's nice to see some
new faces along with those of you who have stuck around.
Thank you for staying out beyond the witching hour. We
opened with a lovely song called 'Black Coffee,' which Ella
introduced a few years back in the movie *Let No Man Write My
Epitaph.*

"I'm standing up here trying to act cool, but it's difficult.
There's somebody very dear to me in the audience and I'd like
to invite her up to sing a song. My daughter . . . Rae Reboulet."

She is sitting at a table three rows back, but he can see her roan-colored head shaking, without its really shaking at all. She doesn't know whether to stand up and walk toward him, or to sink deeper into her chair and try to disappear. Maybe it's a terribly cruel thing to do to her. Maybe not. He watches her stand and push away from the table, as if it were a landing. She is only a little thing standing there, but she is madder than hell. He knows what she wants to say to him: *You sonuvabitch, you goddamn sonuvabitch.*

Never Let Me Go

After she's settled into his public embrace, and the applause has begun to wane, Ronnie kisses her beside the ear. "Are you all right?" he whispers.

"I'm okay."

"You look like you're wasting away."

"I'm fine."

"I like what you've done to your hair."

"I almost match your suit."

"Yeah. Whatever you want to sing . . . these guys are wizards . . . play anything you want. You want me to sing with you? I'd be happy to sing with you."

"How about 'Never Let Me Go'?"

"Beautiful song. Let me know the tempo you want it. You want me with you, I'm there."

He watches Artie wink at his daughter. Lecherous little shit.

Artie milks the moment with a florid vamp that, because she refuses to jump in, seems like it may go on forever.

He puts his hand on her elbow. "This is just a little song we're going to sing, honey. I'm going to lead you in very quietly. You

follow me. I'm going to stay kind of quiet, because I want you
to sing."

It feels like he's throwing a party for her. All the people are
here. Everybody is amazed to see her. They didn't even know
that she existed, but they're waiting for her. They love her
father. They're waiting with their mouths open, like parents
spooning first food into their baby's mouth. Artie is playing it so
slowly that she could go to sleep in the lap of each chord. Her
father nudges her and she opens her mouth. But she is still only
listening, it's him that's singing. His voice is nothing fancier than
a sweet knotty rope that he lets out of his throat.

One time he'd led her up the street, walking as slowly as they
could. Isn't anything to worry about, honey. Nothing to worry.
We're going slow, real slow. Now, shaky-voiced, she joins him.

Life Savers

Quincy is propped up in a chaise lounge by the pool. He looks
like a little man surveying a scene, his dog, Comet, snuggled in
his lap. Betty is in the chair beside them, flipping through magazines. Quincy knows what he's waiting for. He's been told. But
once he gets hot enough he's going to go swimming, whether
anybody comes or not. Betty has already blown up his life pre-
server tube. He calls it his lifesaver. It has a scene on it with
Snoopy swimming around in a great big lake, and he's smiling
like a very happy dog. Pretty soon Comet will see him swimming all over the place with another dog. The Snooper, Betty
calls him, the Snooper.

One time before, Betty bought Quincy a pack of Life Savers
in the hotel lobby. He put a green lime one in his mouth right

before he got in the water. After he sucked it down some, he got it on the tip of his tongue. He wanted to see if he could get the green lime to go around his tongue a little bit, so that he'd have one lifesaver around his stomach and another around his tongue, but his tongue was too fat to get it past the tip.

He wishes he had some candy Life Savers now, but he doesn't. He's hot now. Good and hot. He strokes Comet under his chin where he likes it, picks up his Snoopy, and says, "Goin' in, now." That's all he says. And Betty kisses him on the top of his head, right on the top, and says, "I'll be watching you."

First, all he sees is his grandfather, walking barefoot in his green, snapping turtle swim trunks. He's wearing a long-sleeve pull-it-over-your-head shirt. There she is walking beside his grandfather, except that it's not exactly her. Quincy is shocked to see the way she looks, all skinny with red hair that makes him think of root beer, even if root beer isn't red. There are such things as root beer Life Savers.

He kicks over to the side of the pool where Betty is. Betty is sitting up in her chair real tall like she's standing. Comet has his ears up like he's listening to a radio station that only dogs can hear. Betty is trying to smile. He can tell when she's smiling and when she's trying to smile. When she's just trying you can see muscles in her face that aren't there when she's really smiling.

"What happened to she?" he says.

"She changed her hair, she dyed it red."

"Do you like it? Do you?"

"I think it's a nice change, don't you?"

His mother is coming around to their side of the pool. Someday he's going to learn how to go underwater. There are guys who can swim from one end of the pool to the other, underwater.

"Hi, Quincy!" she says. She is standing beside a palm tree.

"Hi," he says, so softly that only Snoopy can hear him.

Salt

Betty is pleased that Rae's followed her advice—stay close to him, but keep quiet. They've all packed into the Alfa, with a load of knockwurst and Ball Park doggies, buns and marshmallows, beer and pop. Betty cranes her neck to look at Quincy, sitting on his mother's lap in the rear half-seat, Comet snuggled in his lap. They have to sit sideways in order to fit into the rear pocket. The Alfa is not a good car for a family outing—they'd have been more comfortable in Betty's Datsun—but Ronnie wanted to drive the Alfa. It is the only car that he'll drive barefoot.

Betty knows that this is a final excursion, of sorts. Still, it is nice to see Rae's arms wrapped around her boy, as the ocean rushes past their small triangular window. If you squinted your eyes before you took a good look at this clan, they might appear like an ordinary American family: husband and wife, daughter and son, little doggie.

Ronnie has taken the night off from the club. He's been taking off frequently, giving Artie a regular chance to play solo. "That's the way I found him," Ronnie says, "and that's how I intend to leave him." The management isn't thrilled by this development. They want him to lead a quartet, but he isn't into the responsibility. "Screw 'em," Ronnie says, "I've been keeping that dump packed for months."

Ronnie pulls up along a duned strip south of Redondo Beach. It is not a beautiful spot. Betty is surprised to see how prominent the offshore oil rigs are, a little city in the ocean strung with maniacal lights like a giant science project.

They climb over the dunes and walk toward the fringed waterline. An empty beach. The breeze is warm and the dull roar of the waves sounds, to Ronnie, like something cut out of the center of a kettledrum.

"If you stick your arms out on a night like this," he says, "and then lick them, you can taste the salt." He rolls his sleeves past the elbows. Betty and Rae stand beside him. The purpled veins on his arms rise like an elevated highway. After he reaches his arms out toward the ocean, Rae extends hers.

To Quincy, who's been running after Comet, this is a peculiar sight—his mother and grandfather, ready to go flying over the waves like Superman. But he pulls his hands from his pockets and stretches like a boy trying to grab a galloping horse, no bigger than his thumb, from a higher shelf than he's ever reached.

Finally, Betty holds out her arms in a rounded benediction. Each of them is poised at the western edge, receiving the night's warm spirit. Betty lifts her right arm to her mouth, and the faint bite of salt tastes like her desire for him. Tonight she will bathe with him, and lie in his arms, and listen to him hum as he begins to fall asleep.

Breakfast in Bed

The next morning Ronnie is gone. Betty finds a note written very carefully on a piece of music paper. She reads the note and then folds the paper into quarters, eighths, sixteenths, until it occupies no more space than an oversize Chiclet. Nothing to do, she decides, but call room service. She orders coffee and omelettes for Rae and herself, sunny-side-up eggs and extra toast for Quincy, who, among his recent discoveries, has found out how much he likes to make a sandwich out of runny eggs. The breakfast will not be as good as what they'd get up the street at the Pantry, but it will be delivered to their door.

Rae is awakened by the buzzer, and Quincy rouses as the shiny food cart is wheeled into Betty's room by a young Mexican man who looks like a prince in his crisp uniform. Quincy sits up in his bed in the alcove. He watches as the prince nods to Betty and sets a table for two at the foot of the bed.

"Come here, you two," Betty calls. "Come here, you sleepyheads, it's time for breakfast." Odd as it is, it seems right to give them direct orders. "I want you both to wash up and then come and have a nice breakfast."

As soon as they're seated at the table, she sits up high in the bed and tells them that Ronnie has gone.

"When is he coming back?" Quincy asks. "When is he?"

"I'm not sure that he *is* coming back," Betty says. She looks into Rae's moist eyes. "I'm sorry."

"Yeah, I'll be okay. I was expecting this. I have a way of getting people going on their way."

"Hey, you don't get to take the credit, Rae." Betty tries to hold the young woman's glance. "Later today we'll drive back up the coast. We have a nice home to return to. The problem is that some of the plants are going to be in trouble, and some will be dead."

Quincy lifts a side of the stainless steel hat from his plate to peek at his eggs. "Oh, my favorite, sunny eggs and toast."

"And, Rae, I want you to start eating."

Rae nods and lifts the cover, watching the steam swirl off her eggs.

Foreign

For the three weeks before the Monterey Jazz Festival, Ronnie stayed at Murray's estate in Carmel Valley. Murray knew he was using, but didn't make a big deal out of it. Ronnie was taking care of himself. He had a healthy, manageable habit and a good connection. The idea was to practice for a couple of hours a day, take care of his lip, and spend the rest of the time relaxing. Most evenings Murray cooked up a good pasta with fresh clams, or kalamata olives and blue cheese, or capers and artichoke hearts. Ronnie made a point of complimenting the chef extravagantly.

"It's all in the ingredients," Murray said.

"Yep," Ronnie said, "that and mixing them up right."

"What the hell, I like to see what you can do besides a red sauce."

They often sat together in the library after dinner. Murray had a shelf of John Steinbeck novels. First editions. "It's Steinbeck country, after all," he said. Each night he picked out a different novel and read a couple of pages to himself. Ronnie liked looking at the spines lined up together on the shelf. He flipped through magazines and listened to records with earphones on, so as not to disturb Murray.

"What are you going to do?" Murray asked one night, a copy of *Cannery Row* in his lap.

Ronnie had to take his earphones off.

"What are you going to do after Monterey?"

Ronnie lit a cigarette and thought about the question for a moment.

"I think I need to move somewhere foreign. Someplace that

everybody's speaking another language, so that even if they're talking all the time, I don't have to listen to them."

"You going to learn the language?"

"I already know all the language I need."

They laughed together for a moment.

"Foreign," Murray said, opening the novel.

"Yeah, someplace foreign."

Patty Hearst Captured

He hears the news on the radio a few miles out of Monterey as he is driving past Fort Ord. It makes him sad. Not that he knew how she felt. He remembers the baby-white skin above her breasts as she hid herself, without really hiding, in the hot springs near Tahoe. The Asian woman had stood up straight so that he'd be distracted by the sight of her two full breasts bobbing above the water. Not that it had worked. According to the radio, a Japanese-American woman named Wendy was captured with Patty. There you go; the woman with the bobbing breasts.

He's good and loaded and driving north. The thing about driving when you're high is to stay with the rhythm of the traffic. Some guys think that you have to push yourself to drive fast, compensate, because the horse running through your veins is telling you *it's mellow, everything's mellow.* But pushing yourself is an application from outside, whereas the business of staying with the rhythm can only come from within. The traffic doesn't advance like a theory. It has a natural rhythm that you have to feel.

The first time he heard his daughter sing, he knew she was doomed: a grown woman with no rhythm. Rhythm is your innate sense of confidence. It's something that cannot be learned. It can be sharpened, but not to the point that it saves you. He once knew a doomed horn player who spent all day practicing with a metronome. The guy definitely improved. He could read a score by himself in a room, beat perfect. The trouble was he didn't sound natural, but more like a jellied creature who was forced to grow a backbone on the first and third beat of every measure. And when it came to playing with others, he'd revert, just like that, the poor guy'd be back to guessing, tentative as a stuttering child.

The radio makes it sound like the Wild West. "The two women were captured yesterday afternoon in a rented apartment in the Crocker-Amazon neighborhood of San Francisco. Inspector Timothy Casey of the San Francisco Police Department, flanked by several FBI agents, knocked on the door at 625 Morse Street. Casey was overwhelmed by the sight of the famous fugitive, and her Oriental companion. 'Patty,' he said, 'don't make a move.' "

Ronnie doesn't like the image of the two women handcuffed. *Captured.* He hates the word. He has spent his life trying not to be captured.

He and Cat used to have a regular patter on the subject.

She'd say, "Running's not going to get you anywhere."

"Nope."

"You're becoming your own prisoner, is all."

"True enough. But I can't see how staying put will make me a free man."

The benefits of living on the lam are a shifting landscape and and intimate bargain with chance. Nothing more. Shedding responsibility is a mixed blessing, unless you are a sociopath who can travel without the baggage of conscience.

His own daughter has been trying to live a little of her life on the run, but he's afraid she'll get caught somewhere in the middle—neither here nor there. Every woman isn't made to live a suburban life. He likes imagining Rae flying down the highway on the back of a motorcycle, her hair shot back by the

velocity, singing a song that could not be heard even by the man
whose chest she's wrapped her arms around.

Patty Hearst found

Two days after reading about her father's triumphant return to the
Monterey Jazz Festival in the *Chronicle*, the Patty story is everywhere. The September 19 headline reads PATTY HEARST FOUND.

Had she been lost? Rae admits it was a strange part of San
Francisco they'd discovered her in—Crocker-Amazon—a
neighborhood on the way to Candlestick Park, but not one she's
ever stopped in. She'd be lost out there. The paper had a photograph of a chatty neighborhood woman named Rose. "I never
saw anyone go in or come out of the place, I hope to die!" she
said. "To think this happened on our block. I hope to die!"

The large, grainy photograph of Patty on the front page of the
Chronicle shows her right arm in the air and her mouth wide
open, cheering. She is wearing oversize, tinted glasses. She
doesn't look like an heiress, or a fugitive, but like a girl who's
won a sweepstakes, whose boyfriend is the night manager of a
donut shop.

Another photograph shows her parents, Randolph and
Catherine Hearst, embracing. It is an interesting photo, most of
the frame filled with Randolph's large back in a dark suit coat.
Catherine appears almost girlish, with her very white hands
clasped around his back. The mother is giddy while the father is
remarkably restrained. Does he know something more about his
daughter's fate? Rae would love to see a photograph of Randolph Hearst's face. She can guess things from the man's body
language. But are they true? Does Randolph Hearst believe his

daughter has committed a crime? Does he hold himself responsible in any way? Has he really been smoking three packs of cigarettes a day?

Patty Hearst was brought before a federal magistrate, the paper reports.

"The United States of America vs. Patricia Campbell Hearst."

The judge faced her and said, "Madam, is that your name?"

"Yes," she said.

"And your age, please?"

"Twenty-one."

Twenty-one. It's close enough for Rae to feel the breeze.

March 25, 1976

Dear Betty and Rae,

Forgive me for not being in touch sooner. Maybe you've heard it through the vine, but I'm pretty much settled here in Montreal. I've meant to write you a hundred times. Were you as shocked by the Patty Hearst verdict as I was? I hadn't been following the trial closely, so it really took me by surprise. The headline in the English paper had a photo of Patty with a quote: "Did I ever have a chance?"

I don't think she did. I couldn't make out what the French paper said.

Montreal isn't Europe, but it reminds me of it. I live on an international street called St. Lawrence. It used to be the old Jewish neighborhood, now it's everybody. Hippies, raga-muffins, Caribbeans, Vietnamese, what have you. There's also quite a few junkies. This is a decent place for an angel to take care of himself. There's a good supply on the streets and I'm using smartly. Like Popeye says, "I am what I am." Nobody seems to care who I am, up here, though the name goes over well. Je suis Monsieur Reboulet.

Funny thing about this city is that it's got a mountain right in the center of it. It's a hiking mountain, not a climbing one. Whole families go up it all the time. These people are serious walkers.

I miss you both very much. And Quincy. It would be nice to cross over the medicine line for the Bicentennial. By the way, I sold the Alfa when I got up here. Needed a little cash to get established. I don't need a car anymore. They tell me there's a pretty train line—the Adirondack—that runs down to New York.

Take care of yourselves, good people.

Love, Ronnie

Adirondack

Betty recognizes his handwriting as soon as she walks into the kitchen. Rae has attached the letter with a quarter-note magnet to the fridge, and scribbled a commentary of her own: *Sounds like he's looking after number one.*

Betty brews herself a four-cup pot of Kona and sits down to read the letter. After a couple of times through, she gets out the road atlas and traces the probable route the train follows. Yonkers, Poughkeepsie, Kingston, Hudson, Albany, Saratoga Springs, Glens Falls, Plattsburgh. She doubts that she'll ever take the trip, but there is a small pleasure in imagining it.

Rhythm Changes

Once, when she couldn't find a sitter, she brought Quincy along and he sat grinning for two hours as seven amateur singers, including his mother, strolled up to Bernie at the piano, handed over a sheet of music, and launched into improbable versions of "Speak Low" or "Fly Me to the Moon."

Tonight, Quincy sits on a folding chair in the cool church basement, drawing egg-shaped portraits of the faces. Each of the drawings is monochromatic. Rae watches her son choose a grey Crayola for Mai Ling, the breathy whisper singer who specializes in ballads by the Beatles, and tonight offers a version of "Till There Was You" that has everyone leaning forward in their chairs.

Appropriately, Quincy chooses yellow for Rog, the stuttering bus driver who never stammers while he sings, and wears a yellow star pinned to the brim of his Muni cap. Rog adores show tunes from the fifties. Tonight, it takes him nearly a minute to announce his song, "Hi Lili, Hi Lili, Hi Low." Quincy outlines the bus driver's face in a dotted yellow line.

"Lookit . . . lookit, you don't have to introduce the song," Bernie says, "just sing it. You have a fine instrument."

Finally, Rog opens his mouth to a silk-scarf tenor and sings.

Bernie has a knack for attracting singers of small talent and getting them to come back each week to pay their five bucks. The one time Rae asked for an honest appraisal of *her* instrument and potential, Bernie shrugged and pulled on his scrawny red beard. "Lookit," he said, "we sing because that's what we love."

"What the hell kind of answer is that, Bernie?"

His eyes got watery. "That's an answer from the heart."

In the end, she decided the situation was more appealing than group therapy.

As she walks with her music toward the piano, Rae winks at Quincy and wonders what color he will use for her.

Bernie has her working with a metronome, and he talked her into signing up for Transcendental Meditation. For two weeks now she's been going at it twenty minutes in the morning and twenty at night. The maharishi promises a big payoff—Cosmic Consciousness—if she sticks with it. When you reach "C.C.," her meditation teacher told her, you can levitate, but Rae is not so sure she wants to fly.

Rae does not stutter when she announces her song, even though the title may be a lie. She takes a moment to calm herself, then nods to Bernie. He's going to give her an eight-measure vamp. One, two, three, four . . . two, two, three, four . . . three, two, three, four . . . you gotta count it . . . five, two, three, and . . . listen to the . . . song I'm gonna . . . sing, two, three, breath . . . "I've Got Rhythm." Do-bee . . . do . . . ba

Mount Royal

On a Sunday at the end of March, Ronnie sets out to climb Mount Royal. He still can't get over it, an actual mountain, with a steep path to the top, right in the center of the city. Healthy young men and women in jogging suits, efficient people in stripes and pastels, are climbing briskly. He has on a pair of sneakers with black stripes, but he isn't going anywhere fast. He hangs back in the shadows, near the families, not close enough to bother them, yet not so far that he is all alone.

Ronnie prides himself on what good shape he's in. He may be

the only junkie in town to set off up the mountain. His tennies are wet as he steps through a steady stream of melted snow, trying to keep pace with a boy not much older than Quincy. The boy's father, who is fifty yards ahead, turns back to holler at the lad in French. Ronnie can make out only two of the words: "Volkswagen Bug."

At the top, breathless, Ronnie is surprised to find mounds of snow still on the ground. He sits on a damp bench and looks out over the city of Montreal. His father's family, who he never knew, who his father wouldn't speak of, came from here. Bitter people? Good people? Bad? He'll never know. Peasants? Quiet people? Loners?

There are church spires everywhere, and vast bells ringing a garland of hollow sound that makes an open tunnel, it seems to Ronnie, of his ears and his heart.

Acknowledgments

This book has had many generous and helpful readers: Todd Maitland, Brigitte Frase, Cheri Register, Pat Francisco, Philip Patrick, Gloria Loomis, Nicole Aragi, and Paul Slovak. I am grateful to them all.

I wish to thank my parents, for providing a first home filled with books and music. A special thanks to my father, David Schneider, an extraordinary musician, for showing me what it means to hear a thing, and then practice hard enough to get it.

Thanks to Lee Lowenfish, friend and New York jazz guru, for confirming my view that jazz deserves to be heard and celebrated every night of the week. Thanks also to Tom Pieper, master bassist, and his stable of musicians, for letting me play with them regularly.

I am grateful to the authors of the following works, which provided me with guidance and good company during the writing of this book:

Celebrating the Duke, and Louis, Bessie, Billie, Bird, Carmen, Miles, Dizzy, and Other Heroes, by Ralph J. Gleason (1975)

Coming Through Slaughter, by Michael Ondaatje (1976)

Anyone's Daughter: The Times and Trials of Patty Hearst, by Shana Alexander (1979)

Straight Life: The Story of Art Pepper, by Art and Laurie Pepper (1979)

But Beautiful: A Book About Jazz, by Geoff Dyer (1991)

West Coast Jazz: Modern Jazz in California, 1945–1960, by Ted Gioia (1992)

Notes from a Battered Grand, by Don Asher (1992)

Thinking in Jazz: The Infinite Art of Improvisation, by Paul F. Berliner (1994)

My deepest gratitude goes to the countless jazz musicians who have given me far more pleasure than I can repay.